SOPHIE JO

is a writer of YA fiction from the West Midlands, where she lives with her husband and a shy-but-kooky calico cat. Sophie is passionate about making sure teenagers know the difference between healthy love and straight-up-horrible-times-disguised-as-love. She's worked with domestic violence charity Women's Aid to spread the word via the *Sunday Times*, *Cosmopolitan* and BBC Radio 4's *Woman's Hour*. In her spare time, Sophie likes visiting Disneyland, overanalysing cult noughties TV show *The OC*, and writing about relationships – of all kinds – for publications including *Breathe Magazine* and the *Metro*.

OTHER BOOKS BY SOPHIE JO

Red Flags

HEART BREAK ERA

SOPHIE JO

SCHOLASTIC

Published in the UK by Scholastic, 2026
Scholastic, Bosworth Avenue, Warwick, CV34 6UQ
Scholastic Ireland, 89E Lagan Road, Dublin Industrial Estate, Glasnevin, Dublin, D11 HP5F

ISBN 978 0702 33451 1

A CIP catalogue record for this book is available from the British Library.

Printed in the UK.
Paper made from wood grown in sustainable forests and other controlled sources.

MIX
Paper | Supporting responsible forestry
FSC www.fsc.org FSC® C018072

10 9 8 7 6 5 4 3 2 1

www.scholastic.co.uk

For safety or quality concerns:
UK: www.scholastic.co.uk/productinformation
EU: www.scholastic.ie/productinformation

For anyone who's ever poured a little too much love into somebody else and not quite enough into themselves

JUNE

PROLOGUE

The one (forever)

I don't trust a single person on this planet who'd prefer to go out than stay home.

The way I see it is this: home has *everything*. Home has a well-stocked snack selection. Home has cushions and blankets and tartan-print pyjamas with loose waistbands. Home is full of people you actually want to spend time with, instead of people you've been forced to make small talk with at an event you wish you hadn't agreed to attend.

And, for me, home is also where I spend Friday nights with Freddie, curled up in the living room watching old episodes of *Midsomer Murders* with an extra-large margherita pizza.

"Do you think," he says, thudding his left foot into my lap from the other side of the sofa, "that birds believe they're better than us because they can fly?"

I pause the TV and give it a beat of thought.

"No. Birds don't do hierarchies like that." I don't know why I'm so sure of this, because who can say for certain what our avian population is thinking at any given time. "They're too busy. I think they share the planet with us just fine, but they're not, like, smug about their abilities. They've got things to do."

Freddie shoves a handful of jet-black hair from his eyes and takes a second to reflect on this, while I rub at his bare ankle. "Hm. Interesting."

I *love* it when he comes out with questions like this – it's one of my very favourite Freddie Lee traits. The first thing he ever said to me, in a never-ending history lesson three and a half years ago, was, "Harley, did you know there's a potential that some of the oldest sharks in the world were born when William Shakespeare was alive?" The moment he asked me that was the moment I knew. It was like my brain screamed, *This is your person. This one, right here.*

"If you were a bird, would *you* feel superior to humans?" I flit back to him now.

"The thing is, I actually would," says Freddie, and his voice is casual but earnest. "We think we're so great – top of the food chain, leaders of the planet – but we don't even have the ability to ascend into the air at will." He waggles a big toe in the direction of my face. "Had to build aeroplanes for that, didn't we. Pathetic."

"Embarrassing," I agree, and Freddie sniggers. "Was that one from The List?"

"Not this time," says Freddie. He leans to his left to scoop up a slice of pizza, then dangles it into his mouth, taking a bite and half swallowing before he speaks. "I was just sitting here and I thought of it."

The List is a literal list, full of topics Freddie and I think about when we're not together and decide we'd like to discuss at a later date. We used to call it Thought of the Day, until the Thought became multiple Thoughts and the whole thing evolved into something new. And now, The List is really two lists, stored in the Notes app on our respective phones and read out loud when we're reunited again. Things like, *Why is the sky blue and not green*? Or, *If you had to spend the rest of your life as a cat or a dog which would you choose*? Or, *Do you think this hairstyle would suit me (be honest)?*

"Are you two still watching this ridiculous show?" My mum has appeared in the doorway of the living room, a threadbare jute shopping bag in one hand and a flush of pink on her cheeks from the walk home. She jokingly rolls her eyes at the TV, which is still paused for the sake of Freddie's bird query. "It's for old ladies and people with nothing to do."

"*We* have nothing to do," I tell her, and I'm blissful with the knowledge of it. Friday is our night of nothingness – our night of screens and slipper socks and beige buffets. Always has been, always will be.

"I'm well aware." My mum puffs a chunk of dark hair away from her eyes. "And I'm also very jealous."

"You can watch with us, Alice," Freddie offers. He points at the TV with a pizza-wielding hand. "The guy on-screen has just found the dead body in the boot of his car, *but* he's maintaining his innocence, and we believe him because we just saw him have an affair with Mrs Pendleton the chemist, so he has a solid alibi."

My mum shakes her head, but she's smiling. "As tempting as that sounds, I'll leave you to it. I've seen all these before." She leans in to ruffle my hair, and I wriggle away from her. "And so have *you*, Harley. Exactly how many times at this point? Twenty-eight?"

I shake my head at the exaggeration; it's a long show, with enough episodes to keep anyone entertained for at least six months. "From start to finish, three. And I am enjoying it just as much this time around, thank you."

"When Harley was five," says my mum fondly, leaning down to deposit the jute bag on to the floor, "she watched her *Finding Nemo* DVD so many times I had to buy her a new one. She literally wore it out. Freddie, I thought smoke was going to start billowing out of the DVD player."

This isn't strictly true – there was never any smoke risk to contend with, and DVDs don't actually degrade from overuse – but she's right that our family copy of this particular film was loved so dearly that eventually the sticky fingerprints and scratches all over it caused it to give up the ghost during one long, rainy weekend. I have a vivid-yet-hazy memory of my mum frantically trying (and, obviously, failing) to clean the shiny part of the disk, while I burst into panicked tears with a plush Dory in one tiny hand. Later, Dory and I were bundled into the car so that we could secure another copy of the movie from the local shopping centre, and I came home proudly clutching the new DVD case across my chest, like I'd slayed dragons to get it.

Freddie has heard the *Finding Nemo* story several times over the years, but he still lets out a little laugh, stroking at my forearm with his foot.

"Harley just likes certainty," he says, and my heart swells at the warmth in his voice, the way he looks at me like I make *sense*.

There are a lot of uncertainties in life, but here's what I know: Freddie isn't one of them. Freddie is forever.

JANUARY

Seven months later...

1

The break-up

"That's the thing," says Freddie. "This was never supposed to be forever."

From my side of the Ferris wheel pod, I feel red-hot fury that humans can't actually ascend into the air at will. If I was a bird, I could jump right out of here and swoop on home, instead of being forced to sit in a swinging metal box while the love of my life tells me he doesn't want to be with me any more.

Freddie picks at a piece of skin on his ring finger and pretends to be engrossed in the city-centre skyline.

"I'm not saying we can't be friends, Harley. I'm saying this isn't working for me. And honestly, I'm not even sure it's working for you."

It feels like someone – a phantom hand of some kind – has

reached in to grab my stomach and sharply tugged it out of me, straight up towards the sky. Like we're not on a Ferris wheel at all, but instead we're strapped into one of those horrible drop rides where they hoist you into the air and then plunge you down towards the ground at random moments, and your insides feel like they get left behind for a few seconds, as if they're hovering outside your body until they've had chance to catch up with you.

This is our *anniversary.* When I planned this night out in my head I pictured a candlelit dinner at Pizzeria Romano, our favourite restaurant. I pictured Freddie holding my hand across the table, feeding me mouthfuls of spaghetti bolognese and murmuring things like, *Wow, Harl. Four years and so many more to come.* At that point, one of the waiters would overhear us and he'd shout, *Four years, at your age? This is huge! Why didn't you say?!* and then he'd hurry into the kitchen and return with one of those giant tiramisu desserts with a heart and a swirly "4" piped across it in chocolate sauce, and it'd be on the house, and everyone would clap, and even though I'm a long-time hater of sugary snacks *and* being the centre of attention, I'd make an exception because four years *is* huge.

"If by 'this', you mean 'our relationship'," I tell Freddie, fighting a losing battle with my shallow breath, "then yes, it *is* working for me. It's been working for me this entire time, which is why I'm here with you, right now, happily celebrating that fact."

"I think," says Freddie, and I can tell he's picking his words carefully, "that if you were really truthful with yourself, you'd, uh … you'd see where I'm coming from. This is hard – it's hard for me, too – but being in denial isn't going to help anything."

There is no doubt in my mind that he rehearsed this speech at home in front of the mirror. I bet Joshua and Lucas video-called him to offer some helpful you-got-this advice. *Just tell her she's in denial, bro. Tell her she's lying to herself, something like that.*

"I'm *being* truthful with myself," I hiss. "And this is my truth: I have no idea what's happening right now. We're meant to come down from here and go eat so much Italian food that we feel like we're going to pass out at the table. We're meant to go to Resident Retro to play pinball, and *then* we're meant to go back to my house so we can give each other our anniversary presents and do our *Avengers* rewatch."

We're Freddie and Harley. That's what we do.

Resident Retro is the name of our local gaming arcade. It's essentially a pitch-black room with neon lights and spray-painted brick walls, and a bunch of arcade games dotted around the edges. Our favourites are Mario Kart GP – a classic racing game, whoever you are – and the vintage *Doctor Who* pinball machine, which tends to have much less of a queue. Ever since Freddie saw a poster for the grand opening of Resident Retro two years ago, we've been semi-frequent visitors. It's one of the few places that doesn't make me regret leaving the house.

Freddie makes a frustrated noise – a guttural sound at the back of his throat – and the little pod we're sitting in sways with a threatening creak.

"You're proving my point, Harl. *This* is what isn't working. You don't ever want anything to change – you're going to be an old woman, still eating pasta at the same restaurant while life moves on without you."

Who are you, I want to scream, *and what have you done with my boyfriend?* None of it makes sense. Freddie is basically the boy version of me and, other than his need to leave the house on a regular basis to spend time in nature, our interests align perfectly. We're both into fictional worlds – Freddie is more of a sci-fi and fantasy guy, technically, and I'm an all-rounder with a soft spot for cosy crime, but it's fair to say that we both spend the majority of our spare time existing in spaces that *don't* exist. We're both relatively dependent on screens, large and small. We both think that David Tennant's tenth Doctor surpasses all the others, hands-down, and refuse to budge on this point of view. If I'm the old woman eating at the same restaurant, Freddie has always promised to be the old man next to me, reading me lines from his favourite Douglas Adams novels while he strokes my hand.

It's why we're going to university together. It's why we've worked for this long, while other relationships in our year group have crumbled around us.

"What about September?" I whisper. "We're living together. I'm coming with you – we've … we've got a plan."

Freddie sighs. "You can't just go through life picking up a relationship that worked at school and dropping it down in new places like it'll work the same."

"Anything can work, if you want it to," I remind him. That's been our catchphrase for the past however many months, when we've told our sixth-form college tutors what we want to do next year. When the kids next to us have looked us up and down, wondering if we're really planning on showing up to university as a double act. When we've talked about buying a house together in five years' time, and Freddie's mum has smiled at us like we're sweet but ultimately deluded. *Anything can work, if you want it to.*

Freddie hesitates but then shakes his head, running a fist across his dark hair and tugging at the ends. "What if I don't?"

"You *do*," I insist, and I reach over for his hand, even though mine is shaking. "I know that you do. We're going to university together, like we agreed, and it's going to be perfect. We're going to learn and hang out and go on adventures an—"

"Harley, this tacky-ass Ferris wheel is the most adventurous thing we've done in *months*," interrupts Freddie, pulling his hand away and drawing a line in the air to emphasize the word. "If we went to university together in September, do you know what it would be like? Because

I do. It'd be food shopping together. It'd be watching the same three shows on BBC iPlayer together. It'd be rushing home from lectures to hang out in a tiny depressing box room together, instead of meeting new people and immersing ourselves in the experience."

"*Immersing ourselves in the experience*?" I say, echoing him like an angry parrot. "Calm down, Minnie Lee."

Minnie – Min – is Freddie's twenty-nine-year-old sister. She works in marketing and goes to yoga and spends a lot of time filming herself talking about things like *holding space* and *innovative thinking* and *disruptive creativity* for her thirty thousand online followers. Normally, we laugh (semi-kindly, but still behind her back) at this kind of thing. At her buzzword vocabulary. At the fact that the word *Minfluencer* just rolls right off the tongue. Today, I guess … we don't.

"Don't insult Min because she knows what she wants out of life. She's driven! She makes things happen!" says Freddie hotly. "If she just sat around all day reading books and watching TV, do you think she'd be anywhere near as successful as she is?"

"*You* sit around watching TV just as much as I do," I shoot back. It's true. The happiest I have ever seen Freddie was when I found out that an independent cinema a half hour from us was showing the entirety of *Merlin* season one, back-to-back, to celebrate its fifteenth anniversary. I bought us tickets as a surprise and Freddie told me, completely sincerely, that it was the most thoughtful thing anyone had ever done for him.

"No, I *used* to sit around doing that stuff. That's the difference." He shakes his head, combative and sure of himself, and the metal Ferris wheel pod groans as we begin our descent back down to earth. "I'm sorry, Harl, I know this probably feels like it's all come out of nowhere, but it hasn't. People are supposed to change. They're supposed to develop. And I've kept waiting for it to happen to you, but it never did, and now I realize – I'd have been waiting forever. You don't want to do *anything*! You didn't want to double-date with Joshua and Erin—"

"Yes, because Erin talked over me and thought my name was Hayley," I say stubbornly. "That's not my fault."

Erin was a tiny gossipmonger of a girl who dated Freddie's friend Joshua for a few months. She was one of those people who was always in the exact same mood, no matter what – she never seemed to get PMS or feel nervous or just have one of those days where you wake up feeling small and sullen and don't want to talk to anyone at all. It was like she'd been born with an inbuilt level of chirpiness that could never be touched, which I found troubling.

Freddie clenches his jaw. "You don't want to go travelling."

"I don't like hostels."

"You don't want to drink because you think you'll get alcohol poisoning."

"People get it all the time," I hiss. "I read an article about a girl who didn't know she was allergic to alcohol, and then she took three sips of cider, and then she *died*."

I don't know if this is completely accurate – I can't actually remember if this particular girl was allergic to alcohol or not – but she *definitely* died from drinking cider at a one-off party and she would *definitely* still be here today if she'd just stayed home doing a jigsaw puzzle.

Freddie goes to say something a few times but his mouth flounders for words and he lets out a defeated breath, as though he's all out of ways to explain this to me.

"You're … you're so rigid. It's like you don't know how to have fun."

The people on the ground, in the queue, have absolutely no idea that my life is being torn to pieces a mere fifty feet away. They're singing along to the music, making exaggerated teeth-chattering sounds whenever the wind gets a little too brutal, screaming every time the stupid haunted-house carriage wails past them. "Shake it Off" is blaring from the fairground sound system, but I am confident that even my long-term hero Taylor Alison Swift could not shake this off. She would not be *whoo-hoo-hoo*-ing quite so happily if she knew what was going down in pod number three.

I've seen enough break-ups on TV shows, in movies, to know that the person being broken up with will blurt out some very desperate things. They'll beg for the person doing the breaking up to reconsider. They'll start bargaining – promising that they'll do whatever it is they haven't been doing. That they'll stop whatever it is they *have* been doing. And when you're the one watching all that? It's painful. It's humiliating. It could never be you. But when you're the one experiencing the break-up? I can now confirm that it's embarrassing how swiftly all dignity is flung out of the window.

"I'll change," I tell Freddie, and I feel like Ebenezer Scrooge bargaining with the Ghost of Christmas Yet to Come. "I'll go places and meet people. I'll … I'll leave the house after eight. I'll try the hot 'n' spicy burrito in the cafeteria instead of always ordering the plain one."

"It's too late," he says solemnly. "It's too late now."

"But what about our Saturday market trips?" My eyes have filled with hot, frantic tears, and one of them rolls down my cheek in defeat. "What about Eloise and Feng?"

Eloise and Feng are the names of our imaginary future children. Feng – named after Freddie's grandad – is a sweet angel who never eats his vegetables, and Eloise – in honour of my nana – is his doting older sister, who sneaks him dessert under the table.

"What *about* them?" says Freddie, and there's gravel in his voice. "They aren't real. This is what I'm talking about, Harley. I'm eighteen; I'm allowed to not want you to plan our entire lives together."

But I'm eighteen too, and I know Eloise and Feng aren't real. The point is, one day they were supposed to be.

I stand up in the Ferris wheel pod, desperate for the last few moments of this nightmare to hurry up. It wobbles violently and I clutch on to the side, still dreaming of a world in which I could spread my wings and soar my way to safety.

"Si'down, cart number three!" bellows the ride operator, over a loudspeaker. From under thick grey eyebrows, his eyes flash at me. "D'you have a death wish?"

"YES," I yell back, because if there's any time to be dramatic, it's now.

I watch as a girl in the popcorn queue reaches out for her boyfriend's hand. He pulls her towards him, wraps his jacket around her, plants a kiss on her forehead like she's the most precious thing in the world. The sight of them is enough to force me back to my seat.

Freddie softens as we near the loading station. "Please, Harl. I'm thinking of you, too. One day you'll look back at this and you'll understand: this was our first relationship. This was supposed to be the one that was short-lived – the one we learned from before we went on to something else. Not the one that dragged on and on forever and ended up with us resenting each other at twenty-five."

I'm figuratively booted in the shin by the boy who represents my entire teenage existence referring to our relationship as something that was always *supposed to be short-lived*.

He hauls himself to his feet and reaches to pull up

the safety bar from the doorway of the pod, then, with a patronizing closed-mouth smile, waves me out first.

Freddie's chivalry is usually one of my favourite things about him, but tonight it pisses me off. *I don't want to date you any more – I don't want to see you ever again, actually – but here, step through this metal entrance hole before me, because it's still important for everyone to know that I'm a stand-up guy.*

I stomp out, and when I twist to look back at him he grabs me by the hand.

"I leave for France tomorrow – we can talk more when I'm back next week, if you need to, but I've made my decision. Life is more than this, Harley. What do you want out of it?"

But it's a pointless question, with a pointless answer, because the only thing I want out of life is him.

2

The denial, part I

Here are the things I remind myself at 3 a.m. while my mum snores loudly in the room next door and I stare at the ceiling with the night light still on:

- Freddie and I have been together since the brace-faced days of Year Nine. That means we both *had* history together (literally, with Mrs Khan) and *have* history together (romantic history – the kind that means we have in-jokes from two years ago and embarrassing pet names nobody else understands).
- When Min gave birth to Freddie's nephew last year, she referred to Freddie as the uncle and me as the aunt – and ever since then, I have naturally become Aunty Harley to her two children, Rosie and Theo. Regardless of marital status and age, an

aunt is definitely not someone replaceable. An aunt is a permanent fixture – a woman who will be buying birthday presents and attending school nativities in the years to come.

- There are lots of people who have been with the same partner since school – *they* went through bad times, too, but ultimately got through it. There is something deeply romantic about growing with someone and knowing a thousand different versions of them. Freddie and I are a tree, and that tree has solid roots, and if we both take care of the tree then everything we do in the future will grow us a new branch.
- We've already sent off our early applications to university. The Royal Agricultural University, more specifically: a specialist institution on the outskirts of Cirencester, known to its students as RAU. Unless our grades are significantly worse than expected, we're both going to the same place. That's the plan. That's always been the plan. When he thinks about it like this, he'll definitely come around.
- Just because Freddie has a group of single friends doesn't mean he has to *become* a single friend. He could lean into his role as the relationship-guy – the one that every group has. He could be the wise advice-giver: the solid, mature one who knows that the love of a good woman is better than drunken

kisses at Lucas's house party with a girl you'll never see again.

- A year or so ago, when I was crying about something to do with my dad, Freddie cupped my little wet face in his hands and said, "You're so magical that he doesn't know how to handle it, because *he's* not magical at all." There are moments in life, sometimes, where it feels like you've spent ages hiding parts of yourself underneath a really heavy rock, and then someone comes along and carefully heaves the rock off you, exposing all those vulnerable, hidden parts to the sun. That – the magical comment – was one of them. Why would Freddie have taken the time to move my rock away if he was going to leave?
- If I imagine myself as an eighty-year-old woman on my deathbed, requesting songs from my youth while one of my many grandchildren says, *Grandma, was it worth it – only ever being with Grandad your whole life?* I already know what I say. I look them dead in the eye, and I tell them, *Yes.*

3

The denial, part II

"The problem is," says Cassie, "I've got no way of telling if they're nice youths or troublemaking youths."

Cassie is the receptionist at the communal building my mum works in. In its heyday, this building was a church. I mean, it still is a church from the outside – if you walked past it on the street, you'd say, *Oh, look, there's a church.* There's a steeple and a few colourful stained-glass windows, but there have been no religious services in years; not since it got converted to this joint arts and events space.

Shared Universe is what they call it. There are yoga classes here, sing-song parent-and-baby groups, occasional street food pop-ups, craft shops, boutique design agencies and one solitary tattoo studio. My mum works at a small holistic food and vitamin store named Heather's Health. Heather is a tall, sarcastic woman who likes to wear tie-dye dungarees. She has a year-round cough, which leaves me feeling slightly sceptical about the concept of "Heather's Health" overall.

There's a big sign outside the church that says: ALL WELCOME / POP IN AND SAY HI.

The big sign, in my opinion, stretches the truth. If I owned this building, I'd edit it to: MOST PEOPLE WELCOME / BUT DON'T COME IN IF YOU'RE JUST GOING TO MESS AROUND AT THE FREE COFFEE STATION.

Cassie agrees with me, especially since groups of teenagers have now started to congregate in the seating area after 3 p.m.

"It's Phil, trying to keep the religious energy going," she whispers from behind her computer monitor. Cassie has one of those whispers that's just as loud as her usual speaking voice, only hissier. "But as I said to him, this isn't a church any more, Phil. You're a facilities manager, not a minister. You don't even believe in God. And now *I'm* the one left dealing with hooded children and caffeine thieves."

"Mm," I say. "Totally."

Mm, totally is about as much enthusiasm as I can muster in my current state. Nobody ever tells you – or they certainly never told me – that being dumped takes every single little thing you ever enjoyed about life and turns it into a pointless husk of an activity. Showering? An exhausting act. Family dinner? Waste of time. Conversations with someone you previously enjoyed talking to? The most tedious, soul-destroying thing in the world. Right now, everything I do takes so much effort I'm surprised I haven't passed out on the tiled church floor and been stretchered into Heather's Health for an overpriced alternative medical assessment.

"Phil's in Mexico this week, if you can believe it," Cassie continues, oblivious to my internal plight. "And of course he'll swan back in next Monday wanting to know where the monthly reports are, and you know what I'll say to him? I'll say, *Looks like you're going to have to finish them yourself, Phil, because I spent half my damn week chasing* pests *out of your building.*"

We both know that Cassie – famed for her fear of confrontation – will say nothing of the sort to Phil, but I nod to humour her anyway.

"The boys who were here this week just seemed curious," I add. "Bored and curious. I don't think there's much to keep them busy in the evenings."

Cassie lets out a puff of indignant air that wafts the edges of her wavy red hair. "They're welcome to help me with my paperwork, if they'd like."

I say nothing, and use the break in conversation to distract myself with the goings-on of the space around us. The downstairs atrium – the main thoroughfare of Shared Universe – is my favourite part of the church: a huge, airy zone with high, arched brickwork that drags your eyes up to the ceiling. On my right, two women are wrestling with a large plastic board, holding it above their heads in a valiant attempt to affix it to the local artists' display area.

"You're quiet today, bunny," says Cassie, gently prodding me in the thigh with a long purple fingernail. "Quieter than usual, anyway. What's the deal?"

Cassie calls every woman younger than her *bunny*. I don't know what it means, but I've never questioned it. When I see her – usually on slow Sundays like these, or on occasional weeknights when I'm feeling too lazy to walk home from sixth form – I am more than happy to be bunny.

"There's no deal," I tell her. My heart thuds against my ribcage, like it's trying to call me a liar, but I refuse to start using the word *break-up* just yet. "I mean, Freddie was being weird last night, talking about ending things, but I think it's just a freak-out. A temporary panic or something, now that we've hit our four-year anniversary."

Cassie has been happily married since the age of twenty, which is something I've always found very comforting. Her husband, Mike, doesn't seem like the kind of man who ever had a temporary panic – they've both got to be in their late forties or early fifties now, and every time Cassie's phone flashes it's always him on the other end. He sends her photos of their German Shepherd, Luna, on an hourly basis, and she writes back with an enthusiastic wall of pink heart emojis, every single time. Mike calls Cassie *pumpkin*, so maybe slightly unusual pet names are just par for the course in the Dunn household.

"Oh, Harley." Cassie's manicured hand returns to my thigh; she gives it a reassuring pat. "All you've got to remember is – he's young. You both are. He's entitled to a wobble, but he'll come around. And if he doesn't" – she waves a half-joking fist – "he'll have *me* to answer to."

A noise from the stairwell disturbs us – a high-vis guy clutching a cardboard box emerges and nods his way out of the building, closely followed by my mum. She's dressed in her usual Heather's Health get-up: sage green shirt, black straight-cut trousers and a large plastic badge that says ALICE.

"Hi, baby," she says, leaning across Cassie's desk to plant a kiss on the top of my head. "I am *so* done."

"How was the restock?" I ask her. Sundays – the quietest day in the store – are often when my mum and her colleague, Ruby, will be left strict instructions from Heather to unwrap the newly delivered boxes of products in the stock room and replenish the shelves with whatever they're low on.

She grimaces. "If I have to see another packet of porridge oats today, I am going to scream. Other than that … loosely acceptable."

Acceptable is the word we use to describe our days, a lot of the time. My mum always used to tell me to have a *good* day, or a *great* day, or a *wonderful* day, which in my view felt like a lot of pressure to put on the poor day before it had even begun. When I pointed this out, she offered up a new alternative: *have an acceptable day*. It's not good, or bad – it's just manageable. It'll do what it needs to do.

We say our goodbyes to Cassie and head on out to the car together, and I wonder if there'll be a point in the future where my days feel acceptable again.

"Cassie's right," says my mum, tucking her legs to one side on the sofa. Our entire living room is painted in a plummy purple colour, and the worn velvet couch is part of the same palette. "Things are starting to feel real for Freddie – September, living together, the whole deal. That's understandable. Here's my prediction: he'll go on this trip with his family, he'll climb up the Eiffel Tower, he'll think, *God, I miss my beautiful girlfriend*, and he'll come home ready to talk."

She leans forward to blow out the incense stick on the coffee table in front of us, like, *That's that*. One of the perks of working at Heather's Health is the various freebies Heather is willing to give away. I'm not a fan of incense – the scent leaves my nose claustrophobic and desperate for fresh air. But my mum cannot get enough of the stuff, and has stockpiled it in one of our kitchen cupboards.

I take a bite of my banana and speak while I'm chewing. It tastes like glue. Everything I've eaten since yesterday tastes like glue.

"What if that's not what happens? What if he climbs the

Eiffel Tower and thinks, *I'm so glad Harley isn't here; all she'd have done is complain about the exercise and get annoyed by all the people*? What if he meant everything he said last night?"

The thought is so painful – so alien to me – that I feel a brand-new avalanche strike in the walls of my chest. Memories falling down into craters, smashing into smithereens before I can catch them and store them away. Even here, in the living room, there are still reminders of Freddie everywhere I look. The lavender-coloured woollen throw he bought for my mum's Christmas gift last year. The stack of Agatha Christie novels his dad lent me and told me to hold on to because nobody in the Lee household appreciated them the way I did. The drawing Freddie did of me for his Year Eleven art project that my mum thought was so lifelike she took it to the local framers and then nailed it to the wall, even though *I* thought he'd made me look like a long-haired Hugh Jackman.

This is *our* room, mine and his. This is the scene of our first argument, our first slow dance, our first frantic tugging-off of T-shirts when the kisses finally turned into something else.

"If that's what he's decided, you can't stop him," my mum says now, reaching over to stroke my hair. "But trust me, you wouldn't want to, because there is *nothing* less fun in life than a one-sided relationship."

She makes cryptic comments like this every so often, and given that she hasn't, to my knowledge, dated a single man since my dad, I have to assume that she's referring to him. My mum thinks men, for the most part, are a waste of our time. She makes an exception for Daniel Craig, for obvious reasons, and Freddie, I guess because she got to know him. "You've got one of the good ones," she'd always tell me, and Freddie would beam at the compliment, like being *one of the good ones* was all he'd ever wanted to be.

I questioned her dating apathy a few years ago, and she told me that the romantic part of her life was over and done with, at least for now. "Besides, we've got each other, haven't we?" she'd said, prodding my cheek. "You're the *real* love of my life, Harley Beth." I'd thought this was cute, but also kind of depressing, given that my mum is only thirty-seven years old and could probably have many more loves of her life if she just dedicated some time to it.

She untucks her legs now and yawns as she gets to her feet, before padding away to the kitchen in her slippers to switch the kettle on. "Mint, Harl? Green tea?"

I shout back to request camomile, then return to my thoughts, which are mostly made up of Freddie surrounded by French girls named Celine and Marie – girls that represent freedom and the future and aren't sat at home crying in an oversized sweatshirt. *Vive la France*, says Freddie, clinking his champagne glass against theirs, *and goodbye forever to Harley Green.*

No. That isn't Freddie. He's in Paris with family, ready for his cousin's mid-week wedding – he's going to come home with a keyring for his grandma, not a brand-new girlfriend. Not this soon.

Only half convinced, I pull out my phone, click on to Instagram, then wait a second for his profile to load – and what I see makes me let out a wail so painful my mum comes careering back into the room, teabag in hand.

Every single reference to me on Freddie's profile has disappeared. The *HG <3* initials in his bio. The photos from Comic-Con, with Freddie dressed as the tenth Doctor and me as Rose Tyler; the birthday parties at his parents' house, me grinning at their kitchen table with a goblet of orange juice as big as my head. All the images of us posing in front of my bedroom mirror, with Freddie's arms wrapped protectively around my waist.

Deleted. Zapped away from his life, forever.

There's just one new post on the page – a photo of him standing in front of the Arc de Triomphe. The sky is blue; the sun is shining. He's styled his hair – a rarity for Freddie – and tipped his chin up slightly. Here's to new beginnings ☺ says the caption. Three hundred and sixty-two people have Liked it. Multiple people have commented on it to heartily congratulate Freddie on these *new beginnings*.

joshua33222: Yes mate onwards n upwards

lucassmallwoooood: here we GO

priyesh_everywhere: Looking good buddy!!!

Freddie's replied to them all with saluting emojis, except for one – from Minnie's verified MusingsWithMin account – that just says: So proud of you. You deserve the world. To this, he's responded: Love u. Time to go get it!!

There was a time when Freddie would call me his world. Thinking about it now, it's been months since he's used that phrase, but it was a favourite of his for a while. *You're my world, Harl. You're my literal universe*, he'd say as he held me, and I'd smile so hard I thought my face was going to crack. But I'm not his world any more. To Freddie, the world is something else entirely now – it goes beyond my face, my thoughts, my living room. It's exciting and unchartered territory, ready for him to explore without me, like a teenage Indiana Jones.

The avalanche returns to my stomach. I reach forward for the empty fruit bowl on the coffee table in front of me, thrust it under my chin, and vomit.

4

The sign

Not content with taking my boyfriend away, the universe also decides to rob me of my ability to sleep. I wriggle around in bed like a fish in a net: frightened, breathless, desperate for someone to take pity on me and drop me back where I belong. At 3.55 a.m. on Monday, after doing deep breaths to a guided meditation for so long I feel like I'm going to scream, I give up and switch my bedside lamp back on.

"Remember: when we have problems, it's easy to zoom in on them and believe that life is controlled by all our small, insignificant issues," whispers the meditation's narrator, who has clearly never been dumped by anyone, least of all Freddie. "But when we zoom back out again, we can realize that this *really doesn't matter.* Our time on Earth is short; it's as fleeting as a firefly."

"Good to know," I mutter into the ether as I exit the app. I may not be able to sleep, but at least I can now add *Death is on its way for all of us* to my growing list of 3 a.m. concerns.

You hear a lot of stuff about blue light these days, but it's difficult to care about eye health when your boyfriend has decided to delete every trace of you from his personal corner of the internet. I refuse to squint, stubbornly leaning into the masochism of it all, and then shudder as I click back on to Freddie's profile, which has reloaded with fresh updates since the last time I checked it.

freddielee277 7h – Seeing the Champs Eleeyzee was amazing!!

freddielee277 6h – Best meal of my life

freddielee277 4h – We met a French cat lol

Normally I'd Like all three of these posts, one after the other, like a muscle memory. I'd heart-eye react to one of them, partly to be extra supportive and partly to remind the algorithm that Freddie and I love each other deeply. I'd probably reply to the mention of the *Champs Eleeyzee* and lovingly mock his ropy spelling. But today I do nothing.

Do Freddie's family know about our break-up? Why are they wandering around meeting French cats instead of grieving the loss of their future daughter-in-law? Why hasn't his mum texted me? *So sorry to hear the news about you and Freddie. If it helps to know, we all think he's making a terrible mistake, one that will haunt him for decades to come. You're a part of our family, and you always will be.*

I manage to fall asleep just after 5 a.m. and spend a fitful hour dreaming about Freddie. We're on a train together – one of those packed-in rush-hour trains where everyone's standing in the corridor – and it's our first date again, just after we've kissed for the first time. When we reach our stop, Freddie steps off the train and on to the platform, but I get stuck, penned in behind a crowd of other passengers holding shopping bags who won't let me leave. I call out for Freddie – I shout his name, and the twitch of his head tells that he hears me, but the train shunts away from the station and he doesn't do a thing to help. He just shrugs, walks towards the Exit sign, and leaves me behind.

Being at sixth form without him feels like starting at primary school all over again, like I'm a four-year-old with no safety net. I deliberately avoid our usual early-morning stop-off at the campus coffee shop – even without Freddie here, I'd rather not show my face and risk running into Joshua and Lucas.

Lucas has a nervous laugh and Joshua has a large, ostentatious moustache that I can tell Freddie is slightly envious of. He met them both in Year Twelve, within the first few months of us starting at our town's massive sixth-form college. They're not bad people, but if I had to pick friends for Freddie, I wouldn't have picked them. I know what Joshua, especially, is like. He'll pretend to have no idea about the break-up until I confirm it, out of some annoying fraternal loyalty to Freddie. He'll just offer me a patronizing smile and say something snoopy, like, *How's our Frederick getting on in the city of love?*

You tell me, asshole.

It's not that I blame Joshua for any of this. He's not really an asshole, or some kind of evil dictator who's personally responsible for Freddie breaking up with me. He's just an eighteen-year-old boy. It's more that when Joshua dumped his girlfriend – tiny, gossipy Erin – a month ago, something weird happened. We were sitting at a table in the cafe with him after the event, and I'd asked if he was OK, because I wasn't exactly expecting tears but I *was* expecting at least a little emotion, and Joshua had said, "Honestly, I'm fine. She's fine. We both knew it couldn't last – not with *next year* and everything." And Freddie had nodded instantly and said, "Oh, yeah," like he wholeheartedly agreed. Like there was no way anything romantic could ever hope to make it out of one educational institution and into a second.

After that, the concept of *next year* was mentioned from time to time, and I became a little warier when he hung out with Joshua.

Without my normal Freddie-filled routine, I've arrived early today; there are a whole twenty minutes of nothingness to fill before English class starts. I decide to take this realization as a positive: I can eat my breakfast banana, even though it will probably taste just as glue-like as its siblings. I can take some futile deep breaths again, and practise pretending to be a functioning human as I perch in the entrance hall of the English and Social Sciences block. This particular block – affectionately known as the ESS to its wordy inhabitants – is a large slanty-roofed building that's seen much better days but is still somehow clinging on. There's a social space in the entrance hall, complete with cosy armchairs and vending machines, and two large doors – the left one for the English students and the right one for the sociology and psychology classes.

I sink into a squashy entrance-hall armchair, next to a space on the wall that seems to be in use as some kind of community noticeboard. One piece of pinned white paper asks for a French tutor, which immediately makes me think of Freddie and wince. Another is looking for a bass player, for a band that describes itself as: SO, SO BAD, BUT IN A WAY THAT KIND OF WORKS???

And then, in the bottom-right corner of the board, printed out on a bright-red sheet of paper and decorated with glittery hearts, I see something different:

THE RECENTLY DUMPED CLUB
Being broken up with is one of the hardest things a person can go through.

Rejection! Heartbreak! Shock! Anger! Grief! Denial! If you're feeling some – or all – of these emotions right now, you're not alone.

Need support? Come and join the Recently Dumped Club. We're a new group of very nice people in relationship recovery, with one goal: to use positive tips and tricks to come to terms with our pain and enjoy life again.

Meetings: Wednesdays, 12–12.30 p.m. in the P2 psychology classroom. Introductory sign-up session this Tuesday, 6th January, with full sessions starting for six weeks from Wednesday 7th January.

See you there!
Dahlia (Year Thirteen psychology)

I chew on my banana and stare at the red sheet for a while, wondering whether to believe what it's telling me. *A recently dumped club?*

Cassie would call this *a sign from the universe*. She is a big believer in signs from the universe – she gives her colleagues knowing looks whenever the office clock says 11:11 and, once, when an orange tortoiseshell butterfly accidentally wafted in with the postman and landed on her desk, she insisted that it was "almost definitely" her dead father in insect form.

But *is* this a tortoiseshell butterfly-esque sign from the universe? Is this an invisible hand on my back to steer me in a happier, brighter, Freddieless direction? Or is it just … an A4 poster, for a very specific club that has absolutely nothing to do with me?

Maybe I will humour the universe, I think. *I have no better options right now.*

Breathless, I reach out with my phone, snap a photo of the red sheet of paper, then shove the evidence back into my pocket before anybody sees.

5

The persuasion

There's a sad, strange stillness that sits heavy inside of me while I unpack my bag in the English literature classroom. It isn't just that I miss Freddie as a person – although I do, so much it makes my chest feel like it's about to explode. It's the fact that *we*, as an entity, might now be gone forever. It's the sudden, terrifying realization that if this is real – if he means it – then every single little tradition we ever had together doesn't exist any more.

Freddie's never going to make me another badly drawn birthday card and say, *That's me, and that's you,* as he points to the cartoon couple on it. He's never going to delicately tuck my fringe behind my ear when I'm painting my nails and it's getting in my eyes. He's never going to toast one of those supermarket English muffins, butter it and offer me the top part – the lid – because he knows I like that half the best. He's never going to do another late-night drop-in on Christmas Day and sit with me and my mum to watch *The Holiday*, even though he hates *The Holiday* because he thinks that none of the characters seem like real people except for the old man with the ancient film career.

Everything we did together: gone. Evaporated. Like it never even happened at all.

"The boys in this place are out of *control*," says Bella, dropping into the seat next to me.

Bella has a thick, dark mop of pixie-cut hair and a very real interest in angry-girl fiction. She wears bright-red lipstick every day, at the suggestion of her late grandmother, who told Bella as a child that it is impossible for anybody to mess with you when your mouth is the same colour as a cayenne pepper. I made a beeline for Bella in our first ever lesson together because I saw a sticker on her hardback notepad that said HOT GIRLS READ BOOKS, and then, immediately afterwards, another that said DON'T BE A DICK. If I had to spend my time with anyone in that English classroom, Bella seemed like a sensible choice.

"Absolute villains," I say, turning round in my seat, ready to aim daggers at the boys in question. *Villains* is an insult that Bella uses a lot, and it's rubbed off on me. "What have they done now?"

She scowls with both of her brows. "One of them just bashed into me in the corridor and said absolutely nothing.

Not an apology. Not even a backwards glance. Just bounced off me and carried on walking. I *hissed* at him."

"A literal hiss?" I can see it happening. One time, Bella overheard a boy in the cafeteria rating girls in the vicinity out of ten, and immediately grabbed him by the ear so she could deliver him to Principal Withers' office in person. From her, a hiss is low stakes.

"Like a snake," she grins as she removes her phone and a bright-pink pen from her cardigan pocket. "How was your Christmas? Oh shit, how was your anniversary? Wasn't it that whole four-years thing?"

I pull my books towards me on the desk as I try to work out exactly how to answer these questions. We started reading *Atonement* at the end of last term, which I already feel very invested in but Bella can't stand; she thinks it is overly descriptive. "If Ian McEwan sets *one* more scene for me," she'll murmur under her breath as we read out loud, "I swear to God."

"It *was* a four-years thing," I tell her now. My hands have developed a tremor in the last few seconds, as though the mere mention of Freddie is enough to throw my entire body into disarray. "It's now a no-years thing. Freddie decided that the best way to celebrate our anniversary was to take me to a fairground and tell me he doesn't want to be my boyfriend any more. He doesn't want to go to university with me or have sex with me or even eat dinner with me. So. There we are."

Bella is the first person to hear it like this. When I told my mum and Cassie about the break-up, I was careful to leave out the details and quick to throw in protective phrases like, *He seemed stressed*, or, *I don't know if he meant it*, or, *I think the death of his hamster has impacted him more than he knows*. Now, with Bella, is the first time I've formulated my thoughts into honest, scary language – the first time I've actually admitted the truth.

"What?" Bella's eyes widen considerably at this news; she abandons her phone, twisting it over so it's face-down when it reaches the table. "*Why?*"

I lower my voice to a mutter as more students pile into the room. "The summary is that I don't know how to have fun. The longer version is that I am going to be an old woman who's allowed life to pass me by, and the thought of us being together next year in our boring apartment with our boring TV shows and my boring personality is no longer appealing to him."

Bella's pepper-red upper lip curls into a supportive sneer. "Oh, sure. Roughly translated: 'I'm planning to be single in September so that I can contract guilt-free gonorrhoea by the end of Freshers Week'."

"Nobody *wants* to contract gonorrhoea," I point out, but it emerges as more of a shaky question than a statement. "Right?"

"Boys want all kinds of things," she replies dully. "Who knows if gonorrhoea is among them?"

A girl clutching a stack of books flashes us an alarmed look as she enters the classroom; Bella provides her with a mischievous eyebrow raise in return, then remembers the severity of the situation and places a delicate hand on my wrist.

"I'm sorry, Harl. Maybe I'm wrong. Maybe sexually transmitted diseases aren't on his autumn to-do list at all."

The multiple mentions of gonorrhoea aren't exactly bolstering, but her immediate show of support makes me feel a little lighter – a little more understood – so I choose to ask the question that's been lurking at the back of my mind since the Ferris wheel. "Do … uh, do *you* think I'm allowing life to pass me by?"

"No." Bella removes her hand from my wrist and uses it to scratch the tip of her button nose. "You're an introvert, so the rules are different. I think, in your own way, you're actually a big fan of life. Maybe sometimes a little *afraid* of life, but—"

"How can somebody be *afraid of life*?" I cut in. Her too? "Life is not a horror movie. Life is not a ghost train. Here I am, doing my best in the English classroom. What more do you people want?"

Bella holds up a finger to pause me. "But what I was going to say is: do I think that this makes you boring? Unexciting? No. Do I think you're a precious human being who deserves to date someone who thinks her quirks are perfect? Yes, Harley. I really do."

There's a pause while the final students rush in and Karen closes the door. Karen has a pierced septum and a Kermit the Frog mug, which made her my and Bella's favourite teacher on sight. Ever since then, she's only added to our list of reasons. I hear other people refer to her as *Ms Mountford*, but she's never asked for any of us to call her that – so, to our class, she is simply Karen.

"Good morning, Year Thirteen!" says Karen, smoothing her leopard-print shirt. "I hope everyone had a wonderful festive break. I, on the other hand, spent the majority of it helping my brother move house, and now I have a bad back from carrying boxes of comic books into his spare room. But such is life, I suppose, when you're in your late thirties." She clasps her hands together and squints at the students in front of her, crinkling the bridge of her nose with excitement.

"Four *years*," Bella whispers, while Karen tells us about an upcoming trip to the Royal Shakespeare Company. "That's basically a quarter of your life. That's how long it took them to build the entire Golden Gate Bridge. No wonder you feel so hideous."

What I enjoy the most about Bella is how unfazed she is when people talk about things like bad moods and break-ups. There are people out there who push their positivity so hard that it starts to feel like a religion – people who expect you to go through every single one of life's hardships with a large, fake smile plastered across your face. *It could be worse!*

they'll say. *Look on the bright side! No point in letting things get you down!* Bella, on the other hand, will hear someone's story and tell them, *I mean, it could be better. Where even IS the bright side? If I were you, things would be getting me* so *down right now that I would be packing my bags, going to live in Sweden and never coming back.* I appreciate that kind of honesty in a person.

"I saw that there's this lunchtime club," I tell her. "Some free group-therapy thing in the psychology room, where they teach you how to accept being broken up with."

"Jesus, that's niche," mutters Bella, and I nod in agreement. "When I got dumped, all *I* got was a 'these things happen' talk from my mother."

I hate the word *dumped*. The connotations are all horrendous. It makes me think of being bundled into a comedy canvas sack and booted off the side of a cliff. It makes me think of literal shit.

Checking to make sure Karen isn't watching, I reach into a pocket for my phone, unlock it to the photo I took earlier this morning, then push it over to Bella on the table – face-down, like we're in the middle of a covert drug deal. Bella takes the phone, flips it over subtly, and flits her eyes from side to side as she reads.

"Y'know, this actually sounds good."

I shake my head. "It sounds embarrassing. It sounds like an extracurricular lunchtime activity for people who've been rejected."

"No, I don't see it that way," she says, and I can tell from her tone that she means it. "It's not a reject club. Think of it as a … a self-development club. A mental health club." She pushes the phone back to me. "You want my opinion? I say go. I say go, embrace the help and emerge a happier person. What is there to lose?"

At the end of the lesson, as we're packing our belongings back into our bags, a bucket-hatted girl outside our classroom – Bella's friend Riya – waves through the glass in our direction. Bella nods at Riya – *one second* – and then turns back to face me.

"We're going for burgers. Want to come with?"

I shake my head. "I don't feel very sociable right now."

"Girl, nobody ever feels sociable when they get dumped. The unspoken rule is that you have to force it for a while, until you're capable of enjoying things organically again." She swings her shoulder bag over one arm. "C'mon. Not even a ten-minute lunch with me, Riya and some disgusting cafeteria food?"

"Isabella Marchetti," shouts Riya. "If I don't eat in the next thirty seconds I am going to *die*."

"Harley is dealing with some life-changing shit," calls Bella in return. "Your stomach cannot be my priority right now."

"Let's have a little less of the yelling, please, Bella," says

Karen as she rubs at the whiteboard, but I can hear from her voice that she's smiling. Karen once told Bella that she admires her *joie de vivre*, and Bella has never forgotten it.

"I'm a woman in demand, Karen," says Bella, as she bundles herself out of the room. "It's a miracle I can keep up."

Before she disappears, she leans back around the door frame and points at me with an accusing finger. "Next time I see you, you better have signed up for that club." I open my mouth to argue, but Bella shakes her head, pressing the same finger to her mouth in a hushing motion. "Harley. People want to help you. Let them."

6

The embrace

There's no better way to remind yourself that you're alone and unloved, I think to myself on Tuesday lunchtime, *than by turning up to an entire classroom full of people who are also alone and unloved.*

As I head into the ESS building, I try not to picture the scene that awaits me, but I also can't help it. My brain works overtime, providing me with a scene-by-scene reel of what I might be walking into – and in this reel, things are bleak. Thoroughly bleak. Framed photos of ex-partners adorn the desks; mandated trust-falls take place on a regular basis; almost everyone is crying.

The reality, however, is not at all like the reel. I step into a room of around twenty silent, slightly apprehensive-looking students, and a couple of them turn to stare at me from their seats. No one exactly seems *thrilled* to be here – probably because we've all just been brutally discarded by people who purported to love us – but no one is openly sobbing, either.

"Another new member!" yells out the girl who's waiting at the front of the classroom. I pull a thin-lipped, self-conscious smile at her as I gently close the door, and she returns it with a beam. "Hello – I'm Dahlia Kumar. So glad to see you here."

It feels like there's a foreign object in my throat as I swallow.

"I'm … Harley Green."

Dahlia has large dark eyes, hair that moves from jet black at the roots to a letterbox red at the ends, and the kind of deep-set cheekbones I'm always a little jealous of. She's standing in front of a whiteboard, where the words I CAN GET THROUGH THIS peek out behind her in thick green marker. I admire the whiteboard's optimism.

"OK!" calls Dahlia. "I think this might be it, so let's get the whole gang acquainted. Are we all up for out-loud introductions?"

A few people groan, but most of us nod or say nothing at all, which Dahlia takes as a positive sign.

"Cool," she says brightly. "I'll start us off. SO, my name is Dahlia, and I'm eighteen years old. Next year I'll be studying psychology and counselling – so I can be a therapist one day, I hope – and leading these sessions is part of my application. Kinda like group therapy."

She pauses, looking around the room and fixing her grin on a girl a few rows in front of me. "But also, as well as the professional side, I want you all to know that I *get* it. I've experienced it. My friend Kiran and I had our hearts broken at the exact same time, and we realized that community is what counts when it comes to stuff like this. Because, y'know … no man is an island, et cetera et cetera. And it helps to hang out with people who've been through it. People who understand."

"Literally nobody understands," hisses a pink-haired girl in the front row. "My dad keeps saying, 'It is what it is!' and offering me slices of cake, as if that's going to magically fix things."

"This is why you've come to the right place," says Dahlia, bowing a sympathetic eyebrow. "We offer doughnuts, but we also offer practical guidance to help you through. Nobody in this room is going to say the words 'it is what it is' to you. I promise."

The pink-haired girl nods, but doesn't seem fully convinced.

We move around the room for the rest of the introductions. The kid sitting a few seats to my right – Joey – shares that he was dumped in September, right at the start of term. "I thought I was fine after a couple of weeks – I was dating again, the whole thing," he says, still looking at the desk in front of him. "And then I saw my ex for the first time since it all happened and our whole relationship came back to me. Anyway, I instantly threw up on my own shoes."

Instinctively, we all go to stare at Joey's thick-soled trainers. "Not *these* shoes," he groans, his face flushing crimson. As a fellow vomiter in this time of crisis, I feel a pull of camaraderie towards him.

The pink-haired girl's name, I learn, is Lucy – she tells the group that her girlfriend broke up with her last month and has now blocked her on every social media platform going, including Pinterest. "A new low," she says gloomily. "Even for me."

The stories shared are mostly familiar – the classic, well-trodden tales of "everything going fine, until…" and, "it came out of NOWHERE". Nobody says that they expected the break-up. Instead, we're all in shock – bonded by the fact that we were once safe in a snow globe that someone has now shaken and smashed.

"And our final new member is Harley Green, at the back," says Dahlia. "Harley, what about you?"

Addressing rooms full of people is not my speciality – never has been – but I can just about switch it on when I need to. I try my hardest to swallow the lump that keeps respawning in my throat.

"Uh, hey. Like Dahlia said, I'm Harley. I was with my boyfriend, Freddie, for four years – we were each other's first love. First everything, really." I feel heat creep into the tops of my ears as I immediately regret the words that just left my mouth. The subtext of: *we had a lot of sloppy first-timer sex, and now he wants to go and level up with somebody else.* "Anyway, he t—"

I'm interrupted as the door to the psychology classroom crashes open and a tall sandy-haired boy falls through it.

"Shit!" says the boy. "I'm so sorry. I'm so *late*."

He pulls himself into a straighter stance, having crumpled up a little on his way through the door, and brushes something off his tracksuit bottoms. He looks as though he's just run here straight from PE – he's in full sportswear, with a large half-zipped backpack hanging loosely from the top of a bicep, like it didn't quite get the chance to make its way up to his shoulder.

"Better late than never," says Dahlia, who seems to mean it. "Grab a seat – we're just finishing off introductions."

"Oh," says the boy brightly. "Well, in that case."

He spins on the floor and then heads for the seated group members, raising his chin slightly into the air as he searches for a chair. There's still a spare one next to me and he clocks it, squeezing himself through the gaps between the desks, offering further apologies when he accidentally bashes Lucy in the head with his backpack, and then, finally, settling in, seemingly unaware of the silent classroom of people observing him.

"I'm Seth," he says loudly, shimmying the bag strap down his upper arm and prodding a sweatshirt sleeve back into the half-zipped compartment. "I like basketball and athletics and … well, I guess all sports, really. Apparently I'm an Aries, which is probably important if you're into that sort of thing. I have a very old dog named Mr Wilson. He's a great guy." He pauses, scratching at a chunk of hair. "It's, uh … it's good to meet you all."

The silence continues while the group members try to work out what to make of this newcomer. Lucy, still rubbing at her head, scowls at him in disbelief. Another girl, whose boyfriend has recently moved to New Zealand to intern for his cousin's tech startup, nods encouragingly. Seth, apparently oblivious to all of it, deposits his backpack on to the carpet, humming a tune under his breath.

"Sagittarius," says Dahlia diplomatically, pulling a mini curtsy. "So good to meet you, Seth, and we'll *absolutely* come back to you in a second, but Harley – right next to you – was actually just in the middle of her own introduction."

Seth gasps at this tactful news. "Oh my God. I'm so sorry." He turns to me and puts both hands in the air, like he's trying to reason with law enforcement or hold back an angry mob, instead of apologizing to a mild-mannered stranger. "Truly, I am *so* sorry. I get nervous, and then I stop taking in the world around me, and then shit like this happens. Please, go on."

"It's fine," I tell him, because it is. "I was pretty much done, anyway. Same guy, four years, first love, blah blah."

"Four *years*?" Seth whacks his hands on the desk in front of him, palms flat out against the table, like he has no concept of the fact that the other members of the club are waiting patiently at their desks while they listen to this back-and-forth. "And then he just … what, out-of-the-blue ended it?"

I nod to confirm, semi-grateful for the validation, but his energy is so chaotic that I feel a little like I've been winded.

Seth shakes his head in supportive disbelief. "Good *grief*."

I aim a desperate smile at Dahlia to show her I'm ready for the group's attention to move swiftly away from me, and she gives me a decisive thumbs up.

"Back to Seth – our final *final* introduction. What brings you here, Seth?"

"Well, it wasn't four years, but it *was* a full fifteen months," says Seth, resting his right foot on his left thigh so his legs make a triangle shape. "Which is still a long time, in my book. Her name was – is – Genevieve. Gen. She dumped me on Christmas Eve, right as we were supposed to do our gift exchange, so …" He lets out a huff of disappointment. "Here I am, I guess."

He looks at the floor now, abruptly shutting down, like one of those coin-operated kiddie rides in a shopping centre. I feel like I know him from somewhere, though I have no idea what that somewhere might be. Maybe he's one of Freddie's forgettable science classmates, the ones that always wander over to our table while we're eating lunch and invite him to weekend events without looking in my direction. I really, really hope not.

Dahlia nods. "Welcome. I'm so glad to have you

here – to have you *all* here. First up, I need to go through some ground rules – nothing too serious, but just to make sure everyone feels safe to be vulnerable."

She opens a pale-pink laptop in front of her. It's covered in stickers – a collage of them take over the entire front of it. From my seat on the back row, I make out an especially large glitter-bordered sticker that says YOUR FUTURE THERAPIST.

Dahlia begins to scroll, reciting as she goes. "OK. The first rule of Recently Dumped Club is: do *not* talk about Recently Dumped Club." There's a snort of quiet laughter from Joey – shoe-vomit guy – and Dahlia gleefully crinkles her nose in his direction. "Movie references aside, I really do mean it. You can tell people that you come here, obviously, and you're welcome to invite other people to join when we reopen next term – this isn't a secret group – but anything that's said within these four walls needs to stay confidential. This is a safe space for us to talk openly and try to heal. Do we all agree on that?"

A few people – myself included – nod or murmur quiet yesses of agreement.

"Do we all *agree* on that?" says Dahlia, a little more forcefully this time, like a children's party entertainer who's looking for some slightly more confident *woo*s. When she's finished her rule-sharing, she gently snaps the stickered laptop closed. "Now. We meet as a group, but a lot of our tasks involve working in pairs. So, let's get you sorted." She reaches down for the clipboard she was holding when I first walked in. "Uh, Reyan? You're with … Sara."

A sleepy-looking boy with broad shoulders and dark stubble stands up, ready to go sit with the girl whose boyfriend has moved to New Zealand.

"Oliver, you're with Nav. Maryam … you're with Daisy." She pauses, glancing back down to the clipboard. "Harley?" I wave, and she carries on. "You're with Seth."

Wonderful – saddled with the boy who interrupts everyone and can't even manage to show up on time. If anyone is going to be able to help me overcome the painful complexities of my break-up, I can guarantee that it is not going to be him.

The boy in question jolts back to life at the sound of his name and swivels to face me. "Dream team. Harley and Seth. Should we have a team name? Perhaps 'Sarley'. Perhaps 'Heth'. *Or* maybe we come up with something inspirational, like … FORTITUDE. What are your thoughts on FORTITUDE?"

He beams, like a dog waiting for its walk, and I stare at his mouth. I always notice the size of people's teeth – some people have shy, tiny things, like little pearls hiding behind their lips. Others have giant, confident teeth. Seth's – white and alarmingly well-aligned – look like they should be applying for drama school. There's a tiny smattering of caramel freckles on his nose, the kind that look like somebody flicked a paintbrush and somebody else was in the way.

I glance down at his knee, which has been bouncing up and down like there's some sort of mini trampoline in his shoe. "I don't love FORTITUDE, to be honest with you."

"That's fine," says Seth, bringing the knee to a halt. He speaks like an auctioneer – sped-up words crammed into a sentence, with a little pause until the next one begins. "Neither do I. It was a blink-and-you-hate-it idea. What abou—"

"Do we actually need a name?" I cut across him. "I mean, I think just knowing we're a couple is fine." He raises an eyebrow, and I let out a tiny sigh of embarrassment. "A *pair*, I mean. Knowing we're working together is enough."

"Sure." He stretches back in the chair and raises his arms above him, clasping his fingers together and breaking into a yawn, which he immediately cuts short in order to blurt out a brand-new thought. "Hey, what about a motto?"

"I don't thi—"

"*Rejected but not dejected.*" He thrusts his hands out in front of him, like he's holding up a banner. "We could get it on a pin badge."

"Speak for yourself," I tell him haughtily. "I'm incredibly dejected."

Other pairs in the room seem to be getting on just fine. Reyan and Sara are deep in conversation; Joey and a boy whose name I can't remember are high-fiving over a shared interest in shōnen anime. I, on the other hand, am sat here discussing mottos with a boy who seems to think we're applying to be contestants on *The Apprentice*.

He slumps down from the imaginary banner-holding, finally taking the hint, and flashes a look of irritation my way. "You don't say."

"Well, this is the place to say it," I shoot back. "I'm rejected and dejected, I don't want a team name, and I don't require a motto. This isn't the football club. I just want to learn whatever it is we're going to learn here and then be on my way."

Seth makes an *mm* sound, like it all makes sense now. "I see. A classic *no need*er if I ever saw one."

"I am not a *no need*er," I protest. I have no idea what a *no need*er is, but it feels like an insult, and I refuse to take insults from someone I'd never heard of ten minutes ago. "What do you even mean?"

"It's what my mum calls my dad when he says, 'There's really no need, Pam.' You're, like, the anti-effort police; everything is too much for you. Christmas decorations up on the front of the house? *No need.* A complicated meal that takes three hours to make? *No need.* Crochet a little hat for the dog just because it'll look sweet? *No need.*" He grins at me. "Group name? *No need.*"

I don't return his grin. "Well, for this there *is* no need. I fail to see how that's any kind of character flaw."

He shrugs. "It isn't a character flaw. It's just funny."

I cross my arms over my chest as Dahlia calls out to the

group, waving her hands to get everyone's attention. "Stick around if you've got questions for me – but if not, meet back here for our first proper session tomorrow. And remember the golden rule: *sit in your pair, get ready to share.* This is where it gets interesting."

"Well, see you tomorrow," says Seth. He leans down to collect his rucksack, then glances back over a shoulder at me, his green eyes twinkling. "I'll make sure to bring your pin badge."

I side-eye him so aggressively it actually hurts a little. "Please don't."

From the other side of the room, Dahlia throws me a thumbs up of encouragement. I echo it, with absolutely no enthusiasm at all.

7

The start of it all

Seth, unsurprisingly, is late again on Wednesday. He misses Dahlia's instructions, a tearful entrance from Lucy the Pinterest girl, and a large flapjack platter, courtesy of Joey's dad.

"I'm here!" he yelps, slamming the door closed behind him. "I'm here, and I'm ready to learn." He grabs a flapjack on his travels, thrusting it into his mouth as he zips towards our back-row seats. "I phomithe."

Everyone else, already deep in conversation, gives him a look that says, *Shush.*

"We've got a task to do," I hiss, while Seth takes off his jacket and hangs it on the back of his chair. It's dark red, one of those cosy-looking plaid things that's like a shirt has joined forces with a jumper, and underneath it is a black T-shirt with the word BARISTA printed in a bold white font. I point at the word. "Do … do you work in the sixth-form coffee shop?"

He swallows the flapjack bite. "I do. One morning a week, during my free periods."

I snap my fingers together. "*That's* where I know you from."

During one of my and Freddie's many early-morning trips to the coffee shop, a sandy-haired barista had spilled apple juice over Freddie's biology textbook and apologized so many times that Freddie had to pat him on the arm and say, "Please, buddy, these things happen."

Seth's eyes are blank. "I have no memory, sorry. But I do serve a lot of people. What do you order?"

"A mint tea," I tell him. Heather (of Heather's Health) showed me an article about the perils of caffeine six months ago, and I can't unlearn the knowledge I picked up. "That's my usual."

"*Oh*," he says, as though he suddenly understands something new. "Well, that'll be it. I remember the fussy kids who ask for an extra-hot decaf vanilla latte with sugar-free syrup and almond milk, mostly because of the trauma they cause me. You're a mint-tea girl. You're very low maintenance, and therefore very forgettable."

"Great. Thanks."

"Trust me, it's a compliment. If I remembered you, it would be a bad sign." He uses both hands to ruffle his hair forward, so that it sits more messily at the front of his head.

"Do you remember *me*?"

"Well, I didn't, but I do now," I say. "I just needed to place you."

Seth raises both of his eyebrows, like, *Well. There we are then.*

I take a moment to flatten the sheet of A4 paper in front of me. "We're supposed to be talking about our relationships. The ones that have ended, I mean. Dahlia wants us to go back to the beginning together and … y'know. Dive into the backstory."

Those, to be fair, were Dahlia's exact words. "People don't often take the time to process after a break-up," she'd added. "They try to move on too quickly without actually acknowledging the hurt that they're feeling or the impact the relationship had on their life."

So, today, we're starting at the start. We're acknowledging the hurt and the impact.

Seth's face falls at the idea of it. The faint lines under his eyes – the ones that come into play when he smiles, which is a lot of the time – disappear immediately.

"That sounds hideous. I thought this whole thing was about us *moving on* and *feeling better*?"

"I don't know what to tell you." I nudge my head towards the front of the room. "Dahlia has a plan."

Dahlia is kneeling down next to Lucy's desk, offering up a small box of tissues. Lucy takes one and blows her nose with ferocity. I point at the whiteboard behind her, where

Dahlia has written down three questions for us to discuss in our pairs.

When and where did you meet?
How did you first know you liked them?
Tell your partner about the first date...

"Why don't you tell me … *when* and *where* you met your ex?" I ask him, holding a pen in one hand and deliberately sticking to the script.

Seth turns to me with wide eyes and flared nostrils, like an animal about to bolt. "Genevieve?" He shifts uncomfortably in his seat. "Well, I met her here, at sixth form. I saw her from across a crowded room, literally, and … I guess I just knew."

I write *GENEVIEVE* on the paper in front of us, taking a moment to ponder the order of the I and the E. "Knew what?"

"That she was the woman for me. She has the kind of face you don't really see very often … like an angel, if an angel decided to visit central England. Anyway, way out of my league. So far out of my league that it hurt. But I ignored all that, and I set myself a challenge: 'Gen will be my girlfriend by the end of the month.' And she was."

"How'd you manage that?" I've picked up one of Dahlia's doughnuts, so the words come out smooshed-up as I chew.

"Self-belief and determination," says Seth. "Gen would

call that *manifesting.* I started smiling at her, every time I passed her in the corridor. And she started remembering me – I could see her eyes flicker when she saw me, like, 'Oh, that guy again.' And then one day there was a fire alarm, just after lunch. I was late leaving the sports hall because I'd been in the changing rooms, and so had she, and we literally walked out of the doors at the exact same time, like something from a film. And then she looked to her left, and she saw me, and she said, 'Hello, you.'"

He pauses for a moment, staring dreamily into the distance as if he's playing the whole thing back in his head. *Hello, you.*

"That's all it took to get you a date?" I ask him, genuinely curious. "Some smiles and a fire drill?"

A few months ago, Freddie had told me that his friends thought I could be "cold". I'd asked him what it would mean to be "warm", specifically, and he'd said they'd noticed that I don't laugh at many jokes and that I have a tendency to ask difficult questions with a straight face. "So, uh, the opposite of that, I guess," he'd offered.

At the time, I'd asked my mum if she agreed with the assessment. She'd shrugged and said, "Better cold and honest than warm and fake." I don't like tattoos, but if I ever got one, I think I'd probably have that sentence etched across my skin forever.

Even so, I make a mental note to ramp up the warmth, for Seth's sake.

"You haven't let me finish my story yet," he protests. "So, we exited the building together and we talked for ages while we were waiting to go back in – it was that day there was an *actual* fire, do you remember? Something went wrong with the toaster in the staff room… Anyway, I made her laugh and…" He glances down to his lap. "She liked me."

"And you were together for a year?"

He shakes his head. "Fifteen months."

The correction feels needlessly specific – like when Cassie refers to her granddaughter as being "twenty months" instead of just "one" or "almost two" – but I decide not to push it. I guess those extra twelve weeks mean a lot to him.

"Well, fifteen months is a long time. Why did she break up with you? What did she say?"

"Oh, she said a lot of things." He lets out a bitter laugh. "I knew it was coming. I always say I didn't, but I did. She used to love hanging out – she wanted to see me all the time, you know? Then all of a sudden – done with it. Can't do Mondays because she's got extra dance rehearsals. Can't do Tuesdays because she's got homework. Can't do Wednesdays because she needs to do sage-burning and *hold space for herself.* Rest of the week … well. You get the idea."

I try to think warm thoughts. "That sounds like it would've been … very hard to handle."

Seth nods a few times in a row. "It *was* very hard to handle. It still is. How can a person just change their mind like that? How can they look you in the eye and say, 'Seth, I can't see myself with anyone other than you,' and then wake up one morning and think, *actually, false alarm, I CAN*?"

"Freddie did the same," I say. "Checked out overnight because he decided I wasn't fun enough for him."

"It's scary how quickly people move on these days." He lets out a sigh of disapproval, like he's a seventy-year-old man who's seen it all. "You think you can finally get comfy and then, BAM, there they go. Galloping off into the distance with a boy named Jake."

I must look as confused as I feel at the mention of Cowboy Jake, because Seth opens his mouth to explain.

"She's seeing somebody new already. And all *I* can think is, *When did this happen?* The first week after a break-up isn't the time for realizing you want to date your friend from dance class – it's the time to stay home in your pyjamas because your life is an outrageous mess. So, I weighed it up, like a detective, and the only logical conclusion is this: Jake Jenson was lurking in the background all along, biding his time. And now he's pirouetted in, with his Ford Fiesta and his ability to grow a beard, and he's stolen my girlfriend."

"He has a beard?" I'm picturing a mean-spirited, ballet-dancing Santa Claus.

Seth glowers at the ceiling. "No. He has what I'd call aggressive stubble. But he *could* have a beard, if he wanted to. He has the means." He sniffs. "Anyway, tell me about Freddie. How'd you two meet?"

I keep my hand on the pen, using one thumb to flick at the lid. "He was my first and only boyfriend. *Is.* Was. I don't even know. We sat next to each other in history class to begin with – it was all boy-girl, boy-girl, to try and keep stuff quieter. I was super shy, so he didn't get much back from me, but he'd always try."

He did always try. He was even more of a nerd than me in those days; he had a giant, well-stocked pencil case and a *Stranger Things* badge that he kept clipped to his blazer at all times. I found it hopelessly cute. He'd spend entire lessons talking incessantly about *Doctor Who* and asking me for my personal views on the space-time continuum, of which I had many. If I was too shy to answer that day, he'd just tell me his own.

"We went on this school trip," I continue, "to a museum, for history class. It was kind of easier to talk to him outside the classroom, so I did. And … I don't know. I guess it went from there."

There had been something about being away from school, something about being away from the kids sitting around us who'd have likely eavesdropped on every word if we'd had any in-depth conversations in their presence. And so, I relaxed. I stopped worrying so much about getting things wrong, or whether the angry red acne on my chin was as obvious to Freddie as it was to me. I joined in with life, instead of just observing it.

A few weeks after, Freddie pushed a note over to me

as we were packing up to leave our lesson. It said, want 2 hang out soon? I still have the note, buried away in my box of Freddie memories; we used to get it out sometimes and laugh at how far we'd come. Occasionally we'd still text each other: WANT 2 HANG OUT SOON??

And of course, as soon as I saw the note, I said yes. We went to the cinema on our first date, and he held my hand as we waited for the train back home. It was cold outside, but his palm was warm and sticky, like he was immune to the weather, like he had a whole little Freddie ecosystem ready to share with me. We stood in silence and I thought it might be a good idea to get closer to him, to position myself against his chest somehow without making it too obvious that I'd never done that before. Then I saw him lean in towards me with his eyes closed.

The kiss was different to how I expected it to be. I'd hoped for world-changing; I got minute-changing. Hour-changing, maybe. People in books and on TV had always made out that the first kiss would be the most special kiss, but I felt differently. For us, it was only when we'd had a chance to really get into it that I felt like the universe had shifted. After that, I wanted to do it all the time. I found that I missed his mouth when it wasn't in the vicinity.

"And four years later … here you are," says Seth, interrupting the kiss montage playing in my mind as he leans over to take the plate of flapjacks that's being passed around the room.

Four years. Our anniversaries felt like the most important day that anyone had ever celebrated. We did monthly nods to the third, the day we'd first got together – anyone who knew us also knew that the third of each month was out of bounds. It was *our* day; it didn't belong to the rest of the world. They would never understand the third in the same way we did.

Freddie and I grew up together. We watched TV together, played video games together, went Christmas shopping together, ate together, showered together, laughed together, planned together. We even wrote our personal statements for university together. I was actually the scribe of both of these personal statements, mostly because I knew I was the superior writer and I didn't want Freddie to fall behind on account of his haphazard approach to apostrophes, but Freddie was in the room with me, yelling out things he thought might add to the overall effect. We applied early, in November, and both got conditional places. I started making lists of all the things we'd need to buy. I pictured the way our books and DVDs would look together, merged in one space – *our* space. I turned up to his house with an IKEA colander and a three-pack of plastic chopping boards one weekend, way before we'd even sent our applications off, and Freddie picked me up, spun me round in the air, and told me he'd never been so excited for anything in his life.

And now, here I am – sitting at the back of a psychology

classroom, discussing my relationship like it's some ancient artefact, while a strange boy who knows nothing about me eats baked goods with his mouth open.

"You want one?" he asks, offering the platter to me.

I shake my head, feeling tears prickle at the corners of my eyes. "No."

"Are you sure? Because I consider myself to be a real flapjack connoisseur," Seth pushes, "and these are something else. I'm a firm believer that it's all in the golden syr—"

"I said no," I snap. "Thank you."

Seth mutters something under his breath about me missing out, but still backs off, his shoulders drooping a little.

We sit in silence for a while, studying the rest of our group. Oliver and Nav are hunched in a two together, whispering solemnly while Oliver takes notes. Maryam has just said something that's made Daisy laugh out loud, and Lucy – who's stopped weeping – is now tentatively picking at a flapjack while Dahlia strokes her hand.

I try to return to the Freddie flashbacks, but the moment has passed and I can't reach them any more. My memories turn to ribbons and float away.

8

The idea

The rest of the week, I try my hardest to stay busy. I revisit my comfort programmes. I reread my favourite books. I scroll on my phone for hours, staring at video after video until I realize I'm not even taking in a single thing that the people on the screen are saying, and my brain twitches in a way that feels dangerous. I go out on walks, but it's January, and it's dark, and I don't want to be murdered on my way to buy Doritos.

The thing about being part of a couple is that everything boring still somehow counts as a plan. Watching movies? A plan. Eating pizza together in your comfiest, least fashionable clothes? Another plan. The kind of thing you could call *just a quiet one* if anyone asked about it the next day.

When you're single, it's different. It isn't a plan. It's just killing time, without someone to love you.

"I need your complete and total honesty here, bunny," says Cassie, bringing me back to reality as she stands to my left with her hands on her hips. "Is it edgy, or is it just bad?"

I step back to study the six-foot canvas in front of us, and try my hardest to dredge up some enthusiasm. "I thought art was subjective. Can either one of us really call this *bad*?"

The giant piece of work, entitled "Modern Love", was submitted for this weekend's Shared Universe exhibition by a local artist who simply goes by the name GREGOR. Cassie is not a fan of GREGOR; she decapitalized his name by accident when she printed out his bio and he sent her an angry email about *the importance of respecting artistic vision.*

GREGOR's canvas is covered in large dark-red swathes of acrylic paint, like thick dried blood, and on top of the paint is a selection of printed-out screenshots from text conversations. Some say things like, *So sorry to cancel our date! I just don't think it's a good time for us to do this*, or, *I appreciate that, but like I said, I don't feel we're a good fit.* One, which GREGOR has placed in the bottom-left corner, says, *Please respect my decision. I know it's hard but you can't call me at 2 a.m., G, it's not fair. Let me know when would be good for me to come and collect the rest of my stuff. A x*

I wonder who A is. As pretentious as GREGOR might be, I still feel a pang of solidarity towards him – he has known the pain of rejection in the same way I have. He has known the humiliation of lying around his house, desperately contacting somebody who used to care about him, and knowing that anything he says will only add to the reasons they no longer do.

Cassie seems to sense my mood and catches herself, throwing a benevolent arm around my shoulder. "Poor guy. There's nothing wrong with getting dumped a lot. Or at all. We've all been there, bunny."

"I *am* there," I tell her sadly, squinting at GREGOR's crimson canvas. "Right now."

I leave Cassie and the artwork alone together and make my way over to the Shared Universe cafe – a family-run place called The Independent Bean. The logo of The Independent Bean is an illustrated coffee bean named Coco, who's shown wearing a backwards cap and strutting down a long, winding road, which I've always taken to mean that he is *so* independent he's learned how to walk and go on important journeys.

From my usual spot next to the interior window, I pull my phone out and scroll through the last few unanswered messages I sent to Freddie, clutching my mug in my other hand and enjoying the warmth against my palm. Really hope you're having fun, I told him at 1.37 a.m. on Wednesday, not meaning a single word of it. When can we talk?? I asked him at 5.55 p.m. on Friday. Both have been seen, neither have been responded to, and even reading them back is enough to make me shudder with shame.

And then, as if he's somehow listened to my thoughts,

Freddie appears online and a reply – the first he's sent me since the Ferris wheel – instantly comes through. It's the kind of message that's very obviously been drafted in a Notes app and then pasted, and the second he sends it he immediately goes offline.

Today 15:25

> **Freddie:** Had a good time thanks. I'm sorry Harl but I've said what I needed to say and I gave you a chance to do the same. Theres nothing left to talk about now and your just making it harder for both of us.

I abandon my tea and focus on the message, reading the words so many times my eyes begin to blur as I zone in on words like *nothing* and *sorry.* What did I expect? That he was going to say anything different? That he's been AWOL all this week because he was painstakingly concocting the perfect *let's get back together* response, ahead of a jubilant return to the UK, flowers in hand? I thud my elbows on to the table and cradle my chin, letting tears run straight down my cheeks.

There's a loud, expectant knock on the window of The Independent Bean, right next to my head. I startle, then glance up, expecting to see Cassie or my mum, but the face that greets me is freckled and beaming: Seth.

"Not *you*," I whisper under my breath, like a disgruntled ventriloquist.

If he's noticed my crying, he doesn't let on. Instead, he offers me a jovial wave, then gesticulates via some large arrowy shapes to let me know he's heading inside. I watch, helpless and snotty, as he floats over to me.

"Harley Green!"

He's dressed in a pair of long black shorts and a white sleeveless T-shirt with the classic Nike tick on it, and he doesn't look at all chilly. People who wear shorts in winter creep me out. Our neighbour Gareth *lives* in them, no matter the weather. I once saw Gareth shovelling snow off his drive in a pair of cargo cut-offs and flip-flops, as though he was about to head out to catch some waves.

"What are you doing here?" I ask Seth, dabbing at one eye. For a second I have a little surge of terror that he's organized an impromptu Saturday RDC meeting, just for the sake of it, and now Dahlia and the rest of the group are outside with a large flask of coffee, waiting to talk.

He jolts his head in the direction of the pet shop. "I need to buy fish food, and this is my store of choice. Why are *you* here?" He studies my face for a second, and winces as one solitary tear drops on to the wooden table. "Are you OK?"

I ignore the second question and pat at the tear-patch with a sweatshirt sleeve. "My mum works in the health store."

Seth raises an eyebrow, as though mildly impressed.

"Your mum works at Heather's Health?"

I nod, surprised. "You know it?"

"*My* mum buys her lentils from there – she's got one of those Health is Wealth loyalty cards." He lowers his voice. "Have you met Heather? She coughs *all* the time. Like, maybe drink some of your own lemon and honey tea, Heather. Maybe crack open some of that overpriced vitamin C."

Despite everything, my mouth betrays me by curling upwards in agreement. "I'll pass that on."

"Nicely, of course," says Seth. "She might be ill. But if she's not, here's my customer feedback: *Heather, you sound like a smoker from the 1980s, and it's harming the brand.*"

I pull my hand up to my head in a salute motion. "I'll see what I can do."

Neither of us speak for a few seconds. Seth nods his head in time to the beat of the song playing on the cafe's radio, not seeming at all embarrassed by the awkwardness I can feel circling the table.

"Don't you … need to go get your fish food?" I ask him, when the song hits a lull.

He blinks. "I mean, not this second. They were fed this morning; they'll wait for me."

"Well, I'm kind of in the middle of something here." I point at the duck-egg blue teapot on the table in front of me. "So …"

"Yes," Seth deadpans. "You do seem rushed off your

feet as you sit staring into space by yourself at the local community cafe."

I give him a withering look. "Just because I'm resting, doesn't mean people can *thrust* themselves into my day."

"What if I got my own drink?" he counters. "Could I thrust then? Could I rest with you? Would that be such a crime, Harley?"

I sigh in surrender. "I guess nobody would arrest you for it."

"That's what I hoped."

He disappears, returning a minute later with a glass bottle of orangeade, a striped paper straw and a large chocolate chip cookie. After depositing his haul on to the table, he pulls out the chair opposite mine and sits, catching me off-guard with a long quizzical look. "The weekends are hardest for me, too, if that helps."

"It doesn't," I say, which is true but feels pointlessly mean, so I soften. *Warm thoughts.* "I'm sorry. Why are they so hard for you?"

"Because it's lonely," says Seth. He takes a slurp from the straw. "All of a sudden you realize that your friends are out doing stuff with whoever they're dating, and you're stuck at home in your pyjamas like, *No, don't worry, go on without me!*" He adds a sarcastic little wave. "And then I'm just lying there, thinking, *Is Gen out tonight? Is she having fun? Is she with Jake? Does she like him more than she liked me?*

Don't answer that – of course she does. Has she met his family? Are they as sophisticated and worldly as him? Has she had sex with Jake yet? Is he better at it than I was? Don't answer that, either – of course he is. Do they do it and then lie there afterwards laughing at my lack of experience and the fact that I don't know how to drive?"

His breathing has quickened; his Nike-covered chest is shuddering as he breaks the cookie in two.

"I … I really don't think they do that," I tell him.

He gives me a look of disdain. "I assure you they do."

"If I want to torture myself with what Freddie's doing, turns out all I need to do is pick up my phone," I say, grimacing at the thought. "When we were together, he posted once a year or something – normally for our anniversary. He didn't care about that kind of thing. Now it's, like, a daily occurrence."

"I'm posting more now, too," he says, and the tips of his ears turn pink.

I put down my mug and stare at him. "Why? Why do boys do that?"

"I don't know. I guess when you get comfy with the right person you don't share anything online because you never really wanted to share anything online in the first place, so it's like, why bother? You've got what you wanted. You're happy."

"So you're saying Freddie's *not* happy now?"

Seth shrugs. "I'm saying he's been absent from the world for a while. He's probably just trying to remind it that he's returned."

"And he wants everyone to know it. He wants *girls* to know it." I twist at the teabag string, tugging off its damp paper label and rubbing it between my finger and thumb. "God, it's like a caveman mating ritual."

"Not necessarily. *I* don't want girls to know I'm single. I want Gen to think I'm having the time of my life, so that at some point in the near future when she's lying in Jake Jenson's bed she won't laugh at my lack of sexual expertise but instead will think, *Ew, who is this imposter? I miss my* real *boyfriend, Seth*." He looks me in the eye with such intensity that I break the gaze, returning to the teabag label like it's an urgent task. "It's not for other people. It's for her."

"You want to get her back?" I ask, eyes still down.

"Harley," says Seth, thudding his glass bottle down on to the table with resolve, "I would do literally anything to get her back. I mean, I wouldn't commit murder, or become a member of a cartel, or …" He pauses, probably to run through an imaginary list of scenarios in his mind. "I would do anything legal to get her back. Within reason. Don't you want Freddie back?"

"Of course," I say, in a *duh* voice. "But I don't think it's really up to us. Gen has a new boyfriend. What do you think you're going to do, hide him in a cupboard and hope she forgets about him?"

Seth snorts. "I've considered it."

I shake my head. "We have absolutely no say in this matter. We have no power whatsoever."

He holds up a hand to shush me. "Please. Faint heart never won fair lady. Or fair man. Or fair anyone." He takes another slurp of orangeade and swallows it, letting out an appreciative *ah* noise immediately afterwards. "You know, we could easily join forces here. You're single – so am I. You're newly emotionally devastated – wow, me too."

I blow a puff of air up into my fringe, bewildered. "And as desirable as those qualities are, I don't think Nick Fury's planning on giving us a call any time soon."

Seth – clearly unseasoned in the sphere of Marvel references – gives me a blank look. "No, I'm saying we're stronger together. So, we stop spending our Saturdays crying in coffee shops and we *start* showing our exes that they were wrong about us, by pretending to be a couple." He claps his hands together. "How would you feel about that?"

What? I study him as he takes a large, satisfied bite of the cookie.

"I'd feel very uncomfortable about it. Deeply uncomfortable."

"Why?" says Seth, in between chomps.

"Uh, because it's weird? Because it's forced? Because it's *lying*?"

He swallows the mouthful and wipes his lips with the

back of a hand. His forearms – oddly tanned for January – have a scattering of golden hairs across them, the kind that probably glisten in the sunlight when he's out playing whatever sport he plays. "But don't you think it'd change Freddie's mind if he got back from Paris and realized he didn't know you as well as he thought? He said you don't have fun. He said you're missing out on the opportunities that life has to offer you. Well, here's an opportunity, straight from life itself. I'm Freddie… I see you grasping the opportunity… Oof. That's hot."

Is that really what Freddie would think? I try to compute it all in my head. I'm pretty certain that he'd write off *Harley with a new boyfriend* as chaotic. He'd think it was rushed, uncharacteristic behaviour, and he'd be right about that. What difference would it make to anything?

"I don't know what world you live in," I tell Seth, monotone, as I pour out the final dregs of my tea. "But in the real world, stuff like that doesn't work. If someone doesn't want you, they just don't want you. It doesn't take them seeing you with another person to change things. Nothing changes things. They're just … done."

"You don't get it," he says, leaning back on his chair. "Freddie didn't dump you because he didn't love you any more. He dumped you because he thought you were allergic to fun. Gen didn't dump *me* because she went off me. She dumped me because …" He falters, and the skin on his cheeks, under his swoop of freckles, reddens.

"Well, for a specific reason. All I'm saying is – there's a huge difference between falling out of love with someone and just wishing they'd change a little bit. If we can show *we've* changed…"

"But I haven't changed," I point out. "I'm going home to eat leftover pasta and watch *Midsomer Murders.*"

"Doesn't matter," says Seth simply. "What matters is what he *thinks* you're doing. And then, when you guys are back together … dip a toe into the fun pool every so often to keep him happy. Go bungee jumping one weekend or something. Down a shot of tequila in plain view. Use your imagination."

In front of us, on top of the cake counter, sits a large rectangular sign that says WHY NOT TRY SOMETHING NEW TODAY? It's supposed to be advertising The Independent Bean's new range of coffee-flavoured desserts, with a limited-edition Coco the Bean simpering as he promotes confectionery made of his crushed family members, but my eyes zoom in on the words while Seth's offbeat suggestion circles around in my head.

"I can't make a decision on this right now," I say. "I need to sleep on it."

"Sleep on it. Meditate on it. Mull it over while you watch your murder show, then come and let me know," says Seth. He pulls a pen out of his pocket and scribbles his number on my Coco the Bean napkin, in a little speech bubble that he draws next to Coco's beaming mouth. Then he shoves his chair backwards and gets to his feet. "All I'll say is this – if you picture your future, maybe ten years from now, who's with you? Is it Freddie?"

I nod without having to think about it.

He shrugs as he heads for the door. "Then why wouldn't you fight for that?"

9

The change of heart

It's my mum's idea to do something different on Saturday night.

"Instead of being sad that your usual routine with Freddie isn't happening," she says, forcibly removing my phone from my hand and setting it down on top of the fridge, "perhaps you could be happy that Chinese takeaway night *is* happening. With me. Your loving mother."

She's trying her best and I really don't have the heart to tell her that the thought of doing anything remotely sociable this evening is not at all appealing to me, so I nod, and she ruffles my hair. A moment later, she's pulling out the takeaway menus from the kitchen cupboard and making a big deal of reading out the names of dishes she thinks I'd like, even though she's well aware that it's a waste of both her weekend *and* mine.

"Nothing can beat sweet and sour chicken," I remind her. "And that's just the way it is."

Freddie never cared about my dedication to certain things – food and places and people – until recently. He was protective of it; he'd put Min straight whenever she had questions or judgements. *I just think it's a shame that there are such lovely things on this menu and you don't want to try any of them,* she'd say sometimes, when we went out for food and I chose the exact same pizza topping as always. Her voice would be full of condescending kindness, like she was genuinely concerned for me and my experience of life, which in turn would make *me* concerned for my experience of life, like I was inherently damaged and different for not losing my mind at the idea of a specials menu. And Freddie would roll his eyes and tell her to shut up, and I'd feel my face turn pink at the thought of being the cause of a small Lee family dispute, but I'd also feel such a rush of love towards Freddie for sticking up for me. For knowing me. For getting me.

What business is it of yours, Minnie? Freddie would snap. *How does Harley's choice of food this evening impact you in any way whatsoever?*

He wouldn't say that now. He'd watch me ask for the same unadventurous meal as always, and he'd probably be the first to wince.

My mum – a long-time critic of getting food delivered when you can just collect it yourself in half the time – drives us to pick up our order and waits in the car while I run in. The man working on the front desk this evening tells me to take a seat, so I perch on the end of the black leather sofa, next to a poster about the Chinese zodiac. This year, I learn, has been the Year of the Snake, which – frankly – makes a lot of sense.

The man returns with a small bowl of prawn crackers in one hand, which he places on to the glass table in front of me.

"And some crackers for you, too?" he asks a woman who's just arrived. "I'm sorry – we're one down in the kitchen tonight, so things are moving a little slow."

"Oh, yes please." She shakes out her umbrella on to the doormat, speaking with her back to us. "That'd be terrific."

There's only one person I know in the entire world who uses the word *terrific*, and it's Freddie's sister Min. She whirls round, umbrella in hand, thick ponytail swishing in perfect movie slow-motion behind her, and I feel my entire body tense up.

"Oh!" she exclaims as she spots me. "Harley!"

Break-ups probably aren't so bad when you're long distance. I'm sure they're still terrible, but at least you'd have the added comfort of knowing that your town or city is just that: *your* town or city. At least you wouldn't have to worry about passing your ex on your morning run, or bumping into them at the supermarket, or seeing their shiny-haired sibling in your local Cantonese restaurant.

I offer her a tight-lipped grin that I hope looks friendly but sad at the same time. Woefully mature. Depressed, but still dealing with it. "How was Paris?"

"Paris was incredible, and the wedding was *such* a beautiful display of love," says Min, forgetting about any potential awkwardness and lowering herself daintily on to the sofa next to me. A pair of wide-leg zebra-print trousers peek out from the bottom of her trench coat. "The whole trip was rejuvenating – a real experience."

This is what I mean about Min. This is what Freddie, especially, used to find infuriating about Min. Nothing is ever just *good* or *fun* or *great, thanks*. Everything is *magnificent. Restorative. A truly invigorating time.*

The man from the front desk returns with a fresh bowl of prawn crackers. Min calls him an "absolute superstar", removes her phone from her pocket to snap three or four photos of the crackers from different angles, then places the bowl down on the table in front of her without eating any of its contents.

"And how's Freddie?" I ask, while she flicks through her photo gallery.

"He's doing really well." She nods, offering me a smile so proud you'd think her brother had just returned from a trip to the moon. "I … I know things are probably very hard for you this week, Harley, but for what it's worth, I think you both made the right decision. You can focus on yourselves now – fresh start. New traditions." She throws her arms up into the air. "You can be *teenagers*!"

I bet this is what they thought all along. I bet they all used to sit around the dinner table talking about how cautious and annoying I was, how much I was dragging Freddie down. I bet now he's ended things they've all patted him on the back and said, *Well done, champ – that takes guts.*

"How have *you* been feeling?" Min says as she smiles again – and it's generous, because Min's often generous, but it's also expectant. Patronizing. Like I'm going to break down any second and tell her that *of course* I'm not doing well, and she's going to send me home with a takeaway bag, a breathing exercise and the numbers of three recommended local therapists.

Something shifts inside of my brain, and I decide not to let that happen.

"I'm better than ever," I tell her casually, leaning back on the leather booth. "I'm actually … I'm actually seeing someone."

I'm actually seeing someone? The statement darts around the room while I wait for it to land and make its impact, and my shoulders immediately brace from the ridiculousness of my impromptu lie. I remind myself of what Seth said – the stuff about faint hearts and fighting for the things you want – but the thought of Min rushing home to tell Freddie the news still makes my stomach lurch.

"You're dating again?" Min's dark eyes are large and judgemental, almost scandalized. I'm calling it now: at some point in the next few weeks she will post a fifteen-minute MusingsWithMin video called TOO SOON? THE DANGERS OF MOVING ON QUICKLY AFTER A BREAK-UP.

"If it seems sudden, that's because it is," I say, using a prawn cracker to scoop up some sweet chilli sauce and casually crunching down into it, like I haven't just told the biggest lie of my entire existence. "But you can't plan these things, can you? Life is an adventure, and sometimes we just have to jump in and go for it. That's what I'm learning."

Min's mouth hangs open, and I'll admit – the sight of it is kind of glorious. I watch as she blinks at me, short-circuiting over the idea that her younger brother's wallflower of an ex has secured a brand-new boyfriend in the space of one French holiday.

How's that for fun?

As if conjured by God himself for the sake of my plan, the old guy behind the counter emerges with a well-loaded white plastic bag. "Order for Green?"

"That's me!" I call. I take the bag and thank him, before turning back to Min, food in one shaky hand, swinging house keys in the other. "It's like you said, Min – time for some new traditions. Now, if you'll excuse me, I'm late to meet my boyfriend. Bye!"

And then, before she has a chance to respond or I have a chance to backtrack, I pace out of the restaurant, my legs moving so quickly you'd think I'd robbed the place. As soon as I reach my mum's car, I slot the bag between my feet, pull out my phone and send a two-word message to Seth:

I'm in.

10

The fun-loving, legitimate couple

It's early Monday morning and we're huddled together in the squashy-chair reception area of the ESS building, plotting. Seth's clutching a tiny leather notepad in one hand and a pen in the other, which he chews when he enters a moment of particular thoughtfulness. It's my pen, actually, and I've seen enough to know that I won't be asking for it back.

The plan, so far, is this: we'll take today to get to know each other and suss out the logistics. Then, when Freddie walks in to the coffee shop as usual tomorrow morning, we'll be waiting – ready to prove that we are a fun-loving, legitimate couple. The question is, how?

"Well, as far as Gen and Freddie are concerned, we're both technically single," says Seth. The word makes me flinch. "So that means we're each other's rebounds, and rebounds are naturally fun. They're not serious. They laugh a lot. They make out a lot. They—"

"I will not be *making out* with anybody," I say loudly. "So please cross that point off your list right now."

I spout a lot of stuff about *believability* and *realism*, and Seth nods approvingly, but what I really think is that the thought of kissing somebody – anybody – who isn't Freddie would be enough to make my entire body revolt.

Seth tilts his head to the left, like an owl. "I get it; it's weird. It's weird for me too. Not that there's anything wrong with you – I'm sure you're a wonderful kisser, the best of the best, but …" He trails off. "Well, I haven't been with anyone since Gen. So."

I feel a pang of sadness for him, a jolt of solidarity in my abdomen. "We're on the same page, then – we need to be one of those minimal-PDA couples that take things slow."

He snorts, but not unkindly. "Sure. Get ready for our hot 'n' heavy eye contact to leave Freddie *weeping* with envy."

"I'm not saying never," I add, even though I absolutely am. "I'm saying as of now: no kissing. None whatsoever. Write it down."

I watch as he removes the pen from behind his ear and scribbles **NO KISSING (FOR NOW)** in the notepad. He adds a bunch of exclamation marks and a black-haired grumpy face that looks remarkably like me, then underlines the whole thing. I roll my eyes, and we're both quiet while we weigh up our options.

"There's probably a middle-ground choice," I say eventually, offering up a truce. "Hand-holding. Arm around the waist. Something like that."

Seth nods. "Maybe we need a code word, like they have in the movies. Like … I don't know, *butterfly*, or something. If it gets too much, one of us says the word and we both take a break."

"Butterfly," I repeat.

"Yeah. Butterfly."

He busies himself writing in the notepad again, and I take a swig of water. "What do we tell Gen and Freddie, when they ask how we got together? Are we vague, like, *Oh we just found each other*? Or do we have a full backstory?"

"Ooh, this is fun," says Seth. "This is where having a fake boyfriend who's studying drama is going to really come in handy for you. Where did we meet? What did we think, upon meeting? Who introduced us? *Why* did they introduce us? Was it me who kicked things off, or did you swoop in to pop the question? Have you met my dog yet? Do—"

I shoot him the same look I gave him when he offered to bring me a pin badge in the RDC classroom, and he takes the hint.

"Let's say we met … because you came into my place of work." He twizzles the pen like a baton. "I served you a tea made of hemp, or whatever it is you drink, and you said, *Wow, you seem fun and I really like your green eyes. I'm fun, too – wanna date?* And I said, *Sure. Just so you know, I am currently reeling from a recent and heart-wrenching break-up, but if that doesn't put you off then I guess nothing will.* And you said, *Works for me, stud*, and then we started hanging out."

I blink in his direction, straight-faced. "I would never have said that. I would never have said any of those things."

"Fine. Maybe I was the one to do the asking. Maybe I slipped you my number when I handed you your hemp tea."

"I drink *mint* tea," I remind him sullenly. "I do not consume hemp."

Seth waves a hand, like, *same difference*. "That storyline's more believable though, right? The me-asking-you thing?"

"Much more. Let's go with that."

"Cool," says Seth, scrawling SETH ASKED HARLEY AT THE COFFEE SHOP, HARLEY SAID HELL YEAH on the page in front of him. "There we are, then."

"What about consistency?" I ask. "Are we going to tell *everyone* that we're dating? Or are we just saving that for Freddie and Gen?"

Like Seth, all I can compare this to are movies and books where the main characters pretend to date. And normally, in my limited experience, those characters spread the news far and wide. That's basically the point.

"Why would we tell *everyone*?" says Seth, anxious leg-bounce in full swing. "That's unhinged."

"We tell everyone because that makes it stick. If people know, they tell Freddie. They tell Gen. If they don't know, they don't say anything, and it all takes a lot longer."

Seth makes a *hm* noise. "I didn't think of that. I say … let's be discerning. Like, I'm not going to tell my best friends that I have a new girlfriend. They wouldn't believe me; they're too concerned about the fact that I spent last night creating a playlist called SETHEVIEVE FOREVER. I'll tell them the truth. Same with our families, right? They can either be let into the plan or told nothing at all. Everyone else? Full steam ahead."

He pauses, biting on his lip. "Actually, what about the Recently Dumped Club? What if they see us together?"

I feel a tug of worry at the prospect. It all feels a little too devious, like we've both joined the vegan society but are still making secret plans to meet up and eat hamburgers together.

"If somebody from the RDC sees us, we tell them the truth," I say decisively. "If anyone would understand, it's them."

The bell rings, and I see Bella hurry through the entrance hall, hovering an A4 ring binder over her head as a makeshift umbrella. She spots me, waves with one hand, and mouths something about saving me a seat in the English classroom.

Seth snaps his notebook closed. "We're making good progress here. My dad always says, *Fail to prepare, Seth, and you prepare to fail.*"

I feel myself smile. "That's cute. My dad always says,

Harley, maybe if you went outside and saw the world more, you wouldn't be so bothered about fictional adventures."

"Always" is a bit of an exaggeration, given that I haven't seen my dad for several years, but the *fictional adventures* quote is a real one, burned into my brain from the last time we hung out together. It was just me and him – not his wife Elsie or either of their children, which made me feel like he'd warned them off me, like he'd told them, *Don't bother, stay home; it probably won't be worth your while anyway.*

I remember going home from that meet-up, sitting with Freddie and my mum in the kitchen, and thinking, *Who cares about that man, when* my *people are here with me in this house?* I remember Freddie clutching my hand under the table, feeling my hurt right alongside me, like it was his hurt too. For a split-second, that exact same emotion shunts back into me, like a camera flash in a dark room.

Seth studies me, eyes piercing, like he's trying to peer through a wall. "Forget your dad's take on adventures. Just think of it like this: we're having our own."

11

Video (interview): Seth Whittaker and Harley Green

Monday, 12 January, 4.32 p.m.

SETH: Oookay. There we go.

HARLEY: Recording?

SETH: Recording. *So.* Like I said earlier, let's think of this as some kind of speed date thing. We talk, then we watch it back later for revision. I want you to tell me everything you think I'd need to know about you, were we in fact boyfriend and girlfriend.

HARLEY: Like what?

SETH: [Sighs audibly] Like … parents' names?

HARLEY: Alice. And Drew.

SETH: Drew? Sounds like he works on a ranch.

HARLEY: He's an optician. So. Not really the same.

They're not together. What about yours?

SETH: My mum is Pam. My dad is Walter. Very much together. All the time, actually.

HARLEY: Do you call your dad Walt?

SETH: No. He specifically avoids it, because depending on the person, you either get into Mickey Mouse territory or you get into *Breaking Bad* territory, and that just makes it weird for everyone. I also have three sisters – Olivia, Ash and Wren.

HARLEY: [Making notes in her phone] Olivia. Ash... Wren. Are you the eldest?

SETH: Middle-y. Olivia's the eldest – she's twenty. She wants to become a print journalist, which is kind of sad, because by the time she's finished studying I don't know if print journalists are even going to exist any more. Not in the same way, anyway. But you have to keep the hope, right? Then there's me. Ash is fifteen, and very much in her leave-me-alone phase. Wren is twelve and very much in her spend-every-day-with-me phase. It's a busy house.

HARLEY: It *sounds* busy. Like, what if you wanted to go home and speak to no one? Is there always somebody there? [Frowns]

SETH: Well, yeah, but I like that. It's the kind of house *I* want to have one day. Never a dull moment. We also have a dog, Mr—

HARLEY: Mr Wilson. I remember.

SETH: [Offering his hand for a high five] Yes! *That* is the kind of energy we need here. Mr Wilson. Our golden retriever.

HARLEY: [Goes to give the high five, misses, and tries again, slightly more awkwardly] Does he … like to retrieve?

SETH: Loves it. Cannot get enough of the retrieving. Proud owner of several stuffed animals that he likes to carry around the house and show to visitors.

HARLEY: I wanted a dog when I was a kid, so we had one for like a week – Betty – but it turned out my mum's allergy was worse than originally thought, so we had to rehome her.

SETH: God, that's so tragic. Do you get on with your mum, dog-abandoning aside?

HARLEY: We didn't abandon her! She went to live with my uncle. And yes, I do. We're very close.

SETH: That's cute. What about friends?

HARLEY: [Turns slightly pink] Um. Freddie was my best friend.

SETH: I know, but your boyfriend doesn't count. I hate it when people are like, *Oh, my girlfriend, my girlfriend, my very best friend in the world*. It doesn't mean anything. He was your *boy*friend. Who are your *friend* friends?

HARLEY: Well, there's Bella, from my English class. I like

her a lot. And, uh, I'm very close with my mum, like I told you.

SETH: [Silence]

HARLEY: What?

SETH: No, I just … Do you … do you not have a group of friends?

HARLEY: I literally just told you about my friends.

SETH: Dude, you told me about a girl from English class and your *mother.*

HARLEY: [Silence]

SETH: What are the names of your friends from school? Who do you … I don't know, who do you hang out with at the weekend?

HARLEY: Freddie. And Freddie.

SETH: Oh, no, no, no. You're saying that this boy has been the source of all your social interactions since you were fourteen years old?

HARLEY: Not *all* of them. But we spent a lot of time together! His family were my friends!

SETH: Ew.

HARLEY: [Blows up into her fringe] We're getting off-topic. What else do we need to talk about?

SETH: Well, I'm supposed to tell you about my friends, but now I'm scared I'll look like a show-off.

HARLEY: [Scowling] Go ahead.

SETH: My top priorities are Nate and Joy – they don't go to

this sixth form, but they're definitely my favourites. Nate's real name is Nathaniel but if you call him that he'll hate you forever, so don't. Joy is his girlfriend. I set them up. She's not what you'd expect – from the name, I mean. Not overly joyful. You'd like her. Then I've got my class-friends, like Larna and Henry. And my hobby-friends, li—

HARLEY: What the hell is a hobby-friend?

SETH: [Sits forward in his chair, agog] Uh, it's a friend you make through hobbies?

HARLEY: Does anyone have hobbies, really, in this day and age?

SETH: I have a plethora of hobbies, Harley. I like fish, for starters. I have twelve of them in a tropical aquarium, and my favourite (don't tell the others) is a rainbow fish named Jonathan.

HARLEY: Why Jonathan?

SETH: Why not Jonathan? He looked like a Jonathan when I met him. I also enjoy Lindy Hop, which is a kind of dancing they used to do in the nineteen-somethings. I like basketball. I like running. I grow plants. I do improv. I learn French with the Duolingo owl from time to time. I build stuff out of wood.

HARLEY: [Moves back in her chair] You're a little too wholesome. You're like if a parent made a teenager in a lab.

SETH: [Grins with one side of his mouth] Who said it was

wholesome to enjoy things? You know, the author Kurt Vonnegut always used to try all these different kinds of hobbies, but he wasn't very good at them, and he hated that, but one day he met someone who told him that it isn't the being good at the hobbies that really matters. It's the trying them that matters. That's what makes a person interesting.

HARLEY: I refuse to believe that attending thirty-eight different after-school clubs is what makes a person interesting. If anything, I'd say it makes them exhausting.

SETH: Well, maybe the two go hand in hand. You're just jealous you haven't met Jonathan. He's a blast.

HARLEY: No doubt.

SETH: What's your favourite food?

HARLEY: Pizza.

SETH: Season?

HARLEY: Winter.

SETH: Why?

HARLEY: Cosy.

SETH: Favourite smell?

HARLEY: Freddie's pillow.

SETH: Yawn. Give me something else.

HARLEY: [Silence]

SETH: Favourite smell.

HARLEY: The … [swallows] um.

SETH: What is it?

HARLEY: I—

SETH: TELL ME.

HARLEY: [Desperately] I like the smell of candles when they've just been blown out! OK? It's like … It's like a mix of excitement and nostalgia and hope and comfort, and it makes me happy. It always has done, even when I was a kid.

SETH: Finally! There you go. Nothing to do with Freddie at all. Was that really so hard?

HARLEY: Yes. Can we take a break now, please?

SETH: Sure, but you didn't ask me *my* favourites. Lasagne, summer, and my grandma's house.

HARLEY: What does your grandma's house smell of?

SETH: Come over sometime and you'll find out. *She'll* be your friend. In fact—

HARLEY: [Reaches over to stop the video recording]

12

The return

"You need to sip more confidently," whispers Seth, as we begin the coffee shop stakeout on Tuesday morning. "You look like a medieval woman waiting to be executed."

"Nobody is a confident *sipper*," I say. "Let me live."

"I like to think I drink my hot chocolate with at least some self-belief. Look."

He picks up his metal flask, grabbing it with one hand and raising it to offer me a *cheers* motion. Then he tilts his head back and takes a glug, which he immediately chokes on.

"Ow. Shit."

"Too hot?"

"Too hot," says Seth in a muffled voice, suddenly zipping from arrogant drink-gulper to wronged little boy. He picks up a napkin and pads at his chin. "Hurt my tongue."

I blow on to my own drink a touch more smugly than before.

The sixth-form coffee shop is separate to the main cafeteria, and far less intense to visit. The walls are painted in a deep shade of maroon, and there are large pieces of canvas artwork stuck up on the walls, which were created by actual students a few years ago. My favourite is a black-and-white drawing of a long-haired girl who's curled up inside a flower. There are usually people here first thing, working on open laptops or reading through library books before class starts. It's not exactly Starbucks, but it gets the job done.

"Oh my God, is that Freddie?" says Seth, so loudly it practically reverberates off the walls.

"Keep your *voice down*," I hiss, jabbing him in the ribs with a wooden coffee stirrer.

It pains me to admit it, but no-girlfriendhood kind of suits Freddie. He's striding confidently into the cafe, grinning like the weight of the world has been lifted off him. It takes me no time at all to realize that he's wearing a jumper I've never seen before: an oversized dark-green sweatshirt with varsity writing stitched on to it in bold white letters. A few weeks ago, we'd have had a Freddie fashion show the moment he bought something like this. Freddie's insecure with certain stuff, and this extends to his clothes. *Do you like it? Do you think it's too try-hard? If you saw me wearing this and you didn't know me, what would you think?*

Today, I think it's too try-hard.

"Put your hand on my leg," I say sharply, staring as Freddie leans across the counter to place his order.

"What?" says Seth, who's waggling a sachet of brown sugar around like a maraca.

"Put your *hand*. On my *leg*."

Seth drops the sugar and obliges, reaching over to rest a hand on my right thigh. It feels warm – not completely hideous, but alien, like I've walked up to a total stranger on the street and asked them to touch me. I take a deep, courageous breath.

Freddie steps away from the counter a few moments later, dangling a brown paper bag precariously between forefinger and thumb.

"His blueberry muffin," I say out loud without thinking, because Freddie is also a fan of a go-to order, even if he likes to pretend otherwise.

We watch as he heads towards the seating area in search of an available table – and then, as his hovering gaze lands on us.

"Harley?"

I don't know why he says my name like it's a question – as though I'm going to say, *No, actually. A doppelganger. A figment of your imagination. A ghost of girlfriends past.*

"Hi." I try to make the syllable as breezy as my desert-dry throat will allow. Min once told me that the trick to a successful business meeting isn't to say as many words as possible, because that makes you seem frantic and unsure of yourself. The trick is to say few words, but to make sure those words are all valuable.

I have no idea if a *Hi* has any value at all, but I decide that it's a good place to start.

Hesitantly, Freddie moves closer to us. His eyes flit from me to Seth, who he stares at for an elongated second, before moving back to me. Seth takes the thigh-hold to more of an encouraging thigh-rub at this point, and I can't tell if it's for Freddie's benefit or for mine.

"Who's this?" says Freddie, nodding in the direction of Seth's fingers.

I keep Min in mind. I ignore my thudding heartbeat and my shaking hands, and I aim for the high-value words – the ones that will get me what I want.

"This is Seth. We're seeing each other. Just casually."

"Just … casually?" repeats Freddie, with about as much enthusiasm as the time I told him I didn't think Joshua was the comedic genius everyone else believed him to be. "We broke up" – he counts on one hand – "ten days ago."

The way he's looking at me makes my entire torso clench in on itself. He doesn't appear to be devastated, exactly – there are no tears rolling down his cheeks and certainly no immediate declarations that he still loves me and has made a gigantic, foolish mistake – but his dark eyes have filled with a blend of confusion and something I can only assume is hurt. It hurts me right back.

"It isn't—" I start, but Seth interrupts me.

"A lot can change in ten days." He flashes me a *don't mess this up* look. "Especially when you meet someone as fun as Harley."

"Riiiiight." Freddie's eyebrows have developed a thick, dark, disbelieving line between them, the kind that I know him well enough to roughly translate as: *respectfully, what are you talking about, because* I *used to date that girl sitting next to you and her idea of "fun" is a three-hour Mirror Mode* Mario Kart *session.*

Say it, I think. *Get it out of your system. Say that you don't care whether I'm fun or not, because you love me and we're supposed to be together and this new blonde guy is clearly deluded anyway.* I want so badly for Freddie to throw his muffin on the floor, drape himself across the table and reach over to grab my face and kiss it. But he doesn't.

It stalls my confidence. "Well, we met last week and got talking. About … Abou—"

"About everything," interrupts Seth again, removing his hand from my leg and using it to whack the table in emphasis. "You ever meet someone and think, *How were you not in my life before? How have I gone this long – how have I traversed so many lonely days – without knowing you?*"

"Uh," says Freddie. He shoots me a look that my brain translates as, *Seriously? This guy?* "I guess."

"Then you'll know what I mean." Seth turns back towards his now not-so-piping flask of hot chocolate and takes a satisfied sip, swallowing loudly. Then he leans back in his chair, casually leaning one arm around the back of mine. I feel his hand brush my shoulder, twisting a little strand of my hair. My neck tingles, and I silently thank it for knowing how to play along with us.

Freddie fixes his attention on to Seth. "I've seen you before. You work here, right?"

"That's me," says Seth, still playing with a soft loop of hair at the nape of my neck. His voice is a little grainier than usual – and slower, like he's received the exact same how-to-succeed-in-business advice from Minnie. The act is not completely unbelievable. It's confident. Almost territorial. It's *very* un-Seth.

Freddie isn't finished with the questions. "And now you're just out here … making coffee and dating Harley?"

"Looks like it." Seth twitches his freckled nose as he grins at me, scrunching it up as if I'm the cutest thing he's ever seen. Baffled, I try my hardest to mirror the expression, like we're the kind of couple that sends each other baby animal videos in our spare time, instead of two relative strangers who entered into a sham relationship three days ago.

"Frederick, let's go!" Joshua appears with a coffee cup in each hand, his footsteps becoming more hesitant when he realizes who Freddie's talking to. He nods at me, then at Seth, then at Freddie.

Freddie squeezes the paper muffin bag, strangling the

empty part of it with his left hand. "Looks like Min was right. I didn't need to worry, because clearly, you're doing great." He backs away from us, like a baffled moonwalker. "You two enjoy your day."

"Impossible not to, with this girl," calls Seth. He rubs my shoulder with one hand and leans to the side so I can nestle into his neck, positioning myself under his chin. He smells tropical: sweet and clean and warm.

As soon as Freddie is out of sight, I tear myself away from Seth's body. "Do you think he bought it?"

Seth stares at the empty space I've just vacated. "He seemed nicely ruffled. I'd say there's a fifty-fifty chance he's headed outside to weep into his muffin bag. Did you like how fun I said you were?"

"Yes, but we need to do better than that. We need actual, concrete examples, like …" I circle one wrist in the air, using my hand to try and pump ideas into my head. "*She's throwing a party tonight. She shoplifts on the weekend now, just because she can. She has a local weed connection.*"

"You're confusing 'fun' with 'criminally minded'," says Seth. "It's not that deep. Just … think of the most fun person you know. What are they like? What makes them that way? Why are you drawn to them?"

I sip on mint tea and think about this for a little while. "My friend Bella is pretty fun. She's very sociable – she has a lot of friends and she's rarely at home."

This is true – Bella always seems to have plans that

involve leaving the house and not returning for several hours. It could be a weekend brunch event, a Thursday-night cinema visit, a last-minute trip to get matching piercings with a girl from her statistics class.

"This is good, this is very good." Seth nods encouragingly and pulls out the same small notepad from his bag, writing SOCIABLE, TIME WITH FRIENDS on one lined page like a journalist. "Keep going. What else does Fun Bella do?"

"She's confident," I say, leaning into the task at hand. "She doesn't get nervous to speak in front of a class. Uh, she's funny. She's spontaneous."

"Oh, spontaneity is *definitely* fun," agrees Seth. I roll my eyes and he rolls his right back at me. "You're honestly telling me that a last-minute plan doesn't make you feel alive?"

I shake my head with vigour. "It makes me feel annoyed. If someone wants to see me, they'll care enough to plan it in advance, not dump the idea on me with an hour's notice."

"Good *grief*." He scrawls SPONTANEOUS (!!) on the paper in front of him. "I didn't realize it was this bad."

"It isn't bad," I tell him hotly. "It's just my way of operating. Lots of people feel similarly."

"Yes – my ex-girlfriend included, actually – but for the purposes of our plan, *you* can't feel this way at all any more," he bats back. "Knock it off, because we need you to channel your inner Bella, and Freddie needs to meet spontaneous, sociable Harley Green. Think of it as a temporary alter ego, called … uh, I don't know. *Carly Dean*. Is she in there?" He leans back over to me and knocks gently on my head. "Yell if you can hear me, Carly Dean. I'll save you."

"Oh, she's in here," I confirm. "She wants me to tell you to leave her alone."

"Nonsense, she wouldn't say that. She'd say" – he puts on a sultry voice – "*You bet I'm in here, Seth. Let's do cartwheels out of the coffee shop and then speak to three new people on our lunch break, just because we can.*"

I laugh, and I can tell from Seth's smile that the sound is a surprise for both of us. For all his anxious leg-bouncing, for all his excessiveness and his beaming intensity, there's a little part of him that's growing on me.

"That, genuinely, sounds like the worst thing I've ever heard," I say.

"I need you to take the word *worst* and swap it out for the word *best*." His eyes glint. "And then, I promise, we'll be on our way."

13

The reflection

Dahlia stands at the front of the room on Wednesday, holding a large cardboard sign that says WHAT PART DID I PLAY IN MY OWN BREAK-UP? She clears her throat, and the hum of chatter dies out.

"When a relationship ends, it's pretty normal to wonder what we did wrong. And a lot of the time, we didn't do anything wrong at all – a break-up can come about because the other person has grown and changed, maybe, or because they met someone else, or because they wanted some space to get to know themselves."

"Or because they were a soulless ghoul," says Lucy from the front row.

"*Or* because they were a soulless ghoul," echoes Dahlia in a sing-song voice, giving Lucy an *I'll come check on you later* look. "But sometimes – in fact, almost all the time – we have our own part to play in a break-up."

"Like what?" says Reyan, with suspicious eyes.

"Yeah," adds Lucy, crossing her arms. "What if they just changed beyond all recognition and became a horrible person? What would your *own part* be in that?"

"Well," says Dahlia diplomatically. "This wouldn't count for abusive relationships – if someone was an abuser, we'd view that differently. But for a more equal relationship, where no abuse was present, I guess we'd have a think about how our own actions or beliefs might have affected things."

Lucy mutters something about blame, and Dahlia shakes her head gently. "It's not about blame. Sometimes we can't even work it out until years later, but we all bring our own baggage to relationships." She pops the lid off a whiteboard marker and draws two smiley-faced stick people on the board in front of us. "Right. Give me two names."

"Marmaduke," says Lucy, in a slightly combative voice.

"Ethel," says Reyan, echoing the energy.

Dahlia pauses. "You know what, sure." She writes the two names on the board, next to their respective stick people. "*So*, supposing Marmaduke – our guy here – dates Ethel for six months. And then one day Ethel breaks up with Marmaduke, totally out of the blue. She tells him she just isn't feeling the same any more and she doesn't think they're compatible." Dahlia uses the side of her hand to rub out Marmaduke's smile and draws in a replacement sad face. "In this imaginary scenario, did Marmaduke do anything wrong?"

"No," says Lucy firmly. "He was just minding his own business, trying his best. It's Ethel" – she shoots a supportive grimace at Reyan – "who changed her mind and decided to mess everything up."

Dahlia's mouth twitches. "I see. But what about if you spoke to Ethel about her side of things? What about if you had a conversation with her a few months later, and she told you that Marmaduke could be really selfish, or that he didn't make much of an effort with her family, or that he came out with comments sometimes that hurt her feelings?"

"She should have told him," says Reyan. He's shaking his head in disbelief, as though he'd like to find imaginary Ethel and make her see sense. "She should have communicated, so that he could do better."

"What if she did?" says Dahlia simply. "What if she tried, but Marmaduke laughed it off, or he didn't listen? What if she didn't feel confident enough in the relationship to tell him? What if she didn't really understand that she *could* talk about it with him until a while later, because she grew up in a family that didn't ever discuss problems and just brushed things under the carpet every time? Who's the bad guy now?"

The room is silent.

Daisy – a shy girl with long auburn plaits and a freckled nose – coughs gently. "It's kind of … both of them?"

Dahlia points at Daisy with gusto. "Ding ding ding! Absolutely this. And, really, it isn't even about both being bad, or both being good. I'd say it's more about both being human. Either way, my point is, there isn't always an angel-slash-villain scenario going on when people break up. There's usually one person who's hurt more – the one who's surprised – but if you take a step back and think about it, you might be able to recognize the part you've played. And that can be really empowering, not because it *blames* you, but because it sets you up for your next relationship. It helps you to learn.

"When I had *my* heart broken," continues Dahlia, holding one hand over her chest, "I realized afterwards that I was a huge people-pleaser – except, the people were not pleased." She pauses. "Like … I'd have plans with my girlfriend, and then my mum would tell me about a family event on the same day, and instead of just saying, 'Sorry, Mum, no can do,' I'd think, *How can I manage this without letting anyone down?* So I'd rush from one event to the other and leave both of them upset. I thought I was this incredibly selfless person, but honestly – I had my own issues that I brought to the relationship, same as everyone else."

Seth, sitting next to me in a mustard-yellow beanie hat, pipes up. "What did you do about it?"

"I tried to stay aware of it. And then, when I was feeling sturdier, I took some action to make sure it wasn't an energy I was going to bring to the table the next time I dated someone." Dahlia offers the room a brief grin, like she's self-reflected a little too close to the sun and is ready to stop talking about herself now. "Anyway, that's today's task: get deep in your pairs and really have a think about the part you played." She waves her hands from side to side to try and dredge up some ideas for the group. "Were you emotionally unavailable? Were you a pushover? Were you too rigid? Were you so distracted with lacrosse club that you never organized dates?"

"Shit," says Joey, the kid who threw up on his own shoes. "I actually think I *was* pretty distracted with lacrosse club."

"Great!" calls Dahlia. "Well, not great, but great that you're able to recognize it *now.* Keep that self-awareness going for your pair-work, Joey!"

I think Dahlia will make a very good therapist one day.

The room is loud and I feel too emotionally delicate to start rehashing my relationship issues within earshot of everyone else, so I direct Seth out to the comfy chairs in the ESS entrance hall.

He throws his bag down on to the floor, tugs off his hat, and pulls his legs up on to the seat beneath him.

"I don't like today's session," he says. "It's basically, *Let's talk about how terrible we were, so we're less terrible in the years to come.* I already know it, Dahlia. I don't need reminding."

"I don't mean to blow my own trumpet," I tell him, "but I don't think I *was* terrible. Other than the whole minimal-fun thing, I think I was an incredible girlfriend."

It's true. I can see what Dahlia is saying – all the stuff about learning, and growing, and recognizing – but I feel like there must be at least *some* relationships where it wasn't a faults-on-both-sides deal. What about my relationship, which was an almost-perfect-until-my-boyfriend-changed-his-mind-out-of-nowhere deal?

"Examples, please," says Seth. He's drumming a beat on his knees with the palms of his hands and speaking in time to it. "Seeing as you are now my fake girlfriend. Tell me what I'd have to look forward to, if we were legit."

I clear my throat. "Lots of stuff. I made an effort with his family. I always remembered little things about him – tiny things he'd mentioned in passing. We'd walk past a T-shirt in a shop and he'd say how much he liked it, but then he'd overthink the whole thing and get overwhelmed by whether to buy it or not, so I'd go back for it at the weekend and surprise him. Oh, and I helped him out a lot. With writing – his design tech essays. His personal statement." I feel a spark of embarrassment to share this with Seth, as though it might sound like Freddie thought of me as an unpaid life-admin assistant, instead of a girlfriend. "He's one of the smartest people I know," I add quickly. "He just struggles with words. They're not his friend."

Seth raises an interested eyebrow. "But they're *your* friend?"

I nod as I untuck a sheet of hair from behind my ear, using it to cover a little more of my face. "They're basically family. It's like … I *get* words. I feel at ease with them. I'd rather type out every single one of my interactions than say them face-to-face, because I know they come across better that way. *I* come across better that way."

He blinks. "You come across just fine to me."

"Thanks." I pick at a piece of cracked rubber on the side of my shoe. "What about you? Were you a good boyfriend?"

Seth slumps in his chair. "I thought I was. Now I look back on it all and I think … maybe I didn't try hard enough. Maybe I got too comfy too quick." He sighs. "Gen always said I had a *floaty energy.* Which is right, you know – I do. I'm sure you've noticed it. Everyone else does."

A floaty energy sounds about right. In the few minutes we've been sitting here, Seth has already changed his seating position three times and started a valiant mission to peel the sticker off the plastic bottle he's holding in one hand. It's not so much that he's distracted – I assume that he's taking in everything I'm saying, and he's not done anything to make me think otherwise – but I can see how people could read his mannerisms as *floatiness.* I nod slowly, trying to make sure my face gives off some warmth, so he knows that I'm not judging him for it – that it isn't a negative in my eyes.

"Yeah, well," he says. "She hated that. Here's an example for you: we went to Dublin together last year and Gen planned it out in advance – she wanted to do all kinds of stuff. The castle, the Botanic Gardens, whatever." He abandons the bottle, grabbing the worksheet in front of us and drawing a little heart with a jagged crack down the middle of it. "Anyway, we flew there, and she had it all organized – ten a.m. here, eleven a.m. there – then halfway through the trip she told me we were going for lunch at this little cafe, and I said, 'Could we just wait a while and go for pizza instead? I feel like pizza.' And she was like, 'No, no, we're going to the cafe at midday. It's what we agreed on.' And I'm there, floating around, like, 'We agreed on it two months ago, Gen. Things change, let's have a pizza, what does it matter?' And she lost it."

"Lost it how?"

"She told me that she was the only person who'd put any effort into planning the trip and that I expected her to take care of everything and *who did I think I was*, poking holes in her decisions even though I hadn't cared enough to be a part of them at the time. Then she stormed off and left me alone on a park bench until she'd calmed down." He sniffs. "I made friends with an old man named Brendan, so it wasn't all bad. He was a plumber. He said I had the soul of a high-quality tradesman."

I fight off a smile. "And what else did Brendan have to say about all this?"

"Brendan was on my side, actually," says Seth, holding a hand up to his chest. "He told me it was just a classic 'Type A meets Type B' situation, not unlike his own relationship with his wife Sue. Nothing to worry too much about. He said, 'You're a young lad, Seth; don't overthink it. Just go for the pizza.'"

I wait for the next part of the story, but it doesn't come. "And did you? Go for the pizza?"

"No," says Seth, grabbing the plastic bottle again and using a fingernail to pick at its label. "I apologized and we went to the cafe. But then Gen and I came home and it felt like there was this new awkwardness between us. This new feeling that I was always seconds away from disappointing her in some way. It'd disappear sometimes, but then it'd come back even stronger. The night we broke up – Christmas Eve – we'd agreed to meet at seven. But I was at home panicking because my outfit looked terrible, so that took some extra time. And then I remembered I hadn't written her Christmas card yet, so that took even more time."

"It takes thirty seconds to write a Christmas card, surely," I say. "Two minutes, tops."

"Maybe for you," Seth points out. "I like to write a heartfelt message in mine. But then sometimes I'm not sure what to put, so I draft it out first, to make sure it sounds right. So I did that, and then I had this voice in the back of my head, *Seth, you're going to be late. You're SO late.* Which made me more panicky. And then Gen was messaging me, *You said seven p.m.! It's seven thirty-six! What's happening for dinner?! Why do you always do this to me! Why don't you care?!*"

"It sounds to me like you care a lot," I offer. "You were late because you were choosing a good outfit and writing a festive love letter."

"Yes, but Gen gets very anxious about these sorts of

things, and I knew that. I should've been more organized." He manages to remove the sticker from the bottle, and places it on the sole of his trainer for no reason at all. "Anyway, by the time I arrived, she had my Christmas gifts in a bag by the front door. She said – and I remember this, because it felt particularly hideous – 'There are thousands of men out there who'd prioritize me, so why do I keep wasting my time on a little boy?' And that was it."

He leans back and gazes up to the skylights in the roof. His top teeth are nudging at his bottom lip, biting at it in a way that looks painful.

"Ouch," I say, like I can feel his hurt somehow, the same way Freddie used to be able to feel mine.

"Ouch," agrees Seth. "And obviously I went into full, humiliating *let's salvage this* mode. Stood there on her front porch desperately trying to remind her of all the good times we had together. All the good things I did. And then eventually her dad came out of the living room, like an awkward bouncer. He turned to me, and he said, 'Come on, kid, I think it's time to head home.' *Kid*. Like I was some wayward twelve-year-old who'd wandered in off the street."

Students have started to slowly drift into the ESS reception in preparation for afternoon lessons, and Dahlia pokes her head out the classroom door to remind us to wrap things up.

You good? she mouths, and I nod. She disappears back inside.

"You're not a kid," I tell Seth, but he doesn't look at me. "You're not."

He drags his hands over his face. "Maybe not to you."

"Not to any of us in the RDC." I realize it probably isn't my place to speak on behalf of an entire group, but it definitely feels like my job to keep us on script, to bring him back from his sadness. "Hey. Dahlia asked us to think about the part that we played. What do you think?"

"Ugh. Tell her I played the part of Weird, Floaty Boyfriend." His head is still tipped back; I study two particularly prominent muscles in his neck. "People like it for a bit, but then it gets annoying, and then they end up replacing you with Serious Boyfriend Who Wears a Watch and Knows How to Parallel Park."

"No," I correct him gently, steering my eyes away from his throat. "I mean – what was your role in all this? Looking back on the relationship, what lesson do you think you learned?"

"The lesson I learned?" says Seth, snapping back to life and heaving himself to his feet. The bell rings and he offers me a hand, tugging me up to stand alongside him. "There are thousands of men out there who've got their life together and know how to prioritize her. I need to prove I'm one of them."

14

The keeper

Bella cackles when I tell her that she is the unofficial inspiration for the Freddie-themed part of Operation Get Gen and Freddie Back.

"Because I'm *fun*?" She takes her coffee from the barista, her red lips parted in a wide grin.

I nod as we walk to find a table, praying Freddie isn't anywhere in the vicinity. "You are, unquestionably, the most fun person I know. Seth actually refers to you as Fun Bella."

"Oh, he's hot, by the way." We slide into a two-seater booth, and she reaches into her shoulder bag to pull out a small tub of olives. "So that alone will add a little salt to Freddie's wound."

The words *Seth* and *hot* don't really connect in my mind. *Seth* and *athletic*, maybe. *Seth* and *conventionally attractive*, sure. But anyone can be conventionally attractive, objectively speaking. Storefront mannequins can be conventionally attractive. The worst people in the world can be conventionally attractive. Ultimately, it doesn't mean much.

I pick up an abandoned teaspoon and twist it around in my fingers. "How do you know what he looks like?"

Bella shrugs, nonchalant. "You told me about him. I check these things."

"And you think that'll help stuff with Freddie?"

"Put it this way: I don't think it'll hinder," she says, smirking. "You ever see *The Notebook*? My assessment: it's like if that guy had a brother. A happier, weirder younger brother, who liked to play sports. Right?"

I take a moment to consider this unsolicited Ryan Gosling comparison – to think about Seth's sandy wave of hair and his tanned arms and his tiny golden freckles. The way he smells like a coconut incense stick.

"I mean …" My swallow turns into a gulp. "I guess so. If someone really wanted to make that comparison, then I guess they could."

Bella snorts. "Would you please just admit that your fake boyfriend is good-looking? The police aren't going to storm in here. The world isn't going to end. You can notice other guys and still be rooting for Freddie."

She selects a bulging green olive, places it into her mouth and wipes her hand on the knee of her jeans as she chews, before returning her accusing gaze to me. She is *definitely* enjoying this.

I blink at her. "He's … He's …"

I'm still working out exactly which non-committal adjective to insert after this opener when Bella stops, rigid, and points a covert finger at a short, slender girl with a choppy brown bob who's just settled into the table next to us. This girl means nothing to me, so I shrug. Bella lets out a sigh of frustration before reaching for her pen and scribbling down a message on a paper napkin.

THAT'S GEN

And then:

SAY SOMETHING GIRLFRIENDY!!!

Gen, sat to my right, blows on her coffee and scrolls on her phone, while Bella hurries me along with urgent, masterminding eyes. My brain lets me down; it loops on the same opener as before, stuck on the Seth-descriptors. *He's … He's …*

"He's pretty," I spit out, my words stumbling across each other. "His eyes are the same colour as the ocean." Bella writes **I KNEW IT** on her napkin and holds it up triumphantly while my cheeks burn.

"So true. And he just seems *perfect* for you," she chimes in now, with such deliberate feigned enthusiasm I'm surprised the entire coffee shop doesn't hear her. "Like, if I had to create a man and deposit him into your life, Seth Whittaker would be that man."

Out of the corner of my eye, I see Gen freeze at the shameless mention of Seth Whittaker. Bella and I pretend not to notice, and continue our fake conversation as though we're completely oblivious.

"Totally," I agree. "He's sweet, and funny, and … and *so* organized." My brain flits straight into storytelling mode, the same way it did when I was little, hosting one-woman puppet shows for my mum. "I mean, he plans every single date for us in advance. He's always early, no matter what. He even baked me a cake for our one-week anniversary."

This is a straight-up lie; I have no idea when our one-week anniversary would even *be* – and, if it's been and gone, there was definitely no baking to mark the occasion. But at short notice, knowing what I know about Gen's love of orderly boys, it's the best I can do, and I'm certain that Seth will appreciate it.

Bella sighs wistfully, as though securing a man who knows how to make a mean lemon drizzle is something reserved only for the very luckiest among us. "That, my friend, is what we call a keeper. You'd be out of your mind to let someone that thoughtful slip away."

Next to us, I hear a sharp intake of breath and the sound of chair legs scraping against the floor. Both of us watch, silently victorious, as Gen paces out of the cafe, leaving an untouched mug of steaming coffee behind her.

Bella scrunches the napkin into a little ball and throws it into her empty olive pot in a slam dunk. "And the Oscar goes *to*..."

15

The ambush

"I don't care what anyone says," Seth tells me on Friday lunchtime, as the rain batters against the rickety art-block windows. "It isn't an ambush."

He holds out a hand for a fresh paintbrush, and I place the cleanest-looking one into his outstretched fingers. He provides me with a grateful, wide-mouthed smile, resting his tongue between his teeth.

"We're showing up to your ex-girlfriend's dance show, uninvited, in the hopes that she will somehow be persuaded to date you again," I remind him. "I'd call that something of an ambush."

"You're thinking of it the wrong way," says Seth, dipping the brush into a dollop of yellow paint and swirling it into a neighbouring blue. "As far as anyone else knows, it's a completely coincidental drop-in. *Oh, hi, Gen! Wow! What are the chances!* I've heard that Lucy from the RDC is also performing, and I think it'd be a crying shame to miss out on that."

"You've barely spoken to Lucy," I point out. "I don't even think she knows our names."

"It says here that she and her fellow performers want to take us on 'an electrifying journey through dance, showcasing a wide variety of genres'," he says, reciting from the bright-purple flyer that's laying on the table we're sat at. "So who are we to stop them?"

I pick up the flyer and stare at it. "If I agree to be taken on this electrifying journey, I'm going to need some tips. How do we do things tonight? How aggressive is our approach when Gen is involved?"

Seth thinks about this. "Not an exaggerated, draped all over each other, pissing up a tree kind of an energy," he tells me eventually. "That's childish. The vibe tonight is more of a … calm elegance. We're comfortable. We're mature. We're happy. We're exactly what Genevieve wants."

The mention of his ex's name reminds me of yesterday's coffee shop encounter. "By the way, Bella and I saw Gen, and we made sure she overheard us talking about how thoughtful and organized my new boyfriend is. I said – very loudly – that you plan every single date, always show up early *and* baked me a cake for our one-week anniversary."

His jaw drops as he stuffs the paintbrush into its water

jar. "*Harley.* Above and beyond. What did she say? How did she seem? Which flavour did I choose?"

The question-jumping makes me laugh. "She said nothing – she just froze in shock and then ran away. And as for the flavour … I didn't get that far into the detail. Do you have a preference?"

"For you" – he pauses – "I like to think I'd have opted for a classic Victoria sponge."

"Why?" I demand. I can't tell if this is an insult – more unwanted *no need*er-style commentary.

His eyes fall to the table, back to the paper in front of him. "It does what it says it'll do. It's not like red velvet, masquerading as something it's not. It's nothing too avant-garde, like carrot cake." He lets out a low cough. "A nice, honest Victoria sponge. Some would say the Victoria plays it too safe; I would disagree. I think it knows what it's about."

It knows what it's about. No one has ever described me this way before, but it's true.

"Thank you," I say, and I deliberately dart my eyes up to meet his.

"I mean it," he replies. "And, had I made this cake, I would have iced it with a message, like, *Happy one week of love*, or, *Harley, you are never far-ly from my thoughts.* Would you have eaten it?"

I shake my head at him, laughing at the terrible rhyme. "I'm sorry to put an end to the imaginary dessert-making, but I don't really do cake. Or any sweet stuff. I'm more of a savoury girl."

"So if a boyfriend – real or fake – wanted to make you a cake to profess his feelings, he just … couldn't do it?" says Seth, blowing on to his sketchbook. "Or would you be more into, like, celebratory sushi? Perhaps a love-lasagne?"

"I would actually be *very* into a love-lasagne," I tell him. "That would really work for me."

Seth's eyes crinkle as he smiles. "That might be the most fun thing I've learned about you yet."

When we turn up for the dance show, all of Seth's confidence from earlier in the day has disappeared; he's attacking a thumbnail with his teeth, gnawing at the side of it like a beaver with a stick.

"Are you OK?" I ask.

"No," says Seth, spitting out a nail segment on to the ground. "Not OK. Turns out this *is* an ambush, and it's hard to pull off the dress code for a thing like that." He's tapping one heel on the ground, jiggling his entire leg up and down on the spot like a repressed Riverdancer. "Who knew!"

We're approximately thirty seconds away from being the awkward stragglers who turn up after the doors have closed and have to be shown to their seats by a volunteer with a torch, so I grab him by the elbow and begin to frog-march him from our meeting spot to the sports hall. "Try not to worry about it. What you chose looks fine."

"FINE?" Seth bellows. A nearby pigeon flees into the sky at his outburst. "I look like a geography teacher. An elderly one that nobody likes."

I twist my head to the right and take a moment to study him from head to toe as we pace. He's dressed in a starchy black blazer I haven't seen before, on top of his usual jeans and a familiar plaid shirt. His shoes – black and lace-up – are also new. He's right – for someone who cares about their outfits, it isn't exactly fine. Half of his ensemble looks traditional – casual and Seth-like. The other half looks like he just ran out of a corporate job interview and somehow ended up at this teenage arts event.

"It's a little mixed-up, that's all. Why the …?" I gesticulate loosely towards the blazer.

"It was my *dad*," moans Seth, turning his walk into a slow jog. "I was running around the house panicking, telling everyone I needed to look smart for my big Get Gen Back event – which, by the way, they are absolutely confused by. And then Dad comes in like, 'Smart? Smart? I've got just the thing!' and then *he* dashes off to his wardrobe, and *I'm* already late, and then one thing leads to another and before I know it …" He tugs off the jacket and folds it over one arm. "Can we just leave? I'd rather she didn't see me at all than see me looking like this."

There's a little part of me that wants to say yes. To tell

him, *Sure thing. I'd much rather be at home, as always, so let's call it a day and try again later.* But then I look at him – properly, actually look at him, instead of just flickering glances towards his terrible outfit – and I snuff that part out completely. I see the exhaustion in his eyes, his crossed arms, the new embarrassment in his stance. I remember the effort he put into our first-ever meeting with Freddie, his encouraging hand on my thigh, and I hear myself saying, "No."

Seth sniffs. "No?"

I shake my head, the pep talk forming in my throat. "No. We planned this and we're here, so we're not stopping now. Do you want to go home and wallow in your pyjamas? Or do you want to take a deep breath, put your blazer back on, and go show Gen what she's missing?"

He frowns at me, like it's a no-brainer. "The first one. My pyjamas have Pikachu on them."

I take the blazer out of his hands and reach up to drape it over his shoulders. "They sound great, but it was a rhetorical question. We're going for option two."

"That's very adventurous of you, Carly Dean," says Seth limply. "Progress is being made."

The sports hall is buzzing, mostly with parents and younger siblings. We make it in with a few seconds to spare – we flash our tickets at a harassed-looking PE teacher and are advised to grab a seat wherever, although Seth raises the valid point that the nearer the front, the higher the likelihood of a Genevieve encounter.

"Genevieve is a beautiful name," I tell him, as we scurry over to the sea of plastic chairs. It's not the first time I've thought it, but it's the first time I've remembered to say it out loud. "Regal. You can't be called Genevieve and not be beautiful."

"Are you trying to kill me?" says Seth. His face has a new sheen of sweat to it. "Are you trying to cause me some serious pain?"

I blink. "I'm just saying."

"Well, maybe don't *just say*. Maybe just *think*."

Neither of us speak as we "excuse me" our way through rows of parents, before finally squeezing into a spare couple of seats in the middle of the second row. Seth thuds down on to the first one and I follow suit, tugging a paper programme that says A JOURNEY THROUGH MOVEMENT from underneath me.

"I'm sorry," says Seth, more to his paper programme than to me. "I get snippy when I'm stressed. She really *is* very beautiful."

I go to tell him it's OK – that I get it, that sometimes even the mention of Freddie is enough to make me feel like I've been punched, hard, right in the sternum – but as I open my mouth, the lights cut out and a classical music piece starts to play.

"TWO HOUSEHOLDS," yells a girl in

a crimson-coloured jumpsuit. "BOTH ALIKE IN DIGNITY. IN FAIR VERONA, WHERE WE LAY OUR SCENE."

A smattering of students sweep on to the stage in a long line, all dressed in the same crimson costume. They join the yelling girl to continue the opening speech, holding hands and staring boldly at the audience. The audience sits up in their chairs, as if to say, *OK, we're listening.* Seth, to my right, lets out a protracted sigh.

"Is Gen up there now?" I whisper.

"No," he says. "She's up there" – he's looking at the floor but he holds up his finger and counts in time with the foreboding classical music – "now."

Gen, dressed in a crisp white cotton dress and gold hoop earrings, steps on to the stage, and Seth grabs my wrist with such a jerky movement that the woman next to us jumps. Now that I'm sitting here, properly observing Gen instead of hosting a panicked fake conversation from the table next to her, I can see that Seth was right about the beautiful thing. Gen has the air of a girl who has never skipped a hair-wash day because she wanted to sleep in. Gen, I'm certain, has never once bitten her fingernails or been faced with the harsh realities of hormonal acne. She's symmetrical, angular and clean – the kind of beautiful that everyone notices.

It doesn't intimidate me, necessarily, even though I guess technically I'm her direct competition. I'm looking at her more like a science project, like an English literature poem I want to analyse and unpick.

To Gen's left, another dancer appears: a boy with light-brown hair swept back into an exaggerated quiff. He's wearing a black T-shirt with the sleeves cut off, and his exposed, muscular arms grab at her waist, tugging her into a push-pull movement that makes Seth's grip on my wrist tighten.

"*Jake Jenson*," says Seth, in a voice that sounds like he's just unveiled the villain in an episode of *Scooby Doo*.

I stare at the black-vested boy. "I didn't know her boyfriend was going to be here?"

"I told you – this is how they met," says Seth, removing his hand from my arm and using it to cover his mouth, like he's trying to hold himself back from becoming Jake Jenson's very own audience heckler. The rest of his words come out muffled. "Their section is supposed to be a dance retelling of *Romeo and Juliet*. Except in this one, it's modern day. Oh, and Romeo's an asshole."

A man on the row in front of us turns round to shush Seth, who shushes him right back and mutters something about censorship.

We watch the rest of the first half in silence, except for when Seth jumps in to make crotchety comments about Jake's flawed footwork or lack of acting prowess. Lucy's segment of the evening is a much happier affair – she and her group perform a jazz piece to an old pop song, followed by a ballet-inspired routine complete with ribbons that they wave around in the air. I try to catch her eye from our space on the second row, but she's too in the zone with the ribbons to notice. I think this is the first time I've ever seen Lucy smile.

The interval arrives at a good time; I'm so uncomfortable from the hard plastic chairs that I need to move my legs, and Seth is so uncomfortable from the thought of Jake's hands on Genevieve's waist that he needs to get some air. We wriggle back out of the row, past parents with popcorn and children with juice cartons, and make our way over to the reception area, where a woman is handing out cups of water and a cool breeze is wafting its way in through the open doors.

"You're doing very well," I tell Seth encouragingly as I pass him a paper cup. "You're really holding it together."

He takes the cup and gulps down its contents. "I feel ill."

He looks it, too. Even in the more forgiving light of the entrance hall, the sweaty sheen from earlier has remained, and I think he knows it, because he lifts up an arm and uses it to mop at his brow.

"Seth?"

I pull my eyes away from his glistening forehead and see Gen – who, unsurprisingly, isn't sporting one of her own. Her blunt hair has been pulled back with a claw clip and she's changed from her white cotton dress into a pair of heather-grey jogging bottoms, paired with a black bra top.

"Oh, God," says Seth, as if his thoughts have forced their way out of his mouth. "It's you." He suddenly becomes very aware of his paper cup, waving it around as he searches for somewhere to dispose of it. I offer out a hand, like a mum with a sweet-wrapper-discarding toddler.

"Of course it's me," says Gen, her forehead crumpling slightly. "You knew I was performing tonight. What are you doing here? Why are you dressed like a funeral director?"

Seth ignores the second question and takes one step closer to me. "Our friend Lyndsey—"

"Lucy," I say, cutting across him.

He waves a hand. "Lucy. Our good friend Lucy was performing, so we wanted to come along and support, didn't we? Show some school spirit."

Gen makes a questioning sound and narrows her eyes.

"That's right … pookie," I say, grabbing the crook of his arm like he's an old lady I'm helping into a car. Why I opt for *pookie*, I have no idea, and I'm guessing Seth doesn't either, because he flashes a pained look in my direction and simply mouths, *No.*

"Greaaaat," says Gen, stretching the word out like it's the first time she's ever used it. She turns to look at Seth, twisting a gold hoop between finger and thumb. "Seth, are you doing OK? After … everything. You seem a little frantic."

She's right – he does. I mean, Seth's always a little frantic, but after the way he acted when he met Freddie in the cafe,

I'd expected a direct repeat for Gen. Hair twizzling, low-murmuring, all-the-time-in-the-world energy. This is the total opposite. This is knee-tapping, hands-shaking, teeth-chattering panic.

"Frantic?" He rests a hand on my shoulder. "I'm alive with the glory of love, actually. I'm amped. I'm flourishing."

Gen puts an unconvinced hand on an unconvinced hip and scrutinizes him. "You're flourishing?"

"Of course. If you hadn't ended things with me, I'd never have met my Harley."

Gen flits her full attention to me now; her razor-sharp jawbone rotates back in my direction and her eyes scan me up and down. I don't know what to do or say about this, so I offer her an awkward little bow, like a medieval jester, and immediately regret my decision.

"Hey, Vie, you want a drink?" says a deep voice behind us.

Jake emerges, clutching two metal water bottles and a small towel in his ample hands. He unscrews the lid of one of the bottles effortlessly and hands it over to Gen, who looks at him as though he's just completed a Herculean feat and immediately snuggles into the space between his bicep and his torso.

"Uh, I'm sorry," says Seth, holding an affronted hand out to pause the conversation. "Who is *Vie*?"

"Gene*vie*ve," Gen snaps, from the depths of Jake's armpit. "It's what Jake calls me."

“How inventive,” says Seth. I pinch the material just above his elbow as a reminder that sarcastic insults are not usually renowned for their ability to win back wronged women.

Gen raises a perfectly arched eyebrow. “I’m not sure *pookie* gets a say in this.”

Jake – who seems like a decent enough boy (except for the girlfriend-poaching) from the thirty seconds I’ve seen of him – is looking more than a little confused. He gently drags himself away from Gen’s head and steps back to look at us all, tilting his head, like he’s trying to remove himself from the situation in order to fully understand it.

“You’re Seth, right?” he says, squinting at the sweaty blazer-wearer in front of him and extending out a hand for shaking.

“Don’t *pretend*, Jacob,” Seth pings back, as he takes the hand. “You saw me and Gen together outside the dance studio, many a time. You know who I am.”

“That’s … that’s right. I remember now.” Jake nods, but the muscles in his jaw are twitching. “Just ‘Jake’ is fine, by the way. I really hate ‘Jacob’.”

“Don’t we all,” mutters Seth. I pinch him again, harder this time, and he lets out a yelp. “While we’re doing introductions,” he adds quickly, revving up the volume and looking in my direction with a *ta-dah* expression on his face, “this is *my* girlfriend, Harley Green.”

I avoid the bow this time and opt for a brief smile, which Jake returns.

"Where exactly did you two meet?" Gen's pixie-like face has turned a new shade of fuchsia. "I mean, how did this happen?"

Seth opens his mouth for a silent *ah*. "Well. *There's* a story."

"Is that right?" says Gen in a sceptical voice.

"Oh, that's right, all right," says Seth. He reaches for my hand and squeezes it with such wild intensity I can only read the action as: *help me.*

Gen, unblinking, waits for an answer.

"The guy I used to date was immature," I blurt, and the words are falling out of my mouth before I've even thought about them. "He had no direction, and I was sick of it. When I ended things, I said I wasn't going to date again until I met a boy who ticked all the right boxes for me. And I thought it'd take months, but it was like the universe *heard* that. A few days later, I was walking around sixth form and I bumped into this guy" – I look up at Seth with faux-adoration while I stall for time – "*literally.*"

"Literally?" says Jake. He takes a swig of water and looks at me with interest as I internally flail for the next part of the tale.

"Yup," I tell him. "Literally. You know how it is – rushing to English class, wasn't looking where I was going, then *bam*, right into Seth. Tripped over, Diet Coke down my T-shirt, the whole thing. Would've been a day ruiner, right? But my pookie salvaged it."

"He really did," agrees Seth, but the persistent death grip of his hand suggests *my pookie* isn't currently capable of adding any more than that.

"He bent down to pick me up," I say dreamily, stroking at Seth's terrified knuckle with one thumb. "Put his arms under me, swung me to my feet and said, 'Don't worry, I've got you.' It was like Spider-Man rescuing Mary Jane. Then he pulled out a spare shirt from his backpack—"

"I always carry one," adds Seth proudly. "You never know when you'll need it."

"And he said, 'Here, take this.' So I did, and when I came out the bathroom with it on, he'd cleaned up all the spilled Diet Coke on the floor *and* been to the cafe to buy me a fresh drink. It was like … I just had this moment, you know?" I look Gen straight in her bright-blue eyes. "Where I realized: this is the kind of boy I've been looking for. Someone who actually has his shit together."

There's a moment of quiet while I allow my fictitious meet-cute to properly sink in. Seth's hand has relaxed a little in mine, and I carry on stroking at it, like it's a frazzled cat I'm coaxing down from a tree.

"Wow," says Gen eventually, in a low voice. "That's … I mean, good for you."

"*So* good for me," I confirm. "I like a boy who's done the work, you know? A boy who really knows how to take care of me."

"Likewise," she murmurs. She huddles back under the canopy of Jake's chin and places a hand across his thick forearm.

A tall grey-haired woman in a purple trouser suit strides down the hallway, clapping her hands together. "Break's over, dancers – everyone backstage, please, ready for curtain up."

The hubbub of the sports hall corridor changes course, as performers and audience members alike start to traipse off to their destinations. Gen and Jake loosen their grip on each other and Gen points at the door to the changing rooms. "That's us. We, uh … We should head back in now."

"Hey, maybe we could double-date sometime," calls Seth, as they begin to awkwardly shuffle away from us. "Go golfing. Grab some drinks, then head out to dinner. I know a great little place. Jacob, my man, do you golf? I bet you golf." He points a finger at Jake, waiting for the response.

Jake's eyes are wary. "Uh, yeah, I golf."

"I knew it," yells Seth. "I *knew* it – Harley, didn't I say? Gen, I'll have my people call your people; we'll make it happen."

"I think we'll pass, Seth," calls Gen, ushering her boyfriend through the changing room door with some Year Twelve tap-dancers.

The two of them disappear from view, and with a protective grip on Seth's blazered arm, I yank him in the opposite direction, towards the sports hall's glowing EXIT sign.

16

The debrief

"Before tonight, the most embarrassing moment of my life was when I tripped over my own shoelaces in the end-of-year talent show and dived off the stage into Elliot Armstrong's grandma," says Seth, his words emerging as fog in the bitter January cold. "Now, that pales in comparison. I'd happily go back to that night and do it all over again, even the grandmother-in-the-hospital thing, if it meant I could take back what just happened."

The park bench creaks as he shifts on it. I stay still next to him, taking in the stars that are sprinkled across the dark sky next to a full moon.

"It wasn't embarrassing, exactly," I murmur, which we both know is a well-meaning lie. "It was … Well, it was the first time you'd spoken to her and Jake together, right? There's no world in which that could've gone well."

"Harley, I asked them to go *golfing* with us." He leans back, cradling his head in his hands and squeezing his eyes shut. "Like we're all forty-year-olds with clients and American Express cards."

"I like crazy golf," I offer, but Seth's eyes stay closed.

"How are you getting home?" he asks the sky. "Do you *need* to go home?" He chews on his bottom lip. "Will you … Will you come to my home, instead?"

"Why?" It's the first thing I think and the first word that comes out of my mouth. I picture the full Whittaker house, like Seth told me about – his thirty-eight sisters and his happily married parents and his golden retriever. "Wouldn't it be…"

I don't finish the sentence, because I'm not sure which adjective I'm looking for. *Weird? Pointless? Uncomfortable – probably for everyone but mostly for me?*

Seth shakes his head. "No, it wouldn't. Everyone's out except for my dad and the dog, and neither of them thrive when asked for verbal support. I need to debrief, imminently, and ideally in the comfort of my own bedroom – away from these sub-zero temperatures. Please?"

He opens his eyes, glances over towards me, and waits.

The moment we arrive in Seth's room, he launches himself into a defeated star shape on the bed, before flipping his body over and dangling his head down towards the floor.

I take a tentative seat on a fluffy rug in front of him, with my back against the warmth of the radiator, and decide to do some visual snooping.

The walls of his bedroom are painted a cheerful sky-blue shade, with matching checked tartan bedsheets. In both of the coves on either side of the chimney breast are thick wooden shelves, which seem to house the many accessories for Seth's various hobbies. On one shelf is a badminton racquet next to a large potted succulent; on another is a wicker lamp and a stack of A4 music books. In front of the chimney breast, on top of a squat wooden table, sits Seth's aquarium. I peer at it from my spot on the floor and wonder which of the residents is Jonathan, Seth's favourite fish-child.

If I had to offer up a review of the room at this stage, I'd say that the overall feel is good, but definitely not immune to the frantic energy that Seth brings to the world. The bedside table, for example, is *catastrophic*. Four mugs. Two glasses. Three different deodorants, all in the exact same scent. I lean over to pick one up and shake it – empty.

There's a knock at the door, and a squinting face peeks around it. The face is essentially Seth's in a slightly different font – it belongs to a girl of about twelve or thirteen, who has the same sandy-blonde hair, except longer and pulled back into a ponytail.

"Oh, hey, Wren," says Seth gloomily. "I thought you were out with the rest of them. Wanna come in?"

"Only if you're not naked," says the girl at the door, still squinting. "I heard voices and I thought maybe it was Gen."

Seth's eyes, still upside down like their owner, scan me for a split-second. "Definitely not naked."

I feel my face burn red. "And definitely not Gen. I'm Harley."

"Harley? That's such a cool name!" Wren forgets her shyness and barrels into the bedroom, throwing herself on to the bed next to her brother. He offers her a weak hand; she high fives it.

"You think?" I ask her.

"I love it," says Wren. "Sounds like you're going to wear a leather jacket and beat up some bad guys."

I've always felt conflicted about my name. I overheard my uncle Matthew talking about it once, at my sixteenth birthday party. Actually, he was talking more about me. "Not exactly a Davidson, is she," he'd said, nodding in my direction. I pretended I didn't hear him, but I knew exactly what he meant. *Same name as a motorbike for rebels and free spirits – and, as a result, something of a disappointment to talk to.*

I'd wanted to explain to him that Harley is actually an old name – a really old name – a name that means something to do with hares and meadows. Instead I kept quiet, and let him carry on thinking that my mother named me after an anarchic motorcycle.

"Uncle Matthew called *his* children Jesper and

Persephone," my mum had reminded me afterwards, when I told her what I'd heard. "Case closed."

Wren pokes at Seth's shoulder with a stubby fingernail. "You look depressed. You've got the same face as when Mr Wilson chewed up your elephant socks."

"Oh, this is far worse than Sock-gate," says Seth loftily. "This is ... a whole other gate of its own. A brand-new gate, leading directly to the depths of Hell."

Wren rolls her eyes, then flits them over to meet mine. *Gen?* she mouths, and I grimace in reply before providing Wren with a short summary of the evening, to which Seth makes loud, pained noises in response. When I'm finished, Wren lets out an exhausted sigh.

"Seth, do you not remember what I told you, from my book?" she says. "*The longer you spend obsessing over someone who doesn't want you any more, the longer you keep yourself from experiencing true connection*."

"Do you not remember what I told *you*?" Seth shoots back. "I said, *Thanks for the input, Drew Barrymore, but Gen* might *want me if she saw how different I am now.* That's the whole point."

Wren tuts, like a disappointed grandmother, and picks up a raggedy stuffed bear from Seth's pillow, which she immediately places on top of his face. "You're not different at all. You're just pretending to be."

Seth removes the bear and flashes her a glare as he tosses it away.

"Harley, did you know that Gen never came round here, ever?" says Wren, with a look in my direction that says, *Yeah, you heard me*. "She always wanted Seth to go over to her house, every time, even though she had a car and he didn't. And when she did come over to our house, she wouldn't even talk to us. She just walked straight up to his bedroom—"

"Because she was shy," says Seth.

"She was not *shy*. She was rude. Oh, *and* she was weird about Jonathan."

We all turn to stare at the bustling aquarium, and I once again wonder which of its occupants could be the man in question. I plant my hands down on either side of my legs and haul myself up to a standing position, then wander over to Jonathan's tank, where I spot several multi-coloured fish. They aren't quite red-orange-yellow-green-blue striped, like my brain had conjured up, but their snouts are a dark, sparkling blue and their tails are a shade of golden yellow.

"Are these the rainbow fish?" I ask.

Wren nods. She leans forward, picks up a pen, and uses it to point at one of them. "That's Jonathan."

I lean forward with her and squint to decipher why this particular fish scores so highly in the Whittaker popularity stakes. "How can you tell?"

"He has a slightly smaller tail," she informs me. "If you look, it doesn't have the same width as the others."

I do look, and she's right. Jonathan's tail, the shape

of a splayed paintbrush, is noticeably smaller than the ones belonging to his peers, like the Whittaker family's very own Nemo.

"He's cute," I tell her. "I like him."

Wren nods with relish. "Genevieve said he was creepy."

"Not everybody is into aquatic life, Wren," says Seth in a weary-dad voice. "That doesn't make her a monster."

I wonder how many times they've had this conversation – how many times Seth's swept in to defend Gen while his sister points out what he's missing. I listen now as Wren – who's either alarmingly wise for her age or a devout MusingsWithMin follower – says things like, *If she doesn't like you how you are, then maybe she's not the person for you,* and, *Even if you get her back, what then?*

I freeze at her words, suddenly acutely aware of the reason I'm here in the first place: I'm part of this. I'm no different to Seth in this situation – I'm desperate, shape-shifting, broken-hearted, poised to act like a whole other person for the sake of winning over my ex. And, like Wren says, even if I get him back, what then? Spend the rest of my life pretending to like outdoor activities and overcrowded social events, while Freddie remains oblivious? The undercurrent of it all rocks me. Why isn't the real me good enough?

Seth curls up into the foetal position. "Wren, please. Harley was making me feel better; you're just making me feel worse. I'm already embarrassed enough."

"You're not grouching like this because you're embarrassed," Wren insists. "You're grouching like this because you know I'm right."

Seth rolls on to his front now and looks to me for back-up. His hair's been pushed away from his face, leaving him with two thick, anxious lines on his forehead. A tiny part of me wants to reach up and touch the lines, calm them down a little, coax them out.

I clear my throat, torn between my loyalty to Seth and my urge to tell him the truth. "Gen seems … settled. She's with Jake now; she's happy. And I say this with respect: pretending to have your life together doesn't seem to come very naturally to you."

In some ways, I like that it doesn't come naturally to him. It's as if he can't fake it – as if he's so fully-formed as a person that trying to act any differently just doesn't work.

"It was my first time pretending!" Seth protests, both arms in the air. "It'd get easier, just like you with the *being fun* stuff."

"That's your version of this?" Wren asks me. "You're on a mission to prove you're … *fun*?"

I hurriedly attempt to watch the last six months of my relationship on a sped-up video in my head, the way people say your life flashes in front of you right before you die. I see Freddie and his family trying to encourage me to swim in the sea in Cornwall, and me shaking my head because the sea is cold no matter what time of year it is and I only really like to paddle. I see a house party I'd been dragged to where I felt too embarrassed to dance, so I just stood there, nodding my head in time to the music as a token gesture, while Freddie moved his body around like he'd never been self-conscious in his entire life. I see a trip to the theatre where everyone stood up at the end to do a standing ovation, and I stayed sitting, and Freddie tried to tug me up with him, as if the cast members would come and yell at us after the show if I didn't join in.

I see him looking at me like he wanted to shake me, like he needed me to hurry up and get on board with the person he was becoming.

"Unfortunately, yes," I admit to Wren. "I need to prove to Freddie that I'm confident, and talkative, and spontaneous, with my own hobbies, and that I'm not just the kind of person who spends the entire evening in her pyjamas and then goes to bed at nine o'clock because there's nothing else to do."

Wren blinks a few times, then bristles. "What does *he* do that's fun?"

"I don't know." I realize that I mean it. What *does* make Freddie a more exciting human being than me? His family? His friends? His slightly more cemented career prospects? "I guess his life is fuller now. He's changed."

"So have you," points out Seth. "Otherwise you wouldn't be sitting here planning a fake-dating escapade with me and my twelve-year-old sister."

Wren moves across to Seth's shelves, casting her eye over the various accessories that are stored within them, like Merlin looking for a spell book. She picks up a mug from Seth's desk and grimaces at its contents.

"God, brother, do you ever *clean*?" She holds the mug up to show me – it's a large white thing, with the words YES, AND printed in red on the side of it. "If you really need ideas, how about this?"

I frown at her. "It's … a mug."

Wren shakes her head. "It's an *improv* mug. Seth and his friends do weekly improv sessions, and the whole point of improv is to say, *Yes, and.* You don't say, *No.* You don't say, *But…* You just take what the other person tells you and you run with it. That's fun."

"She's right. You can't do improv and not be fun," says Seth. "It's like saying to the world, *I have no self-consciousness. I'm doing this, and I don't care who sees.* Or, in my case, *I need extra-curricular shenanigans on my university application, and I don't care who knows.* Either way, we're improv-ing Tuesday lunchtime. Full half-hour show in aid of the sixth-form hardship fund, venue to be confirmed."

Wren does a little arm pump of approval and moves over to shake his hand, like my own personal secretary. "Done." Then she moves towards the door of Seth's room, looking back at both of us. "Now, I need to go walk Mr Wilson. I wish you luck with your quests, both of you. But whatever happens, Harley, come back here again sometime." She pauses, then shrugs. "I think you're fun. I think you're both better than you believe you are."

Then she turns and flounces away from us, nudging the door closed behind her.

17

The show

The wavy-haired barista working at the coffee shop counter on Tuesday is a friend of Seth's. She offers him a welcoming smile and free drinks when we reach the front of the queue, and he says something under his breath that makes her cackle with laughter.

"The perks of working here," he murmurs, handing me my mint tea. "You scratch their back, they scratch yours."

The barista, who's piled extra sprinkles and off-menu marshmallows on top of Seth's hot chocolate, waves at him in a way that tells me she'd definitely be down to scratch his back if given the opportunity.

We settle at a different table today, one in the main thoroughfare of the cafe, which makes it easier to spot any unsuspecting exes who may or may not swing by for a latte. From his side, Seth opens up his drama club's termly magazine, the *Backstage Bugle*; from mine, I flick through *Atonement* to make sure I'm up to speed before today's English lit lesson.

After a few minutes, he places the magazine on to the table and studies me over the top of his mug. "Now. Are you, or are you not, still willing to join the improv society this lunchtime? We're meeting in the cafeteria at twelve thirty."

I must look panicked, or at least a little dubious, because he instantly reaches into his backpack to collect an orange T-shirt that says IMPROV SOCIETY – DONATIONS TO THE HARDSHIP FUND WELCOME and then strokes me on the arm with it. "In this group, bravery is rewarded with free branded T-shirts. Does that sway you at all?"

"Hard to say," I tell him, leaving the T-shirt on the table between us.

On the one hand, there's the Freddie element. If Wren is right – which, given the wisdom she somehow seems to possess, I'm hoping she is – then improv is an actual, in-person opportunity to prove something tangible to him. On the other hand, if Wren isn't right, then improv is a gigantic risk at best and a lengthy public humiliation at worst.

Seth picks up the T-shirt again and holds it in front of me, squinting. "One point in favour: orange is your colour. It really makes your hair pop."

"But why the *cafeteria*?" I whine, as he drapes the T-shirt over my arm encouragingly. "Why not a dark corner of the language centre, or a basement nobody uses?"

"We change it up every week," says Seth matter-of-factly, as though it's perfectly normal behaviour to be one sixth of a teenage travelling performance troupe. "One time we performed in the staff room; oh, how they hated it. But this week, I've specifically requested somewhere Freddie and Gen are likely to be. How organized! How fun!"

He takes another swig of hot chocolate. "Look, you don't have to do this. But I'll be there. And you know, it isn't just about *looking* fun or *seeming* fun. I wouldn't have asked you to do this if it wasn't *actual* fun." I hesitate, and he tugs his mouth to one side, newly thoughtful. "How about this: if you hate it, we'll leave. If you hate it, look at me and use the code word. Yell *butterfly* and I'll throw you over my shoulder and announce loudly that we have another commitment to get to, immediately, because we've accidentally double-booked. *That's* how fun we are. OK?"

I shuffle uncomfortably in my seat, avoiding his eyes. "You promise?"

He holds out his hand for me to shake, and I take it. I feel the comforting warmth of his palm, the hard mounds of his knuckles. "Harley. I promise."

The cafeteria is heaving. The queue for food snakes right out of its usual L-shaped line and into the main thoroughfare, where tables are stuffed with students. Artists clutching canvases. Sportspeople wearing tracksuits. To my left is a group of rugby players who are challenging one of their members to drink a small jug of gravy, and I see Joey from the RDC among them, clapping along to the chant. Behind the rugby group, three girls sit with their noses buried in books. I get an overpowering urge to sprint to the book table and beg them all to take me under their wing.

"Remember," says Seth as we walk. "It's very simple. What Wren said was right: your aim is basically to *Yes, and* … your way through it. So, say if I walked up to you and said, *We're about to jump out of an aeroplane and rob a bank*, you wouldn't say, *No, we're going shopping.* Instead, you'd say, *Oh my God, and I've just realized we're running low on fuel!* Something along those lines. You hear the story, and then you take it further."

On a bench midway through the crowd on my right I spot Joshua's moustache – and then Joshua attached to it, and then Lucas, and then, finally, dressed in the burgundy hoodie I bought for his eighteenth birthday, looking so painfully beautiful I feel a little sick, Freddie. I nudge Seth, who nods as if to say, *Got it.* He points a covert finger to a crowd adjacent to the bench, where I spy Gen, sleepily curled up into Jake's arm.

"Seth!" A boy with ear-length locs and a can of Fanta claps Seth on the back. "You ready?"

"Beyond ready," says Seth. "Oh, this is my friend Harley." He places a hand on my shoulder, and the boy and I grin at each other. "Harley, Earl. Earl, Harley."

Behind Earl, tugging on their orange T-shirts, are four more people – a girl with blue hair, another girl who I recognize from my business studies class, and two twin boys who are so tall they could probably touch the ceiling if they put their minds to it. The business studies girl, who I think is called Abby, waves at me.

"You've chosen a good week to get involved," says Earl, who seems to mean it. "Big crowd."

"A little too big, I think," I tell him, but he shakes his head.

"It's all relaxed, I promise. You just gotta remember to raise the volume of your voice – it's already so loud in here, you need to make sure people can hear you. Other than that, be brave and enjoy it. We can start with something simple. Here – Seth, you be on whistle duty." He passes a plastic whistle to Seth, who grins. "Harley, you and I are going to act out scenes to start things off. Seth's job is to whistle whenever he gets bored."

Seth waggles the whistle at me. "Don't make me use this."

"What kind of scenes?" I ask Earl, as nerves snake into my stomach. "What am I supposed to say?"

"Anything," says Earl. "Literally anything. Remember when you were a kid, and you'd play imagination games, and nothing was off-limits? You'd just make shit up?"

I nod weakly.

Earl gives me a thumbs up. "Think back to that."

He takes a deep, shoulder-raising breath, and turns to face the cafeteria audience. "MY DOG IS SICK! CAN ANYBODY HELP ME?"

I freeze on the spot, painfully aware of the students nearby who've turned to stare at us both. This is stupid. This is humiliating. There *is* no dog, and now I have to pretend like there is to a building full of people who just want to eat their lunch in peace.

Earl repeats himself, holding out one hand in feigned desperation. "Please! My poor, poor dog. Can *you* help, lady?"

From the corner of my eye, I see Freddie sit upright at his table in the distance, newly interested. It adds to my dread, but it also jerks me into action.

"I can help!" I say, forcing a loud, confident voice that feels completely inauthentic. "I'm … a prize-winning vet."

"Oh, thank God," says Earl, in a relieved tone. "Here's the thing: he ate my fajita, and he hasn't been the same since."

"Maybe he just likes Mexican food," I offer, and I hear Seth giggle behind me.

"You know," says Earl, "It *would* explain why he hasn't eaten any of the dog food we've been buying him lately. But tell me, what are we supposed to do about him projectile vomiting refried beans?"

"I…" My voice trails off, and Seth blows the whistle.

"You slept with my husband," spits Earl this time,

immediately morphing his voice into a brand-new Cockney accent. He holds up his finger accusingly. "What d'you have to say about that?"

What *do* I have to say about that? I falter for a moment, letting my gaze roam around the cafeteria, so self-conscious I feel like I'm made out of dried cement. One of the girls at the book-reading table gives me an encouraging smile, and as I glance at the open novel in her hands, it reminds me: I *know* how to make stuff up. This is like writing – just out loud, and minus the ability to edit things afterwards. This, if I really think about it, is not a million miles away from the fabricated tale I concocted for Gen in the sports hall. It's scary, but it's also just … storytelling.

"He said you were divorced," I tell Earl, with a new bounce to my voice. "He promised."

"Oh, if you believe that, you'll believe anything," says Earl, wiping an imaginary tear from his eye. "And now, when I'm finally trying to get my life back on track, I hear that you're *pregnant*?"

I tilt my chin up into the air, rummaging around in my brain for a dramatic comeback. "That's right. He's coming to live with me and the baby, *and* he's bringing little Timmy with him."

Earl gasps. "What about our other children, Barney and … Peppermint?"

His mouth wriggles a little at the side, like he's restraining a laugh, and I feel my own do the same. It's ridiculous. It's completely nonsensical, but somehow, it's also not quite as hideous as I thought it would be.

The whistle blows again, and Earl gestures for Seth to take his place on the makeshift stage. They swap over, Seth passing the whistle to Earl as he joins me.

"Dance with me, my darlin'," says Seth, adopting a deep Elvis-like American twang. He places one hand on my waist and wraps the other around my wrist. I wriggle down slightly so that our fingers loop together. "Is it true what they say about ya? That you're on the run from Johnny Law, hoppin' from place to place?"

I try my hardest to look relaxed as I attempt my own accent, mimicking well-spoken Karen, the English literature teacher. "It's true. Oh, I couldn't tell you the things I've done, Larry. You'd never look at me the same."

We step into a slow-dance together, and I nudge my head into Seth's neck, burying it deep in the space between his head and his collarbone. I use it – use him – as a shield from the people looking at us, focusing instead on the heat radiating from the very top of his chest. Our bodies are pressed tight against each other now – I can feel the thud of his heartbeat, hear the mechanics of each swallow as it disappears down his throat. My own swallowing has suddenly become difficult, as though I've just landed on Earth this morning and am learning how to do things for the first time in front of an entire cafeteria full of hungry eighteen-year-olds.

"Try me," says Seth, in the same drawling voice.

"I already know about the Toyota Yaris you stole from ol' Mrs Featherwhistle and her son. That ship has sailed, sweetness." He rubs at the base of my index finger with a reassuring thumb. "You're my girl – ain't nothin' you could say that'd make me walk away now. I don't want you to change for nobody."

As the words wash over me, I let out a murmur of appreciation from the caverns of his neck. "Thank you."

And that's when I realize: I've lost my accent. I've abandoned my character completely. In a moment of ill-considered calm, I've forgotten that I'm supposed to be speaking to Larry, the fictional American man, and instead I've spoken directly to Seth. As if he didn't mean those words for a made-up, car-stealing fugitive. As if he meant those words for *me*.

I pull away from his neck, horrified, and drop his hand like it's on fire. Seth's eyebrows knit together in confusion, and he flashes an urgent look to Earl, who blows the whistle and invites the other group members up to the performance area. We become a group of seven as they appear next to us, and the blue-haired girl yells out to the audience. "Hey, everyone, we need a title for our play! Anyone got anything for us?"

"*The Tale of the Guy Who Wished You'd All Shut Up*," offers one frowning kid, who's hunched over a pizza.

"We'll keep it in mind for next time," calls Earl. "Thanks, though, buddy – appreciate the support."

The pizza guy huffs and returns to his lunch.

"*Beyond the Mortal Realm*," yells a tall girl dressed in a white petticoat-style dress, holding her hands up to her mouth like a loudspeaker.

"Yes," calls Seth. "Thank you, Louise – we can work with that." He turns back to the group and pauses, bringing his hands together into a clasped prayer position. "I was just six years old when I died. How old were *you*?"

"Ninety-nine," says the blue-haired girl, adopting a shaky voice. "I was driving home from work one day and BAM: heart attack at the wheel."

"A *job*, at age ninety-nine?" booms Seth, leaning into it. "My God, Cassandra, no wonder you were ready to go. Tell me, what did you do for a living?"

"She was an undertaker," yells Earl, placing both hands on his hips, "with me."

Seth nods. "And which tasks, exactly, did the two of you undertake?"

"Lucius means that we dealt with the dead," says the blue-haired girl ominously. "We prepared the bodies. Organized the funerals. My whole life … was about death."

"And *my* whole life was about finding out the secret recipe for KFC's fried chicken," Abby chimes in, flitting the story in another direction. "Alas, I died not knowing it."

"Didn't you realize?" I ask her, spotting my opportunity and stepping forward to gesture towards the group. "*I'm* the ghost of Colonel Sanders, and I have the recipe, right here in my pocket."

My eyes meet Seth's as I leave a short, dramatic pause. He squints at me, like he's trying to suss out if I'm OK; I send him a small, scene-breaking smile to throw him off the scent, which he immediately returns.

I clear my throat. "The secret ingredient is …"

"Love?" he says hopefully. "Bones? Paprika?"

I reach into my jeans and pretend to panic. "It's … it's gone. My family recipe is *gone*!"

Earl turns to the blue-haired girl, shaking his head slowly. "You were sticky-fingered in life, Cassandra, and now you're sticky-fingered in death. Hand it over."

After Cassandra has been sent, kicking and screaming, to some kind of improv-afterlife jail, we move on to another audience idea – *The Man Who Lost His Shoe*, and then, finally, *Help! Everyone is Allergic to Air.* When the bell rings for the end of lunch, and we've taken our bows, and the cafeteria crowds have started to disperse, I pull off my orange T-shirt breathlessly and smile at Seth, who's by my side instantly.

"You were *perfect*," he says, and he wraps an arm around me, twirling me in towards him. I hover there for a moment, feeling the warmth of his chest, before remembering what happened last time I did that and forcing myself away. "It wasn't so bad, right?"

I don't really know how to answer this. My gut response is, *Of course it was bad*. It was bad because it was hard, and it was bad because it was embarrassing, and it was bad because I didn't have any idea what was coming next. But among the bad – among the hardness – it was maybe a little bit exciting. It felt challenging, different, like a workout for my brain.

Freddie, Joshua and Lucas have appeared in front of us now, trays in hand, ready to leave via the winding painted pathway on the cafeteria floor. Both Joshua and Lucas pass by without looking in my direction, but I see Freddie run a hand through his dark hair as he shoots me a glance from the side. I ignore him, trying my hardest to pretend I haven't seen him at all, and turn back towards Earl, who offers me a sweaty-palmed high five.

"You did good, Harley. Really good. First one of these *I* came to, I tapped out straight away." He tugs off his own tee. "If you ever want to join us in the future, you'd be welcome."

"Thanks," I say, and I mean it. "If your dog's ever sick again, you know who to call."

We traipse out of the cafeteria together as a group, only a few steps behind Freddie and his friends. I see Freddie turn back to catch a glimpse of us, disguising his action as a generic, sweeping scan of the horizon while his knuckles clench white over his bag straps.

How does it feel? I silently scream at him. *How does it feel to have been this wrong about me?*

18

The movie night

"You don't *look* like a fake girlfriend."

Joy stands at the door to her home, clutching a tartan cake tin and peering in my direction. She's a fellow tall girl, with dyed white-blonde wavy hair that rests on her collarbones, the ends flicking outwards. My eyes flit down for a second and make out a floral-patterned skirt, so long it almost touches the floor, and a crisp white shirt with embroidered bell sleeves. Next to her, in black jogging bottoms, Nate – no offence to the man – is severely underdressed.

"What would a fake girlfriend look like to you, Joy?" asks Seth, gently nudging me into the red brick house and closing the front door behind us. "Made out of plastic? Big sign around her neck that says I LOVE SETH?"

"He tried to make me wear one," I say, hoping my

nervous joke lands the way I want it to. "It actually caused our first fake fight."

Joy laughs. It's a loud, slightly jumpy laugh, the kind that's a little more generous than it needs to be. Nate coughs pointedly. He's leaning against the dark-green hallway wall, next to a metal plant stand with a cactus perched on top of it.

We're here, awkwardly, because the last RDC meeting involved a question from Dahlia about how we could spend time this week with our favourite people. Given that my favourite person is unavailable to me for the foreseeable future, and my other favourite person is my mother, Seth jumped in to declare to the group that I would be joining him and his friends for their monthly movie night. After the session, when I pointed out that Freddie and Gen would have no idea that this event was taking place, Seth yawned and said, "Not everything is about them."

"Sorry," says Joy, reaching out to take my jacket. "I didn't mean to be weird when I opened the door. I won't lie to you – I don't think I fully understand … this."

She gestures towards me and Seth with her free arm.

"Joy, we've already been over the basics, several times," says Seth snippily, as he pulls off a shoe. "Fake dates, exes jealous, blah blah. Your role as my friend is literally just to keep the secret and pretend you believe all this. Join in and help us to maintain the facade."

"I just think it's a little odd that you're getting other people involved in the facade in the first place," says Joy. "Whenever this kind of thing happens in the movies, they tell *everyone* that they're fake dating. Parents, best friends and so on and so forth. They don't make other people lie for them."

"Would you have preferred for us to lie *to* you?" says Seth as he hangs up his coat on the banister. "Would that have been fun and believable?"

Judgemental wrinkles appear on Joy's nose. "Ew. No. What I'd have preferred is for you to accept your break-up and do your French revision, like a regular person."

Nate adjusts his glasses and smiles at me, like he's used to this brother–sister back-and-forth and would just like to watch a movie before it gets too late. *Joy's the talker, Nate's the listener*, Seth has informed me in the past. *It's not that he's shy. He's just a person of few words, which works very well for me and Joy, because we are people of many.*

Sensing a natural lull in the debate, Joy uses her cake tin to point up the stairs. "Fake couple, head on up."

Joy's bedroom is large and cinnamon scented; she's developed an addiction to buying candles that smell like baked goods thanks to her weekend job in a homeware shop.

"We get a thirty-five per cent discount," she tells me as she throws herself on to the bed. It's covered in a pale pink-and-green patchwork quilt that looks like it's been stolen directly from Miss Honey's cottage. "So what am I supposed to do?"

Nate clambers on to the bed next to her, kicking off his shoes first. There isn't an invitation to join them, and I'm suddenly very conscious that those two are an *actual* couple, so I stay standing up and try to keep myself busy by peering around the room. Joy definitely got the biggest bedroom, which makes me wonder if there's some kind of attic conversion upstairs where her parents sleep. The floor is a rustic, stained wood, covered in a dark-blue patterned rug with discoloured tassels around each side. A large desk in one corner of the room is covered in objects: figurines and beach shells and stacks of CDs.

Joy pats an empty space next to her. "Harley, you're welcome to shuffle in with us, but if it's uncomfortable for you to sit on a stranger's bed, I get it. I can also offer you the reading chair, if you'd prefer."

She points – casually, like she has guests over all the time – to a large dark-brown corduroy easy chair to the left of her bed, which I'd also spotted and was secretly hoping I could migrate over to. As I pad across to the chair, Seth stays standing, holding a bag of popcorn under each arm like he's not sure what to do.

"So, Harley," says Nate, speaking for the first time this evening. "Seth says you're in the same situation as him."

"Oh, single and sad about it?" I say, tucking my feet underneath me on the embossed fabric of the chair. "Yeah, I think that's fair to say. What about you two? How long have you…?"

"A year," says Nate. He looks very pleased to declare this milestone.

"A *blissful* year," adds Joy, and Nate turns pink.

"And you knew Gen?"

I don't really know why I bring her up. Probably because it feels like the elephant in the room. Probably because they knew her, or they know her, and they definitely think that what Seth and I are doing is ridiculous – which wouldn't be an incorrect assessment at all.

"Unfortunately." Joy's eyes sparkle.

"Can we please stop with the Genevieve slander?" says Seth, finally placing the popcorn on to the bed next to Nate's foot. He reaches for one of the knitted blankets, taking his time to unravel it. "What did she ever do to you?"

Joy narrows her eyes and then counts on her hand, holding a finger up for each new example. "Insulted my baking. Was incapable of holding a conversation without checking her phone. Twenty minutes early to anything and everything but still huffed at us when we showed up on time, like we were the problem. Oh, and *then* dumped my friend for somebody else and made him cry."

"She did not dump me *for* somebody else," Seth protests. "She dumped me and then moved on very quickly. They're two different things."

"And this," says Joy, smiling in my direction, "is why I really don't understand the whole plan you two have got going on. Your ex might be a dream, Harley, but frankly, Seth's is not worth all this hassle."

I try to remain on the fence. "She seems … fine. I haven't met her enough to comment."

"That's very diplomatic," says Joy, and she seems sincere, like she's throwing me a compliment. "You and Nate will get along. He *liked* her."

"Well, she wasn't the two-dimensional supervillain you make her out to be," says Nate, activated by the sound of his own name. "She was…" He searches for the words.

"Fastidious? Shallow?" offers Joy. I see Seth flinch.

"She was honest," says Nate. "And impressionable. She was also, I think, very anxious sometimes, which made her a little awkward to be around." He rubs at Joy's elbow, then glances up at Seth. "Not unlike some other people we know and love."

Joy scowls, clearly insulted by this comparison, and Nate plants a reassuring kiss on her cheek. Then he turns back to me. "Harley, what do you two *do* in scenarios like this? Are you friends when no one's watching? Like … do you sit together tonight, or is it an audience-only thing?"

"Of course we're *friends*." Seth's voice is defensive, and it brings an automatic hint of a smile to my face. "We're on an emotional journey together, and that means we're going to sit together. Right?"

I gesture to the small amount of space left next to me on the reading chair. "We can try."

Seth makes his way over to me, then attempts to lower himself down into the tiny gap, which would be a tight squeeze for a small child, let alone a sports-playing man. I hold my breath out of loyalty to Freddie as the entire left side of Seth's body brushes the entire right side of mine, and wonder why the hell he didn't just sit on the bed with his best friends and leave me to fend for myself. Desperate, I manoeuvre my own body further to the side to try and free up some space, and Seth's thigh finally judders down into the gap.

The result? I'm not sitting on his lap, exactly, but I'm also not sitting fully on the chair.

"Well, there we are," says Seth in a strangled voice. He swallows. "Seated. Sat."

I try to distract myself – and then not look as alarmed as I feel – by one particular section of Joy's bedroom wall that seems to be made up solely of photographs of tombstones – some moss-covered, some large and regal-looking, but all very, very old. One gravestone, shaped like a house, has lichen spots that sprawl across it like Georgian tie-dye.

IN MEMORY OF MARY SPENCER
DAUGHTER OF JAMES AND
FRANCES SPENCER
WHO PARTED THIS LIFE ON THE
3RD DAY OF OCTOBER 1773
AGED 17 YEARS

"Harley, she was *our age*," says Joy, noticing my eyeline and springing up to point at the photo in a way that tells me this is very much her thing. "Isn't that wild?"

"So you're like … a gravespotter?" I ask. The word makes Seth snort. "You go out and take pictures in cemeteries?"

"Only with permission," says Joy, as if this makes it any more commonplace an activity. "But yes. I find death very interesting."

Seth twists to his left and I make eye contact with his teeth, which are literal centimetres away from mine. His breath smells like peaches. "Joy likes to remind us, regularly, that all this is temporary. It's a really uplifting trait."

Joy objects as she prises open the cake tin. "What could be more uplifting than the knowledge that life is transitory and precious and should therefore be celebrated? What could be more exciting than realizing that people our age – the Mary Spencers of the world – sat here hundreds or even thousands of years ago and had conversations just like ours?"

"I don't know," Seth deadpans. "Literally anything?"

"You're a pain in my ass," Joy bats back, but she's smiling. She brandishes a TV remote at the group. "Now, for this month's movie, we've got three choices. Four, Harley, if you throw your own idea in. I want *(500) Days of Summer*, because I haven't seen it in years. Nate wants to watch some terrible comedy. Seth has requested a nature documentary that isn't even a film."

Seth yawns and kicks back a retort about Joy's lack of

impartial reporting, which Nate echoes. I watch, fascinated, as they bounce off each other, familiar and comfortable. I see Joy parade around happily – pulling freestyle dance moves, pouring out drinks – as though this kind of evening happens all the time. As though anyone would be welcome here.

I wouldn't say I feel *part* of it, exactly – I'm very aware that I'm a newcomer, on the outskirts of a friendship group, knocking on an invisible door and asking to come in. But I can tell, from the way Joy catches my eye as she laughs, or the way Nate offers me the first cake slice of the evening, that the door isn't locked. If I'm brave enough, I might even be able to open it and walk inside.

Nate drops me home just after midnight, even though I live a twenty-minute drive away from him and insist that an Uber would be a better idea.

"Nonsense," he says, like a well-meaning father. "Any fake girlfriend of Seth's is a real friend of ours." He waits in the car as Seth walks me up the drive, keeping the engine rumbling quietly.

"Your house is cute," whispers Seth. He nods at the stained-glass tree that's been part of the front door since before we moved in, then the wooden wind chime screwed into the roof of the porch. "Much more whimsical than I expected."

"It's my mum. She has all the whimsy," I inform him. "It didn't make its way down to me."

I reach into my coat pocket for my house key, but Seth holds an arm out to stop me.

"Hey. Happy two-week anniversary."

He swings his rucksack off his back, on to the ground, and crouches down to tug open the zip. Then he digs both hands into the main pouch, emerging a few seconds later with a small freezer bag, which he teases open to unveil a glass casserole dish. From the floor, he presents the dish to me, like the monkey from *The Lion King* presenting the new baby Simba. "As promised."

I take the dish from him and use my fingertips to carefully peel back the tinfoil on top of it. Inside the rectangular glass is what looks like a lasagne, with the number 2 fashioned out of red peppers on top of the melted cheese.

"You *made* this?"

He nods from his position on the floor. "I did. Full disclosure: I had to call my dad at one point, which honestly I'm not proud of, but the pasta sheets were looking a little dubious and it turns out you need to cook those before they go in the oven. Apparently most people know that." His voice has sped up into auctioneer mode, the same way it did when we met for the first time at the RDC. "And I also wanted to go more adventurous with the messaging, but *you* try making the words HARLEY GREEN, MY TWO-WEEK QUEEN out of tiny bits of vegetable. Otherwise..."

He grins, and lets out a shaky exhale. "All me."

"Thank you." I stare at his creation, open-mouthed. "This is… Seriously, thank you."

I don't know what to do with it. I want to display it in a cabinet; I want to contact our local newspaper and tell them to put it on the front page. *Thank you* doesn't feel at all adequate right now.

Seth coughs as he straightens back up to a standing position. "You're welcome. You told me you'd like it, so I wanted to get it done. Anyway, don't thank me *too* much until you've tried it. You might get food poisoning. You might never speak to me again."

I shake my head, meaning it, and he runs a hand through his hair.

"Do you want me to take a photo or something?" I offer. It's freezing out here, and I shiver from the chilled container in my hands. "You could make sure Gen saw it, or Fr—"

"I didn't do it for Gen," he smiles, and he takes the glass dish from me, carefully slotting it back into its freezer bag. "I did it for you."

19

The sapling

People keep using the word *outgrown*.

Dahlia. Cassie. Min, whose stupid life-coach videos still keep popping up on my phone. Even my own damn mother.

"People do outgrow each other, Harl," she says on Sunday evening, while we're painting our toenails in the living room. "It happens way more often than you'd think."

"You outgrow a pair of *jeans*," I snip. The dark-red polish, which promised to dry in record time, has smudged on my big toe, leaving a crater in my creation. "Not a person."

"Nobody is comparing you to a pair of jeans."

"Well, stop saying it, then."

She places her own open bottle of polish on to the arm of the sofa, balancing it precariously. "What about Debbie?"

Debbie is the name of my childhood teddy bear. There's this whole ancient backstory behind her – a long, sweet tale about me discovering her in a department store as a toddler and holding on to her so tightly they couldn't even forcibly remove her from my clutches. People tried. People failed. Toddler-Harley screamed like a banshee. Nobody can remember why I chose to name my teddy after a middle-aged woman – not even me – but she's been a much-loved member of the Green household for well over fifteen years, and still sits in a wooden nook in my bedroom.

"I don't see what Debbie has to do with any of this," I say, like I'm defending a close personal friend.

"You grew out of *her*," my mum points out. "At one point, you were obsessed with that bear. We couldn't go anywhere without Debbie coming along for the ride. Then, over time, you grew – and Debbie naturally became less important to you. Doesn't mean you never cared about her. Means your life has expanded."

First I was an item of clothing in this analogy, and now I am a stuffed animal.

"Debbie is still *very* important to me," I say hotly. "If that wasn't the case, she'd have been donated in a charity bag years ago."

"I don't really think you're hearing me," says my mum.

On Monday, after we finish our practice exam on comedy and tragedy in drama, Karen gives us the final five minutes of lesson time to kick back and do nothing.

"Do you think it's normal to outgrow someone?" I ask Bella, with the Debbie metaphor still fresh in my mind.

"Uh, I think it's normal to change," says Bella, biting on her pen as she speaks. "Like, what once made you happy won't always make you happy, right?"

A girl at the table next to us puts her head into her hands and lets out a deep, exhausted, post-examination sigh.

"Don't you find that confusing, though?" I ask Bella. "If people always change, how is anyone supposed to find somebody they could be with forever?"

Bella studies me. She's wearing a black tee with Shakespeare's illustrated face tiled across it, and the word WILLIAM emblazoned across the top.

"Maybe when you meet the right person you both change, at the same time, so the balance is never off. Or maybe one of you grows for a bit, but then the other one catches up, and then you swap over again."

I lean back on my chair, fixing my eyes on Karen's Sylvia Plath poster. "I just think it sounds exhausting."

"That's my point," says Bella. "With the right person it wouldn't be. It'd be exciting."

We sit in silence for a few moments. "Are you single on purpose?" I ask her. "Like, through choice?"

She nods. "Uh-huh. *I've* changed a lot, and as a result I'm pretty sure I have outgrown every single boy in this establishment. That's why I'm ready for September. Get me the fuck out of here."

Bella has plans to attend a university in London so she can learn how to be a sound engineer. Her parents are unsupportive of this vision and would prefer for her to be heading down a more academic path, but Bella says this just means she will not be offering them guest-list tickets for any future concerts she happens to be a part of.

Get me the fuck out of here causes a solitary bark of laughter to emit from my throat. "Teach me your ways," I tell her. "I need that energy."

Bella shrugs. "Who says you don't already have it?"

I think about this. "Freddie, I guess. He said he'd been waiting for me to grow but realized I never would. And at the time, he was right. It's weird, because I used to think that our relationship was a tree – like, a tree we needed to nurture together – but I forgot about the fact that *I* was a tree, too. I was also something that needed to be taken care of. And now we're both single, it's like Freddie's still this big tree of his own, and I'm just a tiny little sapling next to him. My growth is delayed. I'm trying *so* hard, but I'm still lagging behind."

Bella grabs my hand, and her dark eyes flash. "Hey. You are not a sapling. Stop worrying about him and start worrying about yourself. What do you like? What do you hate? Who do you want to hang out with? What do you want to do with your life? What scares you? *That's* how you grow."

"I want to hang out with you," I tell her, and it's so brazenly sincere that I feel like a little kid in the playground, hanging around by the swings to book in after-school play dates.

"Well, make it happen," she says, grinning. "Text me. Come rock climbing with me. Invite me to your Fake Boyfriend movie nights. For example … what are your weekend plans? And if you say more *Midsomer Murders*, I am going to punch you in the face." I open my mouth in mock horror, and Bella cackles. "Sorry, sorry. Part of my own growing is not judging other people for how they spend their free time. My therapist has raised it."

"I will introduce you to *Midsomer Murders*," I tell her, laughing. "Then you'll see. You'll be eating your judgemental words. Why, what is Fun Bella doing that's so much more exciting and adventurous than me?"

"Fun Bella is going to an eighteenth birthday party in a hotel, *and* she happens to know Brooke the birthday girl, so she gets extra invite privileges. B-themed fancy dress, well-stocked bar, et cetera." She glances down at her Shakespeare T-shirt. "Wouldst thou liketh to attend?"

"Nay," I say to the T-shirt. "A tavern full of drunken sixth-formers? I think not."

"Come *onnnn*," whines Bella. She scrunches her hand

up into a fist and pokes me on the arm with each count. "One: you're eighteen, so no fake ID required. Two: you don't have any other plans, besides watching twee police dramas with your mother. Three: you can bring Fake Boyfriend and show off your fake fun, which is a sentence I never thought would exit my mouth." She pauses, and her next arm-prod is gentler. "Four: I'm your *friend*, and I want you there."

It dawns on me that part of growing, perhaps, is saying yes to things you would have said no to before. Improvisation troupes. Niche break-up support groups. Movie nights. Turning up to the party of a girl you've never met before, purely because someone you care about asks you to be in attendance. Maybe the price you pay for solid, genuine connection has to be occasional fear, or discomfort, or plain old inconvenience.

But what happens if you say yes to all of it and not all of it feels like *you*? This is what makes my head hurt: how do I know whether I'm developing – pushing through the awkwardness to emerge a stronger person – or just pretending, all for the sake of slowly morphing into someone Freddie wouldn't be embarrassed to bring to a family barbecue?

I give myself a little shake and choose to focus on Bella's final words: *I'm your friend, and I want you there.* Maybe Freddie doesn't deserve my discomfort right now, but Bella definitely does.

"I'll make an appearance," I tell the T-shirt Shakespeare. "For my friend."

Bella's face lights up. The whites of her eyes widen and she lets out a gasp of excitement, like we've just woken up on Christmas morning. The sight of it makes my insides glow – there's a new, warm little orb sitting deep within my stomach, radiating proud heat. She holds out a pinky finger, and even though I'm nervous, even though the thought of going to a party hosted by Brooke – whoever she is – is overwhelming right now, I still reach out and wrap my own finger around hers.

And that's how you grow.

20

The calm before the storm

On the night of Brooke's party, Seth, Joy, Nate and I agree to get ready together, except this time, I invite everybody over to my house. It feels like another courageous, growthful move, and I spend an anxious half hour tidying up before their arrival – arranging and rearranging my Marvel figurines, shoving clothes into drawers. Then I stand in the doorway of my room, trying to imagine what it would look like to a first-time visitor. I see the neat wooden desk and its laptop. The small wardrobe, plastered in Freddie-themed souvenirs that I haven't been brave enough to take down just yet. The dark-blue Tardis bedsheets that haven't been updated since I was nine. If bedrooms could speak, what would mine say? Would anyone want to hear it?

When the doorbell rings just after 7 p.m., my mum is immediately on the case.

"I'll get it!" she calls.

From my bedroom, I yell not to bother – to leave it for me – but she opens the door to the three of them as I'm elephanting my way down the stairs.

They look like carol singers. Joy, bundled up in her usual brown faux-fur coat on the right, has a pink-tinted nose from the cold. Next to her, Nate is dressed in a textured zip-up fleece jacket, and Seth, to the left, is sporting a pair of bright-red knitted mittens, the kind that look like they were designed for a cartoon character without any fingers. My heart does a wholesome little backflip at the sight of them all.

"Let me guess," my mum says, pointing to the trio in front of her. "Joy. Great name, by the way. Do you ever feel pressured by it?"

"More than you'd think, actually," says Joy, providing my mum with a warm smile. "Sometimes it feels like my parents had a passive aggressive plan to stop me from feeling any kind of negative emotion at all." She leans in against her boyfriend, who waves. "Uh, so this is Nate. And that's Seth."

Seth steps forward to hug my mum, who giggles, probably because of the beaming Ryan Gosling lookalike who's just embraced her on the steps of her home.

"Good to meet you, Alice," he says, using the same low, relaxed voice he brought out for Freddie in the coffee shop.

"Come in," she tells them all. "It's freezing out there."

I'm very skilled at reading my mum's facial expressions – and the one she gives me as she wanders back into the living room is fifty per cent *finally, some friends for my misunderstood child* and fifty per cent *why didn't you tell me your fake boyfriend looked like* that?!

The fake boyfriend in question is very interested in my home. He points out the Henri Matisse print on the stairs, wanting to know who it's by, and Joy – queen of art history – tells him without blinking. When we make it into my bedroom, he stands in the middle of the room open-mouthed like he's in a museum, looking from place to place, object to object.

"Take a seat," I tell Joy and Nate, awkwardly patting the Tardis sheets while Seth runs his finger over a plastic Jessica Jones statue that lives on my desk. They sink down on to the duvet, Nate resting a camping bag full of costumes against his leg.

"Who's this?" asks Seth, leaning across to pick up Debbie the teddy bear from her newly promoted spot on my bed.

"Nobody," I say, immediately feeling a mix of hot embarrassment and deep guilt for betraying poor Debbie once again.

"*I'm not nobody*," says Seth in a squeaky voice, making Debbie shake her head with indignance.

"Her name is Debbie," I tell him. I'm suddenly very aware of Joy and Nate in the room with us, watching us interact. "Deborah, to you."

"What's that, Debbie?" Seth takes a seat on my computer chair and holds Debbie's furry mouth up to his ear. "Uh-huh… Uh-huh. Wow, really? Who'd have thought." He places her in his lap and looks back towards me. "She's got some significant gossip to tell me about you. We're waiting until you leave the room so we can really get into it."

I roll my eyes – with the tiniest bit of affection – as Joy chimes in. "Your mum looks a lot like you, Harley. Or, you look a lot like her, I guess." Nate nods in agreement, and even Seth drags his gaze away from Debbie.

"People have always said that about us," I say, and there's a twinge of anxiety in my chest at the thought of discussing this with new people for the first time in years. *Is she your mother or your sister?*

I loved people confusing us for siblings when I was younger; I thought my mum was painfully beautiful, like an English Courteney Cox. I wanted to play into it – style our hair in identical pigtails or something, buy matching sweatshirts – but she was never keen. Being such a young parent left her defensive and desperate to be taken seriously. She didn't want to be my sister. She wanted to be my mum.

"How old was she when she had you?" asks Seth, still clutching on to Debbie's stomach.

"She was nineteen," I tell him. "She and my dad were together at school."

"Drew," says Seth, and I'm touched that he's memorized

the name of someone so absent yet so important in the general scope of my life. "The optician."

"He's an optician *now*. Back then, he was just a boy who got to carry on living his life while hers changed."

"He didn't support her?" Nate's eyes are wide.

"He tried." I shrug. "The story as I've heard it is that his parents insisted it would be a waste for him not to go to university. So he went, and my mum stayed here, because no one thought it would be a waste for *her* not to go to university. And my dad visited every so often, and they carried on being a couple, and then he graduated and moved back home and it sort of just … fizzled out. I don't know. I don't think he wanted to be a dad, and I guess he got put in a position where he didn't really have to be one."

There's a silence while I pick at a hangnail on my thumb and think about what I've just shared with them all. The strange thing is, if *I* go to university – wherever I actually end up going – I will still be the first woman in my family to do that. My nana didn't attend, for reasons I've never asked her about. My mum would have done, if she hadn't been heavily pregnant with me. Even the act of applying, of accepting a place and showing up with a car full of IKEA homeware, would be a family anomaly. It would be big.

"I'll bet your dad has other kids now, though," says Joy knowingly. "Right?"

"Twins," I tell her, surprising myself by the bitterness

that seeps out with the word. "They're blonde and busy and I've never met them. I haven't even seen *him* lately."

The mention of my dad and his other children tugs at something familiar in me: a well-trodden, gnarly pain that I don't want to bring into this particular evening. "He… They…"

"Deborah tells me," Seth interrupts in a loud proclamatory voice, "that she thinks we should start getting ready. She has seen the time, and she's heard all about my complicated costume, and she knows that as a formerly late person I am going to need to start the process imminently so that I can avoid the last-minute meltdown you've all seen so many times before." He holds Debbie back up to his ear again. "Yeah, she says enough chit-chat, thanks."

"*Formerly late*," scoffs Joy, in a tone that's fond but still so disbelieving it's basically one giant tut.

She reaches over to physically restrain Seth's leg, which is so jumpy this evening it's as if it's radiating anxiety right across the room. Seth shakes her off, then looks up at me and mouths, *You good?*

I nod, grateful for the dad-related check-in, and silently bat the question back to him.

He doesn't reply. He just holds on to Debbie's soft tummy, then reaches up to pat her, very gently, on the top of her head.

21

The party

Brooke is definitely rich. The party is opulent – a specially hired two-storey mezzanine in a huge hotel bar, with balloon arches, platters of sushi and tiny cupcakes with the birthday girl's face printed on the icing. I take a bite of her forehead and keep an eye out for Freddie.

"Why is it so busy?" says Seth, who's using one of Brooke's birthday-branded napkins to fan his face. "God, why is it so *warm*?"

"Probably because of … that," says Nate, nodding at Seth's already-sweaty polyester outfit.

We've turned up in our meticulously planned couple's costumes – I'm Villager Belle, in a handmade pinafore and an itchy brown wig. Seth, bundled up in a royal blue blazer with yellow trim, is the Beast. This is because Gen's favourite movie is *Beauty and the Beast*; she and Seth have watched the film together countless times, and Seth is convinced that Gen has a crush on the Beast that she's too ashamed to admit to. Freddie, as far as I know, doesn't feel strongly one way or the other about Belle as a character, but I've tried my hardest to make the costume as convincing as possible. As Harley Green outfits go, this is definitely one of the more interesting ones.

Joy is an all-black bat tonight – she's ethereal, in a long floaty dress with her favoured bell sleeves, complete with pointed black wings and matching eyeliner. To her left, Nate is wearing a loose-fitting baseball outfit finished with yellow face paint and a black patch smeared over one eye, which he tells me is a reference to an old cult movie that he and Joy bonded over when they first dated. He reaches out to rest a nostalgic arm over Joy's shoulder, but she waves him away.

"You'll damage my *wings*."

When we reach the second level of the building – the dancefloor – I shut my eyes and take a breath. The music swells, and I feel as though I'm walking into a new dimension, like Neo stepping out of the Matrix. But when I open my eyes again, nothing is as overwhelming or scary as I expected. There are flashing lights and high-pitched voices and the *thud-thud-thud* of a bassline, but other than that I'm just looking at … people. Normal, everyday people.

At the outskirts of the rabble, dressed in an orange-and-pink minidress, is Bella. She sees me, shrieks and waltzes her way over, leaving a trail of open-mouthed boys in her wake.

"You *came*!" Her arms reach out to hug me and a large splash of whatever's in her plastic cup lands on my foot. "And you're a *Disney princess*. I think…" She takes a dramatic, drunken breath. "I think maybe this is the best night of my life."

"I promised I'd be here," I tell her happily, leaning in to squeeze her right back. I stroke at the shoulder of her dress. "What's your costume supposed to be?"

"Duh," slurs Bella, breaking away from the hug and pointing to her own torso. "I'm *me*. If your name begins with B, why rock the boat?"

She suddenly clocks Seth next to me and grabs him by the blazer sleeve. "Oh my God. Fake Boyfriend!"

"Fun Bella!" says Seth, a small smile materializing on his face that looks like a blend of embarrassment and pride. "How do you feel to know you're the inspiration for our joint project?"

Bella raises her cup in his direction, cheers-ing him. "Undeniably smug." She keeps a hand on Seth's arm, steering his eyeline to different places around the room. "If you're looking for Gen, she's sitting by the gifts table; some random showed up and tried to steal Brooke's birthday presents. If you're looking for *Freddie*, he's…" She sways on the spot, then points. "Ah. There."

My arms tingle with goosebumps as we all turn to

look at Freddie, who's standing at the bar next to Joshua and a couple of other boys I don't recognize, sporting a bright-blue suit with gold bars sewed across the chest and a matching military-style hat. He's clutching a beer bottle and laughing like his life depends on it.

"Your boyfriend's a Beatle," says Nate, from behind me.

"He's not her boyfriend," says Seth quickly. "He's her ex."

I remember seeing something online, probably days or even hours after the break-up with Freddie, that said, *One day this will get easier. One day you'll see them, or you'll think about them, and it won't feel like the world is ending any more.* Today, it doesn't feel like the world is ending, but it doesn't exactly feel like it's thriving, either.

"Come on," I say, grabbing hold of Seth's clammy hand and tugging it slightly. "Let's start with Gen."

Bella gives me an enthusiastic arm-flex as Seth and I wander away as a pair towards the gift table, which is essentially more of a gift *stand* – like a stall at a fairground. There are pale-pink ribbons draped over the top of a plastic structure, and more pearlescent balloons tacked on alongside them. Brooke, clearly, is expecting a lot of eighteenth birthday presents and has set up shop for the occasion.

Sat scrolling on her phone, Gen is a real-life Barbie: pink flares, pink waistcoat, blonde wig and a cowboy hat. She looks beautiful in a way that makes my stomach clench, like she could do or say or have whatever she wanted, just because.

"Oh my god, of *course* Jake is Beach Ken," groans Seth, side-eyeing the couple as Jake sidles up to Gen with two something-and-Cokes in his hands. "Look at his hair. Look at his stupid neckerchief." He cranes his neck to get a better glimpse of the outfit. "Is there anything lamer than a couple's costume?"

"We're wearing a couple's costume," I remind him.

"That's different. We're different." He adjusts his cravat and looks at the floor.

Jake, done and dusted with drink-drop-off duty, plants a kiss on the top of Gen's cowboy hat and disappears. Sensing an opportunity, we approach the table. Seth clears his throat.

"Hey, Gen. This where we drop off the gifts?"

Gen aims a pointed glance towards the large sign above her head that says GIFTS. "Uh, yeah. I can take them."

Seth reaches into the depths of his Beast blazer and produces a large card and a hand-wrapped gift that I know is a small velvet jewellery box with a large B on the front. I know, because Seth spent three hours selecting it on a gifts website earlier this week, narrated the entire thing via text message, changed his mind several times, and then proudly sent me the link to his final choice.

Gen takes the items from him and studies them both. "Are these from you?" She places them down on to the large pile. "Like, you went out and bought this?"

"Of course," says Seth. He's brought out his

lower-pitched voice again, like he's trying to add a couple of years to his vocal cords. "Can't show up to a birthday party empty-handed, can you?"

"I guess *now* you can't," says Gen coolly, shifting her Barbie hat to one side like a literal cowboy, ready for a gunslinging match. "But you had no problem doing it when my uncle Rufus turned fifty."

Seth's shoulders hoist up a little. "Like I said at the time, I'd never *met* your uncle Rufus. Nobody told me I was supposed to buy him an *offering* in order to fit in at his birthday meal."

"Well, nobody told *me* that dating you meant having to constantly apologize to other people on your behalf!" she hisses. "*Sorry he's late; sorry he didn't remember your birthday; sorry he said he'd come to your barbecue but then forgot all about it because drama club ran over and he got distracted by a cat on the way home.*"

"Oh, you *had* to bring that up," says Seth, jutting his jaw out. "He was a local cat, a friend of mine, and he was looking a little peaky that day, all right? I still showed up to the barbecue. I was late, and I'm sorry about that." He relaxes his shoulders and retracts his jaw. "Gen, I'm sorry about that. You deserved to feel like a priority. I'm glad..." He swallows, then glances towards the bar, where Jake is watching this conversation play out from a supportive distance. "I'm really glad you have that now."

Gen's glower falters a little while the music blares around

us. She rests her front teeth on the pillow of her bottom lip, blinking at the table in front of her. "Thank you. That's all I wanted you to say."

"D'you need to talk about it?" I ask Seth as we make our way back to the dancefloor, still holding hands. In the distance I see Bella attempting to do the worm with a girl from her maths class.

"No," he says. "What I need is a drink."

I pass him mine – my untouched second Prosecco of the evening – and he takes it from me, tipping his head backwards and draining the liquid into his mouth while we push past people, slowly moving towards the middle of the crowd. Freddie and his Beatles friends are standing next to the speakers, and when Freddie scans the area over in our direction I remember to nuzzle into Seth's neck just in time.

"I'm DJ Colin, and you guys are looking *gooooood* tonight!" hollers the man at the music desk, gesturing to the sea of people in front of him. He's wearing a sequinned red suit and large matching glasses, which leave him resembling a budget Elton John. "You look like people who are ready to PARTY!"

"We're not," yells Seth, newly morose.

Joy and Nate rejoin us as the DJ brings the music to an abrupt, awkward halt and asks us all to assemble on the dancefloor so that we can sing to the birthday girl. "Brooke, get up here!" he shouts from the stage, sliding in and out of an American accent that's definitely fake, and Brooke – who's dressed as a bee – obliges.

"Thank you for celebrating with me," she coos into the microphone, when the most drunk and/or musically gifted guests are finished elongating the final *you* of the Happy Birthday song. "You're all here because you're my all-time favourite people." There's a loud *woo* from a group at the front of the crowd, and Brooke blows them a delighted kiss. "I love you, and … that's really all I need to say."

I have never seen Brooke before in my entire life so, naturally, I feel like a giant fraud for being named as one of her all-time favourite people, but I still *woo* along with the rest of them. Good for you, Brooke. Enjoy your mountain of Genevieve-approved gifts.

"Now," roars DJ Colin, after he's ushered Brooke off the stage to rejoin her friends. "You're all dressed as something beginning with B, in honour of our birthday girl, and I want to see the very best costume of the night."

He switches on a spotlight, using it to illuminate individuals in the crowd, and points out a bunny, a bride, a Buzz Lightyear and a builder, before fixing a tentative spotlight on Nate and Joy.

"Well, what do we have here? A creepy baseball dude and a…?"

"A BAT," yells Joy, cupping her slender hands around her

mouth. "But not a baseball one. Instead, I represent nature's most misunderstood flying mammal."

"All righty then!" says the DJ, who looks slightly terrified. "And what about these two here next to you?" He shines the spotlight on me and Seth, and I squint under it, immediately feeling my face flush bright red. "Do I see … a princess and her prince?"

"Yes you do, Colin," Joy bellows on our behalf. "Bonus points for the handmade costumes, please."

"A real cute pair," drawls Colin. "Before we return to the floor-fillers, let's hear it for these DIY Disney royals, ladies and gents. Look at 'em go."

The spotlight is still on us, and so are hundreds of pairs of eyes.

"They're looking," says Joy. She's speaking out of the corner of her mouth, and her words sound muffled against the hum of the room. "Gen *and* Freddie. If you want to do something dramatic in front of all these people, I suggest you do it *now*."

Seth's waving at Colin, a smile fixed on his face, but his voice is filled with something that sounds like panic. "What do we do?"

"Do I have to spell it out for you two?" hisses Joy, waving a bat wing indignantly. "Kiss. *Now*."

Seth turns his head towards me, and his eyes ask the question. I think of Freddie. I think of Gen. I think of another version of Harley, off in some parallel universe – a

Harley who'd had several boyfriends by the age of eighteen and wasn't so jumpy at the thought of kissing someone new. I think of all the things I've done in the last few weeks, and how *they* felt scary until I did them, at which point they just felt like accomplishments.

I nod *OK*, and Seth reaches sideways to grab at my waist, pulling me in towards him. As I reach over to wrap my arms around his cravat-wearing neck, I hear Colin say something about a *tale as old as time*. Then, before I can even begin to think about what we're doing here, Seth pushes his lips against mine, and I push back.

It feels so different to Freddie. With Freddie it was all familiar – I knew his mouth like a person. I knew what it wanted. I could predict how his tongue would move, where his hands would go, what his breath would do. With Seth, right now, I have no idea. His mouth is a warm, anxious stranger.

I bring my hands up towards his face, using my fingers to feel the side of it, to get better acquainted with the rough swathe of skin across his jawbone. He breathes me in as he sweeps his hands from my waist, up my back, and settles them on the base of my head, cradling my static-y wig in his hands. The sensation lingers on my spine, like a shiver.

"They saw it," Joy says. "Aaaand … they're now pretending they didn't see it. Gen's doing tequila shots. Freddie's gone satisfyingly pale. Oh, Freddie is *definitely* having an internal crisis." She pokes me on the shoulder. "You can stop."

I break the kiss off, but Seth keeps his hands on the back of my head, eyes closed, like he hasn't got the memo. The music swells again and the dancefloor dwellers return to their activities, cheering and yelling as the evening cranks back up.

"Seth, you can *stop*," repeats Joy, exaggerating the *P* sound in a teacher-voice.

His eyes jolt open, and he falls away from me.

Jake and Gen are, unsurprisingly, crowned king and queen of the costume party. DJ Colin invites them up on stage to collect their plastic prizes, and when they wave at the crowd, Joy lets out a quiet boo under her breath.

The room is hot and claustrophobic, and my mind is full of questions – the most pressing being, *What was that?* The sensation of Seth's lips on my own hasn't faded – it sticks around, like hot breath on a mirror. My stomach lurches at the thought of Freddie watching us, at the thought of *everyone* watching us. What did they make of it? What did they think? I haven't seen anyone from the RDC here tonight, but I squirm even more at the idea of having to explain our way out of baffled questions from a disappointed Dahlia.

I said no kissing. I *always* said no kissing.

Seth follows me to the bar, where I ditch our shared Prosecco glass and collect my coat from the piled table of jackets.

"I need to go get some air," I tell him.

Seth's brows tighten as he reaches up to tousle his hair. "Are you OK? Are we OK?" He looks at the floor. "Was *that* OK?"

"Yes." I smile at him as best I can, ignoring the weight in the pit of my stomach. "Yes, to all three questions. I'll be back."

I exit through the side door and take the spiral staircase up to the rooftop, pulling my coat over my costume as I go. But when I reach the roof, there's already someone sitting out there. Perched on a wooden bench, under a canopy that's wrapped in golden fairy lights, is Freddie.

"Hey," he says. He blinks, and pats the space right next to him.

"Hey." I try to say it as carelessly as possible – like he's one of many people I've spoken to this evening; like he's not that big of a deal to me. I wander over to the bench, shivering from the cold, and take a seat next to him, running a finger over the cheap fabric of his costume. "Which Beatle are you supposed to be?"

"Paul," says Freddie. "He's everyone's favourite, right?"

"I have no idea."

He sniffs. "That's what I heard."

We sit in silence for a few moments, listening to the

noises from the traffic passing by below, the thudding pulse of Colin's 2010s-centric DJ set. The wood of the bench is cold against my thighs, and the feeling of Seth's kiss has now evaporated. I rub my lips together, wondering if I could bring it back.

Freddie clears his throat. "So, the guy you've been seeing… The Disney prince. How serious is it?"

"Seth?" I say, waving a faux-relaxed hand as Freddie takes a sip of beer, as though he could have been referring to any number of boys. "It's casual. I mean, it has to be, with next year and everything. Who knows where we'll both end up."

Freddie stops, mid-glug, and the liquid catches in his throat. "You're not coming to RAU any more?"

A stab of emotion prods me square in the chest, and for a second I read it as relief. *He loves me. He wants me.* But then it prods again – a more aggressive tap at the top of my ribcage – and I realize it isn't relief at all. It's a spiky burst of irritation.

"Why would you still think I'm coming to RAU, Freddie?" I ask him, the burst emerging via my mouth. "Here's a thought: maybe being your university plus-one isn't top of my priority list any more, given the life-altering break-up I've been going through."

"But it hasn't been life-altering for you at all," he says, and there's a genuine cloud of confusion across his face. He places the beer bottle down on the bench next to him. "You got a new boyfriend within the week, Harley. *I'm* the one who can't sleep."

I scoff. "I'm sure you're sleeping just fine."

He shakes his head viciously. "No, that's the thing: I'm not. I *was*, but then I thought about everything. Moving out. Starting again. Leaving everyone behind." He's playing with a button on the shoulder of his costume. "Next year scares the shit out of me, but if we were together, it wouldn't be that way. You've changed, Harl. It's like you just needed something to shake you up a little. And I keep thinking – maybe if we tried again, it'd be different. We'd go out. We'd travel. We could be us again, but … better."

I look at my lap and say nothing. It's confirmation – concrete, verbal, vulnerable confirmation that Seth and I have done what we set out to do. That somewhere along the way, I have successfully proven I'm no longer cautious, predictable Harley. I'm new Harley. I'm Fun Harley. I'm a version of Harley that Freddie actually wants.

It doesn't feel how I thought it would.

"Have you told RAU you're not coming with me?" asks Freddie. "Have you applied somewhere else?"

"No," I whisper. The shivers from earlier have turned into full-blown shakes, and I clench my hands together to try to calm them. Freddie wraps his own hands over my fists. His touch weakens me a little.

"We could do it, then. Me and you." He lets out a

jagged sigh, a breathy, melancholy laugh. "I've missed you so much."

I don't say it back, but I think it. I've missed his smell, and his smile, and the way he gets toothpaste all over his chin when he's brushing his teeth because he never closes his mouth. I've missed hearing his questions from The List, and his irrational long-term hatred of green peppers, and the way he spells *definitely* like *defiantly* even though those are two completely different words. There's a world now where I could have all those things back, and it makes my heart spasm.

"You can't keep doing this," I say, and my voice is small. "You can't keep deciding I'm not enough for you and then changing your mind."

"There isn't a world where you're not enough for me," he says. He reaches for my hand and then he's kissing it: he's kissing it all over, moving up my wrist with his lips like he's missed every single cell in my body, every freckle, every hair, every scar. "You were always enough for me. I just needed to remember that."

I try to pretend that I'm strong, like Bella. I try to pretend there aren't traitorous goosebumps prickling all over my arms. "What if you forget again?"

"I would never. I just … I needed to make sure we weren't stuck in a rut before our lives even started. But we're not any more." He nuzzles into my shoulder, planting tiny kisses up the curve of my neck. "I know you, Harl.

And you know me. Anything else is a waste of time."

That's when I cave. I roll my head down to meet his and he surges towards me, reaching out to grab at my face, pulling me in against him until I can't breathe. We kiss the way we used to, until we're one person again, until we're Freddie-and-Harley again, and finally, I am safe.

22

The distant land of Dullsville

For the first time in a long time, I wake up slow. Calm. The sun filters in through the tops of the curtains and I stretch my arms up above me, grateful for a new day. Last night there was no panicked 3 a.m. wake-up, no shitty meditation app to contend with while I grappled for scraps of sleep. There was just me. And Freddie. There was a midnight walk home, more frantic kisses against the front door as I clung to the back of his neck. And now, on Sunday morning, with a dishevelled wig on the pillow next to me, there's the undeniable knowledge that my boyfriend is back.

"I have very good news," I tell my mum when I pad barefoot into the kitchen, still dressed in my pyjamas. "I have such good news that you're not even going to believe it."

"And I'm very excited to hear that news, but *I* have work," says my mum. She's dressed in her go-to Heather's Health polo shirt, with a banana tucked under one arm, pacing the room in search of something. "Car keys? Any idea?"

"Check your coat," I offer, and she shakes the pocket of the jacket hung on the chair in front of her. A familiar jangle rings out.

"Bingo." She stuffs the keys and the banana into her handbag and leans back to scrape her dark hair into a ponytail, speaking with her chin tipped up towards the ceiling. "Now, tell me this news, before Heather calls and asks where the hell I am."

"We're back together," I say, and I clench my hands into anticipatory fists, bracing for the excited shriek I'm sure is about to come out of her. "Freddie and me."

"Oh!" says my mum, and her mouth makes a literal O shape that takes a while to shrink. "Wow. Well, that's… That's not what I thought you'd say."

She scoops up the coat from the kitchen chair and threads her arms through it without making eye contact.

"Why?" I demand. "What were you hoping for? What better news could possibly exist for me?"

Her face is apologetic. "I don't know. I'm sorry, Harl. I'm in a hurry; maybe I'm not phrasing myself too well. I just…" She grimaces, like she's holding back certain words and letting others filter through in their place. "You've come so far, baby. New friends, and parties, and movie nights. It's like a whole new you."

You've come so far. From where? Monotony? Predictability? The distant land of Dullsville? Her words feel like tiny, familiar pinpricks on my heart, and I cross my arms against my chest as protection. "So the old me wasn't good enough?"

"What? It *was*." She leans down to pick up her handbag and flashes me a warning look. "I just meant … you've been so brave lately. You've seemed like you were enjoying yourself."

"Yes, in order to get Freddie to *notice* that I was enjoying myself," I tell her slowly. "You know that. None of this was because I wanted to do it. I just wanted my old life back."

My mum pulls a facial expression I've never seen on her before – her mouth droops, like an upside-down horseshoe, and her dark eyes fill with concern.

I select my own banana from the fruit bowl and angrily crack the stem. "I don't get any of this. You *love* Freddie."

"Sure. You know what I'd love even more?" she says, and she's striding towards the front door now. "Knowing that you're willing to challenge yourself. Knowing that my daughter wouldn't keep going back to the same guy just because he's all she's ever known."

"That *guy* has been in my life for four years," I yell. I can't remember the last time I yelled at her. It feels wrong, but so does the way she's talking about Freddie. "He's been in *your* life for four years. Are you saying that counts for nothing?"

My mum pauses by the door, resting her fingers on the handle, then turns back to look at me. "You want my advice? The world is always turning, Harley. Sometimes it's better just to let it."

23

The plus-one

At the start of all this, when I'd fantasize about the day that Freddie changed his mind and decided he wanted me back, I had a whole scenario planned out. It was basically like that one scene from *(500) Days of Summer*, after Tom's slept with Summer for the first time, and he's parading around Los Angeles, gleefully high-fiving the locals and dancing with cartoon birds. I could see my mum happy-crying as she welcomed Freddie back into her house with open arms. I could see Seth slapping me on the back like one of his basketball teammates and saying something about how *faint heart never won fair Freddie.* And yet, here I am, with fantasy flipped over into reality, and everyone seems either disappointed or angry at me.

"No, that's not true at all," says Seth, as we wander

out of the coffee shop, reusable cups in hand, on Monday morning. "I'm ecstatic for you."

"Are you sure?" I ask. "Because you haven't smiled all morning, and you called the new barista an incompetent goblin when his back was turned."

"He *was* an incompetent goblin!" Seth's shrug is large and defensive; his hot chocolate almost lurches out of its metal home. "How hard is it to make a cappuccino?"

"Hey." I lay a hand on his arm. "Is this about Saturday night?"

Seth's eyes dart towards my lips. "No." Then, "What *about* Saturday night?"

"About Gen not reacting the way we wanted her to." I keep my fingers where they are, hoping they're offering him some kind of comfort. "I pictured it all happening at the same time. I thought when we finally cracked it, Freddie and Gen would come up to us together or something, having had the exact same epiphany, and then you and I would give each other a celebratory look, like, *We did it.* I feel bad that's not how it worked out."

"Don't feel bad," says Seth, but he slowly pulls his arm away and scratches at the side of his neck. "You got what you wanted. You deserve that."

"But if I could change things somehow, so that Gen felt differently, I would. You know I would."

He placates me with a polite nod. "I do."

We pass the science classrooms, and my heart swells with the knowledge that Freddie – *my* boyfriend, Mr Frederick Lee – is sitting inside one of them right now, doing some biology task he'll tell me all about later.

"God, you're beaming," says Seth. "You're actually beaming. I didn't think Harley Green knew how to smile."

"Shut up," I tell him fondly. "I always knew how. I just paused my ability for a little while. It's like … you know when you were a kid, and you'd had fun on holiday, but you still missed home? And then when your car pulled back on to the driveway, you ran into your house, and you saw your pet, and you ate your favourite food, and that night you slept in your own bed and you felt *so* lucky to be home again. Remember that feeling?"

Seth nods. "Of course."

"It's that," I say simply, and the thought of it is enough to make me shudder with joy. "I'm home again."

Seth does a shudder of his own – a little shake, like a dog shaking rainwater off its back after a walk. "Well, then I'm glad to have been a good holiday for you." He takes a sip from his cup. "Did you remember your letter?"

The letter he's referring to is a handwritten, *nothing is off-limits* piece of writing homework that Dahlia set us last week. "I want you to use this as a chance to get it *alllll* out of your system," she'd proclaimed excitedly to the RDC classroom. "Tell your ex exactly what you want to say to them, and make it as angry and messy and vulnerable as possible. Tell them the truth. Your truth."

This, naturally, had come as an unwelcome request to those of us who have no interest in posting tear-stained communications to our exes via Royal Mail, but Dahlia had shaken her head. "We don't send them," she'd said. "We just write them. Maybe we show them to our RDC partner and talk about them, maybe we don't. Sometimes, the act of venting is all it takes."

So here we are, as planned: letters written, ready to vent.

I don't tell Seth that I almost didn't bring my own letter – that I read it back yesterday after the argument with my mum and came *this* close to ripping it up out of loyalty to Freddie. Instead, I reach into the inner pocket of my jacket, and emerge with a piece of folded A4 paper. As I open it, I make out words like *coward* and *miss you* and I feel a twinge of guilt at the thought of reading anything this slanderous out loud when it doesn't even matter any more.

"You go first," I instruct Seth, holding out one hand to take his cup as we reach an empty bench outside the art block. We settle down on to the wooden seat together and he leans into his bag, pulling out his phone. Then, a moment later:

"Hello, Genevieve. I talked to you a couple of weeks ago, properly, for the first time in a while. Jake was there, of course. Nice perfect Jake, who you always told me not to worry about. I don't know, Gen. Maybe if I'd worried a little more, we wouldn't be in this situation. I miss you.

I miss your smell and your baby voice and your stupid heatless bedtime curls. I miss how I felt when I was with you, like I was worth something. Like people might actually have respected me, just because you did. Wren thinks you're no good for me. She thinks once a fish-hater, always a fish-hater. But she's twelve, and she doesn't understand how hard I worked just to get near you. And I know I never texted back on time, and I know I'm kind of a mess, but I wish you'd realized: that was about me. It was never a reflection on you. Anyway, good luck with Jake. I'm sure his conversation is scintillating. Best wishes from Seth (the person you said you'd love forever but didn't)."

There's a long, sad silence.

"People do respect you," I say quietly, and it isn't a lie.

"No," says Seth. The wind has dislodged his hair, leaving it out of place on his forehead. "They don't. They think, *Oh, Seth Whittaker, what a nice guy. What a quirky guy. Kind of loud, kind of annoying.* And it's fine, y'know – I'm more than happy to be that guy. I just felt a little more impressive when I was with Gen. She gave me an edge."

He reaches back over to collect his hot chocolate, shaking the almost empty cup in one hand.

"Why don't you tell me about her?" I nudge his foot with my own. "All we ever talked about was how to get her back. I don't feel like I ever knew her."

"She had a really specific laugh that she'd only do for me, when we were on the phone," says Seth, after a beat of thought. "It was a real rarity, like a rainbow, but when she did it, it made my insides collapse. It was my favourite sound in the world. She didn't know what I meant when I brought it up, so she couldn't replicate the laugh; it just came out sometimes. She did this cute thing where she called poppadoms 'pompadoms', and even though I told her that she always used the wrong word, she didn't ever remember how to say it properly. She'd be like, 'Yeah, yeah, I know,' but then every time we ordered Indian food: 'two pompadoms, please.' She was bad at singing but she was an amazing hummer – like, note-for-note. I don't know how she managed it. She'd get shy about singing in front of people, but she'd hum really elaborate songs all the time … just wandering around the house with a full orchestra in her mouth. I still kind of miss that."

"Do you still miss *her*?" I ask.

"I don't know." He picks at a fingernail. "It feels … It feels like we were a ship, and now the ship has sailed. Or maybe the ship has sunk, and now it's at the bottom of the ocean, and I've been on this pointless rescue mission, like that man who was obsessed with the Titanic."

"James Cameron?" I offer, and Seth shrugs.

"I feel like I did things wrong, for sure. I wasn't perfect. I'm *not* perfect. But neither is Gen. I can learn from that relationship – and I will do – but I don't think it's fair to keep thinking that the only reason it ended was me." His arms are crossed now, and he starts to tap on an elbow.

"When I saw her with Jake at the party, she was sitting on his lap and they were laughing, and she looked … happy. Really happy. And I thought … *Is this what I've been trying to destroy? Could I honestly make her feel better than he does?*"

"Jake seems sweet," I say, even though I'm pretty sure it's not what Seth would want to hear right now. "He seems … sturdy."

Seth laughs, but it's hollow. "I bet he knows how to make lasagne without calling his dad."

"Hey." I scold with the word. "Your lasagne was delicious; I'm planning on requesting the same again for our one-month anniversary. You put a lot of thought into that. Don't knock it."

He stares into the distance, refusing to blink. "I'm a disaster. I'm an eighteen-year-old boy who's been dumped not only by my real girlfriend, but by my fake girlfriend, too. My pre-teen sister knows more about relationships than I do. My *dog* knows more about relationships than I do." There's a new pain in his voice. "What the fuck is wrong with me?"

"Nothing," I insist, and it doesn't feel forced to say. "Nothing is wrong with you."

"Please. Just tell me the truth. I won't even hate you for it."

"The truth," I say, "is that you're funny. Very funny. You have good hair and nice friends and a thriving tropical fish collection." He looks up at me, listless, and I continue.

"And yes, you have poor time management, and you can't grow a beard, and you don't own a car. Doesn't stop any of the first stuff from being true."

The corner of Seth's mouth jolts, like a tiny smile is trying its very best to form against its owner's wishes. "Good hair, huh? Better than Jake Jenson's stupid quiff?"

"Oh, *much* better than Jake Jenson's stupid quiff," I assure him. "The quiff pales in comparison. I hope that comes as some comfort to you."

"It does." Seth sniffs. "More than you know."

He prods at the paper on my lap, nudging it open again with one finger. "What about your letter?" I hesitate, and he must sense it, because he speaks quickly. "You don't have to read it, by the way. I'm just … I don't know, I got past caring about mine."

"Dear Freddie," I begin. "There isn't even any point to me writing this, because I'm never going to send it, and maybe you wouldn't read it, even if I did."

"Strong start," says Seth, radiating something that feels like pride.

I hold a grateful-yet-serious finger up to my lips to shush him, and he takes the hint.

"I miss you. Remember when we were talking about my dad once, and I told you that it wasn't so bad, really, because he only lives an hour away, and lots of people have zero-effort dads in completely different regions or even different countries to them. Do you remember what you said? You said, 'If anything, I think him only being an hour away is worse. It's like, he could be present – it'd be easy for him to be present – but instead he chooses not to be. For me, that'd hurt more.' I never thought about it like that until then. This feels like that. You aren't dead. You aren't stuck in a country thousands of miles away, pulled from one life to another, missing us. You're a five-minute drive from my house, having a wonderful time without me because you don't want me any more. Living a different life away from me, because you decided I wasn't exciting enough for you. I don't think you have ANY idea how much that hurts. Every time I think about you now, it's like you turned invisible and bit me on the heart. There are holes in it – ragged chunks missing from where you've chewed."

I carry on going, even when Seth winces at the part about my chewed-up heart, even when my voice begins to crack.

"I know you don't think we could have made it work through university," I say, "but I do. I know we could. I can see us living together in our twenties, having kids in our thirties. Sometimes, when I think of you doing all that stuff with somebody else, I feel like I'm going to pass out. We made each other happy. We kept each other safe. And people keep saying, 'One day you'll feel differently! One day you'll meet someone else and it'll all slot into place; it'll be better!' – but it won't. In five years I might be with some new boy, but that won't take away the fact that I loved you and you loved me, and because of that there will always be a piece of you stuck inside of me like a splinter. And even if this new boy loves me too, he won't know every part of me like you did. He won't laugh at the same things we laughed at, he won't know the same things we know. I'll have to pretend with him. And then what if he and I break up too? The same thing will happen again, except in a different way, with different things, and I'll be stuck with another splinter. And what am I supposed to do after that? Just keep getting splintered? Just keep collecting relationships and then having to pretend like they didn't happen?"

There's one final paragraph to go – one where I refer to Freddie as a frightened coward of a man who cares way too much about what everyone thinks of him – but I deliberately leave it out, taking this as my opportunity to wrap things up.

"That's it. That's how I felt. You get the idea."

"Damn." Seth scratches the top of his head. "That was blistering, especially the stuff about splinters. How long did it take you to write?"

"I don't know," I tell him, taking a deep breath to recompose myself. "Ten minutes?"

"It took me two hours to finish mine. That stuff isn't easy for everyone." He nudges my knee with his own. "What else you got to show me, writer-girl?"

I return the nudge, ignoring the twinge in my stomach at the offhand pet name. "Nothing here. I write at home, sometimes. Poems. Blog posts that nobody reads. Fan fiction, sometimes. I always wanted to be an author when I was a kid, so I used to do short stories and stuff, but…" I trail off. "It's never really gone any further than that."

He sits up straighter. "And that's what you're studying next year, right? English lit? Creative writing?"

"No." I shake my head. "I'm doing business management."

"I didn't know you wanted to manage a business."

"I don't, particularly, but Freddie wants to go to a specialist agricultural university and this was the only non-specific degree available there, so … that's what I'm doing. *Was* doing." The uncertainty of it all leaves me jittery.

There was never a big conversation about which university we'd go to. Freddie and RAU always felt fated – a predetermined agricultural destiny – and I never wanted to rock that particular boat, especially because I didn't have a boat of my own to speak of. Freddie mentioned other places I could have applied to: nearby universities like Gloucestershire or Oxford Brookes, but they were all miles away, full of people I didn't know and possibilities I wasn't sure I wanted. In the end, I decided Freddie meant more to me than an abstract future I couldn't see yet.

"It doesn't matter that it doesn't offer a writing degree," I continue. "Business management will probably be way more useful in the long run anyway." I swing my bag back on to my shoulder. "Not the end of the world. Wanna walk me to class?"

Seth spins his body so he's cross-legged on the bench now, facing towards me. "I'm sorry, how can you drop a bombshell like that and then ask me to walk you to *class*?"

I feel confusion commandeer my face, my eyebrows creeping closer together. "What do you want me to say?"

"Uh, *I'm a great writer who deserves to go to the university I want to go to and not get stuck at some second-choice place just because my self-obsessed boyfriend has his heart set on it*?"

"Freddie isn't self-obsessed," I snap. "He's dedicated. He has plans for himself. He wants to make things happen."

"But why is he the only one who's allowed to be dedicated?" says Seth, his green eyes larger than ever, and sad now too. "What about you?"

"I'm dedicated to Freddie!" I say, and I don't like how high my voice has gone. "I don't mind compromising. That's what makes relationships work."

"Does Freddie compromise?"

"Yes."

"In what way?"

"In…" I swallow. "In lots of ways."

Seth snorts. "Such as?"

"You can't just ask for immediate examples. I'd need to think about it."

"Fascinating." He shakes his head. "All this time I'm there thinking mine and Gen's relationship was the unhealthy one, and you're sitting on this."

"Freddie and I are very healthy," I inform him,

placing one hand over my chest. "I've made the choices I wanted to make."

"So, what if it doesn't work out again?" pushes Seth. "What will you be left with then – a university place you don't even want? That doesn't seem like a great choice to me."

The camaraderie from earlier has now completely evaporated. I stand up, taking a few angry steps away from the bench, away from Seth.

"Why are you being so *judgemental* all of a sudden?" I ask him. "I'm trying my best. I'm prioritizing my partner. Isn't that what relationships are supposed to be about?"

Seth blows up into his hair. "Uh, yeah, when you're forty-five and have three kids together. Not when you're eighteen and have the power to do whatever you want."

"Well, this is what I want," I tell him, stretching my arms out into the air while the words fall. "I'm sorry that's so disappointing to you."

The bell rings to signify the end of our free period, and we glare at each other as students around us hurry away to class.

"No, *I'm* sorry," he says eventually, and I feel myself retreat a little. "I guess it's got nothing to do with me. But it still doesn't make sense. I told you already – you're a Victoria sponge. You know yourself; I love that about you." His freckled skin flushes. "Why is Freddie the one thing that stops you from being like that?"

It's not an unfair question, but I can answer it immediately.

"I don't think of it that way." I wander back over to the bench and lower myself down next to him. "It's more like, Freddie *is* one of the things that I know about myself. If I had to map out my entire life – the things that make me *me* – on the back of this piece of paper, right now, Freddie would be one of them."

Freddie would be more than one of them. He'd be the main element, the focus of the whole thing. Going to university together wasn't about me forgetting who I was. It was about me doing whatever I could to keep remembering it.

Seth shrugs. "Fine. I just think you deserve more than to be his lifelong plus-one."

I pick at a rip in the thigh of my jeans. "I'm not a plus-one."

"Exactly. You're not. So why does he get to act like you are?"

"What would you do differently?" I demand. "If you were m—"

"If I were him?" he interrupts, and his voice has a grit to it. "I wouldn't expect you to follow me to university. I'd want you to find a course you were *in love with*, a course you couldn't wait to join, wherever it was. I'd come and visit you at the weekend, but not every weekend, because I'd want you to have enough time to make friends and get properly settled in on your own. I'd watch reruns of your detective shows under a blanket and predict who the murderer might be, and when you were shy about meeting new people I'd hold your hand extra-tight. I'd make you love-lasagne and bring it with me in a Tupperware, and all your new friends would say, *Hey, did you know her boyfriend can cook?*"

He clears his throat, and I look at the floor. "Oh."

"But hey," says Seth, hauling himself to his feet and flashing me a smile I can't quite read. "I'm not him. So it really doesn't matter."

24

The sinking ship

"That," says Bella, as she drops into the seat beside me, "was the hottest thing I ever saw."

I give her a look of total confusion and lean to my right to try and see whatever dramatic event she's just witnessed in the corridor.

"No, no, the *kiss*. God, Fake Boyfriend really went for it," she drawls. She's drawn a little circle under each of her lower eyelids today, in dark-purple liner, and her lips are glossed in an identical shade. "How was it?"

"It was …" An eloquent description evades me, and I tell myself it's because the situation here is weird, no matter which way you look at it. How is anybody supposed to describe a fake kiss with a fake boyfriend that succeeded in winning over an *ex*-boyfriend, who has now returned to his role as *real* boyfriend?

It was acceptable? It was perfectly pleasant? It got the job done?

Bella gasps, flitting a graceful hand up to cover her mouth. "Oh my God, you're blushing. It was good, wasn't it? You *loved* it. You want to grab him by the cravat and do it all over again."

"Says who?" I ask her, silently scolding my overactive blood flow.

"Uh, says anyone who watched that whole thing happen. I'm surprised you didn't ascend into the air like an actual Disney princess, with puffs of smoke and animated birds whirling around you."

I blink at her. Is that what it looked like to everyone who watched us? Is that how it *felt*? I can only remember snippets of it: the tingle of Seth's handprint on my back, the linger of his lips on mine as I walked up to the rooftop, the horror of knowing how many people were looking our way. Of knowing Freddie was looking our way.

"Come on," Bella teases. "I love you, but you're not that good an actor. And, if my sources from the drama department are anything to go by, neither is Seth." She draws a little stick man on a page of her DON'T BE A DICK notepad, adding a triangle-skirted stick woman and a heart in the middle of them. "You *like* him. He likes you. He—"

"Is very happy for me," I butt in, anxious to complete the sentence for her. "Because the plan worked and Freddie changed his mind on Saturday night. And now I've … I've got my boyfriend back."

"Oh." She closes her mouth, drops the pen, and considers this for a moment. "*Oh.* And this is it? This is what you want, for definite?"

I nod, three or four times in a row. "He was so sweet, Bella. He kept saying how much he missed me, how he's the only person who really knows me, how I'm the only person who really knows *him*. I'm pretty sure it was the most romantic moment of my entire life."

Sometimes, when I was a kid and my dad took me out for lunch with him, I'd come back desperate to tell everyone how great a time I'd had. It didn't matter if he'd spent half the meal on his phone, or if he'd given me a look of total bemusement when I'd tried to show him my beloved Captain America origins book. I'd still arrive home beaming, ready to inform anyone and everyone that my dad had shown me the afternoon of a lifetime at our local branch of McDonald's.

This, for some unknown, uncomfortable reason, reminds me of that.

"OK, I don't say this lightly," says Bella, pulling her legs on to the chair so they're tucked underneath her. "But I am *thrilled* on your behalf. In fact, I don't think I have ever used that word before. I reserved it, especially for you."

The boost I've just received from some positive reception to my news – *finally* – courses its way through my body, and I have never been more grateful for Bella.

"I had a plan," I tell her, "and I made it happen. I am

not a sapling; I am an ancient oak. I am a … a giant Sequoia tree."

"Like I always told ya," she says gleefully. "We need to celebrate. Lunch, right after class?"

I nod, relieved that we're out of kiss-debrief-land and firmly planted in celebration-land. "Let's do it."

💔

At the end of the lesson, Bella grabs me by the arm and leads me out of the classroom towards two girls: Riya, with her pencil-thin eyebrows and such immaculate make-up skills I don't know how she hasn't been scouted to go work in a Hollywood studio somewhere, and Lauren, who I now know as the friend Bella was attempting to do the worm with on Saturday night.

"Gals, look alive," says Bella, immediately picking up the pace. "Harley has incredible news to share."

Riya clutches a hand to her chest, like a Jane Austen character who's just received word of her sister's marriage proposal. "Oh my God. Is this about the hot blonde guy who dressed up as the Beast?" I shake my head, and she deflates slightly. "Oh."

"For Harley, it's better than that," says Bella. "I propose we get a large pizza to share and discuss all this on the art block sofas."

She takes me by the crook of the arm again, linking herself to me, and I feel a swell of pride at the thought of being the topic of conversation in a group like this. Of being so important to Bella that she'd allow her lunchtime to be taken over by my news, because she's so happy for me that it's basically her news now, too.

"Harley?"

I jump at the unexpected sound of a boy's voice – Freddie's voice. He's sitting waiting in the reception area of the ESS, a checked scarf looped around his neck, and he gets to his feet as soon as he sees me.

"Freddie!" says Bella, who's never been properly introduced to the man but chooses to skip the formalities and greets him as if I've just announced our engagement. "Congratulations, my guy. Do you even *know* how lucky you are? Are you even *aware*?"

Freddie provides her with an uncertain, distracted grin. "Of course." Then he turns to me, reaching for my hand and shutting the conversation down as quickly as it started, as though Bella, Riya and Lauren aren't even there. "Hey, I thought we could walk into town and get some food. Talk some more."

The silence is long and painful.

"I … I'm supposed to go for pizza with Bella and her friends," I say, eventually, and I immediately regret my choice of explanation. The word *supposed*, as if this impromptu lunch to celebrate my relationship reunion is suddenly some kind of obligation for me. I feel Bella's arm tense in mine.

"What about Lucas and Joshua?" I suggest to Freddie, hoping that this will magically solve the problem. "Aren't they around?"

Freddie uses the toe of his trainer to flick at a pebble on the floor. "They've got football practice." He drops his voice, aiming it only at me again, even though everyone else is still well within earshot. "I thought we'd said we'd hang out? We'd usually do Monday lunch together, right?"

He's correct: we would. But that was before – back when I only had one, boyfriend-shaped option.

"Sounds like you two have a lot to talk about," says Bella, but her voice has an edge to it, like she's challenging me. She drops her arm away from mine and steps towards Lauren and Riya, who are hovering on the outskirts of this conversation with their heads bowed.

"We do have a lot to talk about," agrees Freddie, who doesn't seem to have picked up on the edge at all and actually looks grateful, as though Bella's given us her blessing. "And my lunch break finishes in half an hour, so we've gotta be quick, Harl."

Bella coughs pointedly, waiting for an answer from my end.

"Would that be OK?" I ask her, and my voice is pleading, pathetic. "We can reschedule. I really want to do this, just … maybe tomorrow?" I look at Freddie for calendar confirmation and I hear Bella scoff in disbelief. "I'll buy the pizza."

Bella cocks her head to one side. "Sure. See ya."

She paces straight out of the building, with Riya and Lauren following in quick succession. I wonder if they'll spend the next hour discussing how weak I am, or if they'll just fall into a brand-new conversation that has nothing to do with me, because I was never even part of their friend group anyway. I'm not sure which would be worse.

Freddie – completely oblivious to the situation he's just created – takes my hand, and we set off on the walk through sixth form, across the park and into the town centre together. He tells me he has a burning question for me from The List, which is, *How come the sun is good for you, but also bad for you?* I ask for clarification and Freddie says, "Well, on one hand it's vitamin D, but on the other, you can't spend too long lying under it, otherwise you'll get ill. It's like, can't live with it, can't live without it. If I was God, I just think I'd have planned things better than that."

He asks about Seth, and I say something non-committal about mistakes and how some people are just better as friends. Freddie says that friends don't usually kiss each other on the mouth at costume parties, which I have to take as a valid critique. I ask if he's told Min and his family about us. He says no, but that he will, probably tonight at dinner. He rubs at the black hair-tie on my wrist, the one that lives there in case of emergency, and tells me he thought about this one specific hair-tie every day we weren't together.

"Isn't that weird," he adds. "I never really noticed it before."

We eat our sandwiches and Freddie asks me if I've thought any more about RAU. If maybe I have other plans now. I shake my head. *Still no.* I look at him from across the table and I know that RAU isn't my dream, but the truth is that I don't really have a dream right now. Maybe in the future I will do, and the roles will swap, and Freddie will follow *me* while I prioritize it. Until then, this could work. This is what I thought I wanted, so maybe I still do.

As we walk back to sixth form he perches his chin on the top of my head and wraps his arm around me. I snuggle back into him, basking in the return of his attention, and wait for everything bad to melt away.

25

The apology

My mum slides a paper note under my door that evening, the same way she used to when I was small. Back then, we'd always refer to ourselves in the third person whenever we had an awkward or difficult conversation brewing. It made the words feel easier to say, like they weren't coming directly from us and we were just the messenger, passing on the gist from somebody else. *Harley doesn't like it when your friends come over without telling us first*, or, *Mummy thinks it would be very helpful if Harley helped to empty the dishwasher from time to time, even though Harley finds it boring. Guess what: Mummy finds it boring too, but maybe Mummy and Harley could make a game out of it. Does Harley have any ideas?* Over time, it evolved into an occasional way for us to communicate: *Good morning! Mum wants to tell Harley that she loves her SO MUCH, more than anyone ever loved anyone.*

Tonight, she's written the note in purple felt-tip, with tiny smiley faces at each corner and a whole row of kisses at the bottom of the page.

Mum would like to say that she's sorry for responding badly to Harley's news. She understands that Harley has had a very difficult start to the year, and if Harley wants to be with Freddie, of course Mum will support it. However, Mum would also like to remind Harley that change isn't always bad. It can be scary, but sometimes it can lead to the best things you ever experienced.
(Please just come down and talk to me, I LOVE YOU!!)
XXXXXXXXXXXXXXXXXXXXXXXXXXXXXXXXXXX

I read the note a few times, smiling at the final sentence, and then fold it in two, slotting it into my pocket. When I head downstairs my mum is sitting alone on the sofa, her feet tucked up underneath her and a cross-stitch pattern laid out on one thigh.

"I got your note," I tell her.

She abandons the pattern and pats the space next to her. "I'm glad. Ready to talk?"

I nod, then plod down on to the sofa, keeping my eyes on the incense-laden coffee table in front of us.

"You asked if the old you was good enough," says my

mum, "and I'm here to tell you: she was perfect. I've never, ever wanted you to change who you are – not when you were younger and *certainly* not now."

There's a fierceness to the way she forms the words, like if anyone stormed in here and challenged them she'd happily throw a punch.

She continues. "I'm so sorry if what I said made you feel like I don't want you to be yourself. That wasn't it at all. What I've loved watching is the way you're letting more people *see* you. You're so special, baby." She places a hand on my knee and rubs it with her thumb. "I just wish more of us got to witness that."

"I didn't mean it when I said that everything I did lately was just so Freddie saw it," I say. "I mean, it was, but I did enjoy some of it. And realistically, I don't think I'm an improv girl. I don't want to go to parties every week. But I like my new friends. I like the RDC. I like Seth."

He bursts into my head, the same way he burst into the psychology classroom the first day we met. Frantic. Messy. Endearing, despite it all.

"That's what I mean." My mum's hand is still on my knee, warm and reassuring. "What I wrote in your note is true – that not all change is bad. You were the biggest change of my entire life, and I was so scared to meet you – to know that I was somehow responsible for this tiny baby when I still felt like such a baby myself. But look at us now." She lets out a low, proud breath. "Look at *you*. You think I'd have done anything differently, Harley Beth?"

In an ideal situation, in a perfect world, I'd be able to accept these words as a given. I'd lean in for a hug and my mum would ruffle my hair, the way she always does, and I'd fix it back to normal, and then I would take this whole conversation at face value. But there's a part of me – a large, unrelenting part – that can't settle just yet.

You think I'd have done anything differently? My honest answer is *yes*.

I know my mum's life, and that means I know she's content enough. She likes the town we live in – the park at the end of our road and the blossom trees that flower every Easter. She likes her friends. She likes her colleagues, even coughy Heather. But when I see photos from the 90s and the 00s, her standing there clutching prizes for award-winning history projects and Tudor-inspired dioramas, it still makes my soul sad. In another life, she's a historian, archiving in a museum or teaching an open-mouthed class of children. But she isn't there. She's here, in this life, the one she'd never have dreamed of or picked out for herself at a careers fair, with me.

I've always felt guilty about that. And not the kind of guilt that's motivational – not the kind that would shunt me in the direction of growth and opportunity and self-development, to try and write my own life differently to hers. It's the kind of guilt that's been fused to every single part of me, for as long as I can remember. I wonder now if it's kept me small, because as much as she loves me, as much as I *know* in my bones that she loves me, I also know I'm the person who kept her from doing what she wanted to do.

It doesn't make sense to me. How can I be the best thing in her life, when I'm also the thing that jackhammered it out of all recognition?

"I think if you had the chance to do it all over again, you'd make sure you didn't even look at Dad," I say, in a voice so quiet I can barely hear it. "You'd walk straight past him and leave it alone. Do you ever think about how different it could've been?"

She stops breathing for a second, freezing in place. Then, "Sometimes. On bad days, I'll do the 'what if's. But not seriously. I'll think about it in the same way I'll think, *What if I'd never had this stupid fringe cut in and didn't have to go through the torment of growing it out?*" She exhales, gently at first, then in one long shudder. "This is *my* life, Harl. My house. My job. My beautiful, complicated daughter. You think there's some perfect parallel universe out there where I did everything by the book and was never, ever sad? There isn't. There's just this universe. That's all we have."

I cling to the edges of the sofa cushion, picking at the same piece of fabric over and over again, and I think of Freddie. We used to discuss the concept of parallel universes, way back when I sat next to a smaller, nerdier version of him in history class four years ago. He loved the idea that maybe we could exist in multiple places, living multiple lives, trying out multiple opportunities. At the time, it didn't appeal so much to me – I felt like one existence was more than enough to cope with – but as I got older, I could really see the draw.

I knew I didn't make sense to some people. I also knew that my existence on the planet was almost definitely the result of some ill-thought-out contraception and a bottle of cheap alcohol. The thought of that made me feel precarious – delicate, like my place here was shaky and could be yanked away from me at any second. I started to wonder if there was another universe out there that I was *supposed* to be part of – one where I was easy to understand and had always been included in some bigger plan.

"I wish I could try different lives," I murmur now. "I wish I could test something out for a bit and see how it goes, and then ditch it if I hate it."

My mum's blue eyes blink at me. "Who says you can't?"

"*I* do. Nobody has that ability; you just have to pick a life and live it. That's why everyone forces you to make all these decisions at eighteen: where you want to go, what you want to learn, who you want to be. But what if you change your mind? What happens then?"

"Well, then you change your mind. And what a luxury. What a dream, to have the power to do that." She repositions herself on the sofa, leaning back against the cushions and gently guiding me with her, so that I'm angled against her, nestled with her legs and arms wrapped around me. "Sometimes it's like you think you're a … a feather, or a paper aeroplane or something, Harl. You think you have to just let the wind waft you from place to place, take you wherever it wants, while you observe the whole thing. But you don't. When you live like that, it leaves you vulnerable. It means you're always waiting for someone like Freddie to grab you and redirect your path."

I can't pretend that hearing this analogy feels good for me. It doesn't. But it does make me hold myself differently, straight away. As the words land and make their way into my understanding, I'm so newly aware of any potential featheriness that I feel myself steel against my mum – weighted, instantly alert to anybody who might try and drag me away in a direction I don't want to go in.

Even Freddie.

I thought he was my universe – that he was everything that made my life good, that he was the only one who could leave me feeling truly *known*. And maybe he was, for a while, but now he isn't. There's Bella – fun, bold-lipped, loyal Bella – who deserves a much more committed friend than me. There's Joy and there's Nate, who didn't have to care about Seth's awkward fake girlfriend but still chose to because of the kind of people they are. And then there's Seth. I don't even know what to say about Seth.

"Everything was supposed to be better now." I look

over to Freddie's painting of me on the living room wall. "Everything was supposed to be better, but it all just feels like a mess."

My mum leans her chin down on to the top of my head. "It's lucky you have choices, then, isn't it? Lucky that this particular life belongs to you, and nobody else." Her arms are tight around me. "If everything feels like a mess right now, what are you going to do about it?"

The answer hovers in the air in front of us, somewhere above the coffee table, a little too fuzzy to see.

26

The one that got away

The vibe in the RDC room is different this week. Brighter, maybe. A touch more hopeful. The sun is shining in through the streaky classroom windows and Dahlia – dressed in a plum-coloured scarf and a long celestial-print pinafore that looks like it'd be at home on a vintage TV show about witches – is holding up a new cardboard sign that simply says CONTENTEDNESS.

"That's the name of the game this week," she says, launching straight into it. "Often, when we come out of a relationship, we want to hide away. We don't want to deal with the uncomfortable emotions that are coming up for us. So we distract ourselves with numbing activities, whatever they might be. TV. Scrolling for hours on our phones. Food. Sex. Alcohol. Those things might feel good in the moment, so no judgement from me, but long-term, they're not always the best things to help us actually heal."

"What *did* help you heal?" asks Daisy. She's holding a pen, ready to write down Dahlia's advice word-for-word. If anyone in this club is going to get an A grade at the end of term, it's Daisy.

"Y'know, I went outside a lot, which was unusual for me," says Dahlia. "I went hiking, and swimming, and cycling, because it helped me to remember that other people existed. It helped me to remember that the *world* still existed. Sitting inside of your house, you're like a tiger in a cage. You only think about yourself, and you start to worry that that's all anyone else thinks about, too. Getting outside your house… It's different. There are hills and lakes and birds and trees and none of them give a shit about your break-up or your skincare routine or your grown-out hair dye. They just want to exist alongside you."

She pauses to scratch at her lower eyelid. "When I was at home, I made things with my hands. Coasters and Christmas decorations and jigsaw puzzles and stuff. *That* helped me to switch off. I tried to make a plan with a friend at least once a week, even on the days when I wasn't feeling up to it. I'm not saying I didn't mess up. To begin with, all I did was check my phone, even when I could literally feel it eating away at my brain. You don't have to be perfect with it. But I promise you, even when it all feels pointless, there are things you can do to help you feel content again."

"Why just content?" asks Daisy, hovering the pen over her bottom lip. "Why not happy?"

Dahlia makes a *hm* noise. "I guess because happy feels like a short-lived emotion to me. It's like a spike of something – you might be happy because you got good news, or because you achieved a goal. It's cool, but I like contentment more. Contentment is cosier. It's more embedded." She waggles the end of her scarf at us all. "I felt content when I was knitting this scarf. The act of going back to it every day and sitting there drinking my hot chocolate with the fairy lights on – *that* was contentment. I felt happy when I'd completed it, but I enjoyed the journey just as much. Different things, y'know?"

She faces the whiteboard and begins to write.

Which activities helped me to feel content
before my relationship?
Which activities could help me to feel
content now?

"Take twenty minutes for this one – get thinking, get planning and let's see what we can come up with. Unless..." She twists back towards us. "Does anyone have questions? Thoughts? News?"

Seth coughs. "Harley has news she'd like to share. Big news, actually."

Today – Wednesday – is the first time we've spoken since the awkward letter-reading morning, and I'd expected Seth to show up quiet, maybe a little embarrassed. Instead, he'd arrived on top form: leaning forward across the desk with his torso pressed against the wood, deep in loud, flirtatious conversation with Daisy, who'd seemed slightly bewildered by this new burst of attention. I'd glimpsed a streak of the toned skin on his back, peeking out between his belt and his T-shirt, and shuffled my chair to the left, another few centimetres away from him.

"Big news?" Dahlia opens her eyes a little wider. "Harley, what's going on?"

"I'm … I'm back together with my ex," I say. "We, uh, reconnected at the weekend, and we've decided to give things another go."

The entire room turns round to look at me, and I get a sudden impulse to slide out of my chair and hide under the table.

Dahlia blinks several times in a row. "Oh! Wow. Well … congratulations, Harley." She gives herself a little shake. "I'm sorry – it's just, obviously, you're breaking new RDC ground here. I feel unprepared. Will you … will you be leaving us early?"

I think of Year Ten, when I started attending an after-school writing club in the library and quickly abandoned it when I found it interfered with my ability to text Freddie back on time. Then Year Twelve, when I considered joining a pottery class on a Saturday morning but struggled to sit with the discomfort of knowing it would mean reshuffling our well-trodden weekend traditions. And now there's this. For the first time in a long time, I've committed to sticking with something. Something for me.

Lucy waggles a pen-tattooed hand in the air. "Full disclosure: I feel uncomfortable sharing this space with someone who isn't in the same position as I am." She glances back at me. "No offence intended."

"None taken," I say, but it isn't remotely true.

"Interesting," says Dahlia. She's watching us all like a rapt documentary producer. "What about the rest of us – does anyone else feel like Lucy?"

Reyan, Oliver, Nav, Maryam and Joey each gingerly raise their hands.

"It's not that I don't want *you* here," says Joey quickly, twisting in his chair to face me. "It's more that I don't want anyone here who doesn't get it. It was different when we were all in the same boat. Now you're not in the boat with us. You're just swimming past for fun on your Wednesday lunch break before you float back to your boyfriend."

"Harley, why would you *want* to even come here any more?" questions Lucy, bug-eyed. "You're living the dream. If I was in your position – if my ex changed her mind – none of you would ever see me again. I'd be like one of those cartoon holes in the wall; I'd have run out of here so fast." She turns back to Dahlia. "Again, no offence. I've learned a lot."

"It's more complicated than that," I tell her. "I like being here. And what's Seth supposed to do? We're a team. We were meant to be in this together."

To my right, Seth stares at the wall.

Dahlia shakes her head. "Don't worry. Seth can join up with a pair to make a three; he won't be alone. We'll make sure of that."

"Can I stay for today?" I ask quietly. "I want to say goodbye to everyone."

"Of course." She nods, and her eyes dart towards Seth. "It's a big change for all of us."

When Seth and I vacate the RDC classroom, we head for our regular spot on the comfy entrance-hall chairs, leaving the rest of the group to disperse to their own favourite haunts.

"The end of an era," he calls from the vending machine as he waits for his packet of pretzels to emerge. "Can I interest you in an out-of-date snack to mark the occasion?"

"I'll take some of your pretzels," I yell back. He nods and throws the bag my way. I catch it and tug it open, reaching in to pull out one of the salted swirls.

When Seth arrives back next to me, he thuds down on to an armchair. "OK, final question of the process. Harley Green, I want to *knowwww*: what made you feel content before your relationship?" He thrusts his own hand into the bag, surfaces with a pretzel and begins to chew. "I know you were like, nine years old, but try and think back."

I roll my eyes. "I was *thirteen*."

He shrugs: *po-tay-to, po-tah-to.* "Well, at thirteen, what were you into? What was a Freddieless Harley like?"

I try to remember it. I try to think about a younger version of me, a pre-Freddie Harley Green, who had no concept of boyfriends or commitment or university or anything else. I can see her in my mind: a shorter, more nervous me, with the exact same haircut and thick metal braces across her front teeth. What did she like? What did she hate? What made her happy, or angry, or frustrated?

"I know I liked writing," I tell him, eventually. "Stories, that kind of thing. I wrote a comic book about this girl who could fly."

"Where did she fly to?" asks Seth, mid-crunch.

"It wasn't so much about the destination. It was more the *act* of the flight. Like, that was the story – the fact that she could just kick off from the top of the stairs and then float down to the bottom. She could head up to the sky and help solve crimes, like a human helicopter."

The *Harriet Grant* series still exists in my house somewhere – probably up in the attic. My mum kept them all in a box file and told everyone who'd listen that they'd be worth a lot of money one day.

Seth lets out a little laugh despite himself. "That's so cute. And it made you feel content?"

"It made everything speed up. I'd start typing, and then three hours would have passed without me even knowing it."

It was like magic; no other activity made time warp like that. Sometimes I'd imagine being called for dinner and emerging from my bedroom as an old, wrinkled woman with long white hair, who'd just kept going and going and had eventually written her entire life away.

"To feel content, Harley Green needs to write." Seth jots it down on the sheet of paper in front of us. "Perfect. What else worked for ya?"

"I had this friend," I say slowly. "Rashida. She moved away in Year Nine. Sometimes I think maybe if Freddie and I hadn't started dating, I'd have put more effort into keeping in touch with Rashida. Or maybe just finding new friends. Like … replacement friends."

Rashida was a wannabe detective – I met her in the library because she was trying to unearth information about a rumour that our school had been built on top of an old cemetery. She had a giant backpack – stuffed with books about mysteries and murders – and big, dark eyes, like Bambi's. We promised we'd keep in touch when she left, but we didn't. I think maybe Rashida tried, for a while.

Seth prods a finger at the sheet of paper, where he's written down my second answer. "Putting it out there now: if you don't write some stuff and call a friend this evening, you will have me to answer to. I will be like an

RDC ghost; I will turn up at your house demanding proof of your contentment. I don't care who you're dating – just promise me that you're going to write."

His eyes are determined, and when I look into them it makes me feel too many things at once.

"Harley?" He holds out a hand. "Promise?"

"I promise." We shake on it, and Seth's fingers are tight across my knuckles as he smiles.

"While we're on the subject of promises, *I'd* enjoy some reassurance that you're going to spend large chunks of your spare time talking loudly in front of Genevieve about how much you miss your hilarious, orderly ex-boyfriend Seth Whittaker. Just for old time's sake."

"It goes without saying." I reach into the bag for more pretzels. "He's the one that got away."

Seth makes a breathy noise with his nose, a quick huff of amusement. "He didn't go anywhere. He's right here."

27

The road trip

Min, as expected, is far from thrilled to see me and Freddie back together.

"Harley!" she says when she answers the door on Saturday morning. Her eyes are giant and her smile is stretched, like she's mid-inspection at the dentist. "What a joy to see you!"

The only time I have seen Minnie Lee look less joyful is when Rosie, her daughter, spilled paint all over Min's cream-coloured #ad #gifted jumpsuit before Min had even had a chance to film anything in it.

"Such a delight," I tell her, as I try to restrain a laugh. Rosie appears now behind her mother, peering round at me with both hands clutching Min's waist. "Hey, Ro-Ro!"

"Aunty Harley!" Rosie squeals with excitement. She's dressed in a green mermaid tail – handmade by Freddie's mum – and a large, bedraggled purple wig that's clinging on to her head for dear life. "Have you come to play actresses with me?"

Actresses is Rosie's favourite game. It involves putting on the strangest clothes you can locate, usually found in Rosie's dress-up box or Min's well-stocked wardrobe, and launching into a completely improvised back-and-forth, loosely based around the fact that a) you are famous actresses, b) you are about to go on stage, and c) there has been some sort of crisis that needs to be urgently resolved in the nick of time. We've had fires. We've had cardiac arrests. Last time we played, Rosie's character had just been video-called by a TV executive who demanded she fly out to Los Angeles there and then.

"They need me," Rosie had proclaimed. "And that's showbiz, Aunty Harley."

"No actresses today," I say apologetically, and Rosie tugs her dark eyebrows into an exaggerated frown. "Next time, for sure."

"Mummy said you wouldn't be coming over to Grandma and Grandad's house any more," she accuses. The wig gives up the ghost, and Rosie reaches out to catch it with one hand. "Mummy said, 'Aunty Harley isn't a real aunty; she's more like a friend of the family, and sometimes friends fall out.'" She sticks out her lower lip. "Why did you fall out with us?"

So much for four years of Lee-family adjacency. So much

for the fine-line BE KIND tattoo etched on Minnie's wrist.

"I didn't say exactly that, Rosie, did I?" Min shoots her daughter a frazzled look. "What I *actually* said was that H—"

"Don't worry about it," I interrupt, smiling at both of them. "But you know, Rosie, sometimes friends make up, too."

Rosie nods, satisfied with my answer, and looks at her mother for confirmation. I hover awkwardly on the doorstep for a second, not knowing whether to head straight inside to Freddie's bedroom like I used to, but Freddie appears behind Min and Rosie with a backpack and a water bottle.

He looks *good* today. His hair – freshly washed and still a little damp – is shoved away from his face, with tiny strands of it pole-vaulting back into their usual position the moment he leans down to Rosie for a hug.

"You good to go?" he asks me, straightening back up.

"Ah, the RAU open day," says Min, leaping on to the distraction from her child's honesty, and Freddie nods. Min gestures towards the sky, like she's personally responsible for conjuring up the sunshine. "Exquisite weather for it."

"Well, the world is happy for us, Min," mutters Freddie, pushing past her and rubbing my shoulder in greeting. "It's a shame not everyone feels the same."

Min watches us from behind the net curtains in the kitchen as we walk back down the driveway, like an incompetent detective. I offer her an obvious, passive-aggressive wave while dumping my belongings into the back of Freddie's old Honda, and she jumps, immediately moving over to the cupboard above the kettle and pretending to root around for something inside of it.

"We're really doing this," says Freddie, as he types the RAU address into his phone. He uses his other hand to reach over for my thigh, rubbing at it with a familiar thumb. "Today is, like, a preview of our future, Harl. This is it."

"Great," I tell him, in a voice that doesn't sound anything like mine.

I fasten my seatbelt with shaky fingers, and we hit the road.

"The exciting thing about this particular course," says the woman with the clipboard, "is that it combines so many different elements. Lots of our students come here unsure of where the future might lead them, and that's why we think the mixture of business and environmental sustainability, paired with our innovative technology focus, really lends itself to the generalist degree that you're looking for before you move on to a specialism at a later date."

"That's good to know," a well-spoken boy in a gilet replies.

Freddie nudges me, as if to say, *Isn't this exciting?* and I give him a thumbs up in response.

The campus here is beautiful. Each building we've

walked past or through is old and pretty, like it's been loaned to the university by the National Trust, and there's greenery in literally every direction.

"We go sledging right here in the winter," a student volunteer had informed me and Freddie earlier, pointing out a large grassy verge, and Freddie had looked like he was going to pass out with glee at the thought.

At the end of the session for Freddie's course, we bump into the volunteer again. "I remember you!" she says, more to Freddie than to me. She's wearing a blue bobble hat and has two thin plaits at the front of her blonde hair. Her large flared nostrils remind me of a horse we came across just before lunch. "Finding everything you need to find?"

"I think so," says Freddie, scratching at the top of his head. "But we wanted to speak to someone about accommodation. We're, uh … We're coming here as a couple – we were thinking we'd get a studio flat or a double room or something. How do we do that?"

The girl squints at him, then at me. "There aren't really any double rooms on campus. You could go further out into the local towns, but then you'd be reliant on a car to get you in for lectures. Like, you'd be leaving home super early to get here on time." She wrinkles her nose, as though leaving the house before 8 a.m. would be a higher education deal-breaker for her. "Would that work?"

"I guess it'd have to," I say. "That's what I was expecti—"

"I mean, I wouldn't recommend it, personally,"

interrupts the volunteer. Her badge says VAL – STUDENTS' UNION and not VAL – ESTATE AGENT, so why she's offering us property advice I have no idea. "Why don't you both just apply for single rooms on campus? It's such a close-knit community, so you'll want to be here to make the most of it all. You can still be a couple and live separately. It's not like you're *married*, right?"

She lets out a little whinny of a laugh at her final sentence, and Freddie joins in. "Nope," he says, a touch too enthusiastically. "Absolutely not married."

"So we'd just … live in different apartments?" I clarify. "And hang out at mealtimes?"

"Well, a lot of the socializing takes place as a group," says Val, and I want to grab her stupid bobble hat and throw it into the manure pile I'm sure is nearby. "You probably won't have that much time to worry about couple-y stuff. You want my advice?"

"Not really," I mutter, at the same time as Freddie lets out an emphatic, "Sure!"

She hands him a flyer with the words WELCOME TO YOUR FUTURE emblazoned on the front. "Enjoy the now. You'll be here" – she spins on the spot like a ballerina, lifting her arms to the sun – "and it really is the best place."

"I can't wait," says Freddie. He steps back to fully take in the view of the fields that surround us, breathing in the smell of the outdoors and clasping his hands across the back of his head. "I can't *wait*."

Val trots away to bother some other prospective students, and Freddie turns to me. "What do you think? I know it isn't what we expected, but I'm pretty sure the single-room thing could work. Like Val said, we'd still be together all the time, anyway. Just … in a group."

He leads me over to a wooden bench that overlooks the sledging field, takes a seat, then pats the space next to him. I hesitate, then lower myself down.

"This is very different to what we'd agreed," I tell him in a small voice. "We'd already guessed we couldn't live on campus. That's why we said we'd find a studio flat nearby. I don't see why that's suddenly such a problem."

"It's not a problem," says Freddie, but his voice sounds distant, like he isn't really here with me at all. "I just liked what Val was saying. She made campus living sound fun. And …" He wraps an arm around me, leaning in to inhale the scent of my hair. "I thought you were more about the fun these days."

The urge to slip out from under his arm, sprint into the field opposite us and scream at the top of my lungs is overwhelming.

I give my head a little shake and touch Freddie on the knee. "I think I'm going to go see the business management course leader. Get some extra detail about the modules."

"You want me to come with you?" he asks, but he's still staring out adoringly at the fields around us in a nature-induced trance.

"No," I say, removing his arm from my neck. "You carry on exploring. I'll call you after."

I pace back over to the teaching zone and locate the business management classroom, which smells like rubber and old books. The gilet-wearing boy from earlier is standing inside, next to a proud-looking woman I assume is his mother, and when they see me they wrap up their conversation with the course leader, who shakes their hands and tells them to email him if they need anything at all over the coming months.

"A future business leader?" he says, as he turns to greet me. He has a little pin badge in the shape of a tractor attached to his tie.

"I'm not sure," I say. "Maybe. I have a provisional place here for September. I'm Harley."

"Well done you. I'm Obie. Now, what would you like to know?" He clicks the lid back on to his pen. "We can talk modules, or future career paths. We can even talk pre-university nerves, if you so wish. This is your time."

I decide to get straight into it. "I just … I wanted to ask – is there much writing on this course?"

Obie raises a thick grey-tinged eyebrow. "Writing? Uh, well, I suppose there's some. You'll be expected to write essays and use your abilities to demonstrate understanding of each module, of course, but if writing's a struggle for you, please do rest assured there's support available, and there's a great deal of practical work on this degree."

He gestures to a large display on the wall to his left, which is plastered with images of RAU students doing RAU-y things. One photo shows a blonde girl in a trouser suit, standing in front of a forest with her hands on her hips. It might even be Val.

Obie takes my silence as a sign of literary hesitance. "You'll be networking, taking part in trips, finding out more about the on-the-ground work it takes to manage a business. It's not just words – not at all."

"Oh," I say. My heart takes a nosedive, thudding right down into the pit of my stomach. "What happens if I wanted it to be just words? What would I do then?"

He leans his head to one side and studies me for a moment. "Harley, I'm sorry. I'm not sure I understand."

I laugh, even though it's not funny at all. "Don't worry about it. I'm not sure I do, either."

28

The coward

Bella keeps her head down when I arrive outside the English room on Monday morning. Karen, unusually, isn't here yet, so it's just us two, stood waiting by a locked classroom, together. Bella's arms are crossed over a gingham waistcoat, clutching her A4 notepad; from the gap between them, I see the infamous peeling sticker that says DON'T BE A DICK.

"I forgot about the sticker," I murmur.

Bella's dark eyes snap up to meet mine. "What?"

We haven't spoken since the Freddie-incident last week, since I ditched her to go for tuna paninis with the boy I said was more important than anything. On Thursday, we stayed silent after an hour-long mock exam and walked out of the lesson separately. On Saturday, I wrote out a couple of messages to her: things like, *I shouldn't have said what I said*, and, *Your friendship means so much to me*, but I wasn't sure if I was making more out of something than actually needed to be made, or whether Bella might have forgotten all about it by today. In the end, the messages stayed in the drafts folder.

"I was a dick," I say, using my forefinger to gesture towards the notepad. "And I'm sorry."

Bella's voice is small and sad. "Mm. Well, I'm sure you enjoyed your lunch."

"Lunch was fine." I raise my shoulders then thud them down again, arranging my lips into a shy, polite smile. "But it wasn't the same as pizza with my friend."

She cuts back in, the instant I stop speaking. "Then why didn't you *protect* pizza with your friend? Why didn't you say, *Sorry, Freddie, I've already got plans, so no can do*? You just stood there, Harley. Like you had no power over anything."

I've never seen Bella like this before. I've seen her skip down sixth-form corridors singing both parts of the duets from *Wicked*, full of the *joie de vivre* Karen told us about. I've seen her tip an entire can of cherry Pepsi on to the head of a boy who cheated on Riya during a holiday to Corfu. I've seen her playful and angry and mischievous and morose, but never hurt like this, ever. I don't think I even knew I had the ability to hurt someone like Bella, who's always had such an action-packed life that I suspected I'd have no impact on it at all.

But here she is. Eyes on the floor, breathing heavy. Hurt.

"I'm so sorry," I tell her. "I did do that. And the only excuse I have, however terrible, is that it felt natural to me – that's what I've always done, so I did it again. I don't think I've ever said, *Sorry, Freddie, I've already got plans, so no can do*. Like, the words have literally not exited my mouth."

Bella's gaze doesn't move from the worn-down carpet tiles. "I could tell."

"That doesn't mean they *shouldn't* exit my mouth," I add. "And they will."

She shakes her head, like she doesn't believe me. "I always look out for you, Harley. I ask you to do things, and I check how your weekend was, and I listen to you talk about your boyfriends, both real and fake. I know you're going through some stuff right now, but ..." She catches herself, biting her lip.

"Say it," I push.

Bella releases her crimson lip, leaving little toothmarks in her wake. "We're all going through some stuff. That's life, and you're never going to have more than just a boyfriend if you can't learn how to juggle him with everything else. If all you want is Freddie, fine. Go ahead. But if you want pizza lunches and friendships and growthful shit, *which you said you did*" – she waggles a finger at me – "then you can't pull the kind of stuff from last week." She swallows. "That's not how friends operate."

"You're right," I tell her. She's so right that tears well up in my eyes – fierce and ashamed and full of love. "That's not how friends operate at all, and I promise it will never, ever happen again."

Bella uses the toe of her boot to poke at the space where the wall meets the floor. "It better not."

"It won't," I repeat. "I'd rather head up the sixth-form social committee before letting something like that happen again. I'd rather go skydiving with my dad."

I see a small, reluctant smile sneaking on to her face. "If it happens again, I'm calling him. Don't think I won't."

For the first time in a week, we laugh together.

The bell rings for the beginning of class, and Karen waves at us in the distance. Bella moves towards the door, but I put a hand on her elbow.

"I appreciate all the things you do for me, and I'm going to do those things for you. Freddie's important to me, but he's not the only thing I care about. Not any more."

For weeks, my insides have been collapsing – falling apart day by day without Freddie Lee – and now he's given them exactly what they wanted and they're still no happier.

"It really feels like everything's gone back to the way it should be," he announces as we stroll into the coffee shop on Wednesday morning. He squeezes my hand. "RAU. Us. It's like everything is falling into place again."

I smile, but my strangled palm feels instantly slick with sweat and my stomach churns like a washing machine. It makes me mad at myself.

We join the queue for drinks and Freddie wraps his arm

around me, landing soft kisses on the top of my head as we move with the line.

"Oh," says the server when we reach the front. I pivot at the sound of a familiar voice, and Seth smiles at me with his mouth closed. "Carly Dean. Hello, there."

"I thought you worked here Mondays?" I say, at the exact same time Freddie asks, "Who the hell is Carly Dean?"

"I do," Seth confirms to me, "but Jessica has laryngitis and the macchiatos won't make themselves." He nods at Freddie, and I see a muscle in his neck tense. "Hey."

Freddie stands a little taller and puffs his chest out like a startled bird. "Hey." He takes a moment to look at the menu board behind Seth. "Uh, one caramel latte and one mint tea, please."

"Coming … *up*," says Seth, punching the order into the cash register with a little more gusto than required. He glances at me. "No hemp today, huh?"

"Absolutely no hemp, please," I say. "If I see a single leaf in that mug, I will call the police."

Seth lets out an exhale of laughter as he points towards the card reader. Freddie taps his phone for payment with a force that suggests this particular card reader has wronged him in the past, and Seth moves on to the next customer, a girl with tightly coiled curls who giggles loudly at something he says to her.

"Are you still up for tonight?" Freddie asks me a few minutes later, when we've taken our seats at a spare table.

I lean forward in my chair, blowing on to my mint tea to cool it. Why is the curly-haired girl taking so long to place her order? Doesn't she know there's an entire queue of thirsty coffee drinkers behind her wishing she'd just hurry up and *pay*?

Freddie waves a gentle hand in front of my face. "Harley? Joshua's house? Eight o'clock?"

"I don't even know why he's having a party on a Wednesday night," I say, snapping back to reality. "It's feral behaviour."

Freddie's eyebrow twitches. "I told you – it isn't a party. It's just people and drinks and video games."

"Aka, a party." The girl is still mid-order, leaning right over the counter to look at something Seth's showing her on the specials menu.

"Aka," says Freddie, and he smiles as he leans over to rub my hand, "a low-key social event with my beautiful girlfriend, who likes parties now and will definitely be happy to be there."

I allow my hand to be stroked and try to look like that's true.

29

The den

There are at least twenty people crammed into Joshua's spare room, and if that's not a house party then I don't know what is. Joshua refers to this room as "the den", like he's an investment banker with two kids and a Range Rover, but it's essentially a large upstairs space that's at the top of a separate staircase to all the bedrooms. The walls are a dark, striking green, and the rest of the room is taken up by a large television, an L-shaped leather sofa and a well-stocked mini fridge. Joshua's parents are out at dinner and have probably been instructed to stay there until at least 11 p.m. if the amount of alcohol in the mini fridge is anything to go by.

There isn't enough room for everyone on the sofa, so I take a seat on the floor next to it, picking at a piece of loose skin on a cuticle.

"Harley!" says Joshua, circling me from above like a bird of prey. I make eye contact with his moustache, which I realize now is the only thing I find interesting about him. "Wine? Vodka? Beer?"

"Whatever the host is having," I tell him. "Thanks."

Joshua pops open the mini fridge and pulls out a can of Strongbow; he cracks the ring-pull and hands it to me. "Done."

We drink and talk for a while as a group, which – as usual – involves a lot of shouting and not a lot of listening. The Strongbow tastes like sour petrol, but it gives me something to do with my hands, so I keep up with regular sips, trying my hardest not to gag as I swallow. Joshua tells everyone that his life goal is to own a house on Grammercy Road, which is a long street opposite the cricket club, renowned locally for its mansions and swimming pools. Freddie high-fives him, even though Freddie once told me that owning gigantic gated houses is something for people with no morals and even less personality. Thirty seconds later, some new guy named Benedict says that he doesn't want a girlfriend because he can get all the benefits elsewhere anyway, without any of the hassle. Freddie falters at this, but still manages to plaster a compliant grin on to his face. He gives me an expectant look, willing me to join in.

I don't.

While the party continues around me, I get a text from Seth.

Today 21:03

Seth: I'm at one of Joy's gravespotting nights. There's a whole group of them here and a man wearing a monocle has just asked me for my thoughts on the Highgate Cemetery (I have none)

Seth: To summarize: it is very cold and I am out of my depth

Harley: Google says Karl Marx is buried at Highgate. AND Douglas Adams

Seth: Harley, YOUR FRIEND SETH will be buried at Highgate if they don't get me inside and warm soon

Seth: Please tell me you're having a better evening than I am

Harley: Sorry to disappoint, but no. I'm at Freddie's friend's house – turns out Minecraft is very dull to watch and cider tastes like sadness

Harley: Can I come meet the monocle man??

Seth: I can tell you without even asking him that he would love that, and so would I. Where are you? I can walk to you??

Harley: The house is next to the train station, Park Hill Road

Seth: You're literally 10 minutes away. Hang tight, Carly Dean, I am coming to you

"You're leaving?" says Freddie, when I tell him my plan. He's still holding the controller in both hands, but he swivels his neck, speaking to me over one shoulder while he plays.

"Just for a while." My voice battles with the music and loses. "I don't feel like you need me for" – I gesture towards the room – "all this."

"I *do* need you for it." Freddie throws the controller to Lucas and takes my hand, leading me out of the den and on to the soft carpet of the landing, where he closes the door behind us. "I want you to be here."

I soften a little at his touch. "I'm sorry. I'm not going for long – my friend Joy has this thing, and Seth just told me about it, and I'd li—"

Freddie's mouth droops, like a plant left out in the sun for too long. "But we have plans."

"Yes," I agree, "but those plans don't really seem to include me. I'm a plus-one to this event. You're the main character and I'm your good-natured animal sidekick. I'm Flounder, or the little raccoon from *Pocahontas*." He says nothing to reject this theory, so I carry on. "I'm not saying we can't do stuff like this together. I'm just saying that right now, this particular activity is not doing it for me."

"But what would do it for you, Harl?" says Freddie. He doesn't sound angry. His dark eyebrows have met in the middle and he's chewing at the side of his mouth, like he's processing. "Because when we said we'd be different, this is more or less what I expected. Hanging out with friends. Socializing. I thought that's what you wanted now, too."

"You thought *this* was what I wanted?" My voice comes out screeching and urgent. "You thought I'd suddenly lose my mind to spend the evening drinking cans of *whatever this is* and watching you and a bunch of moustached misogynists move blocks around on a screen?"

The noise from Joshua's den has lessened and I'd put money on the fact that Benedict and co are gleefully listening to this argument unfold on the other side of Joshua's solid-wood door. *Go ahead*, I think. *At this point, I don't even care.*

"Uh, Minecraft is the bestselling video game of all time, and you know that," says Freddie coolly. "If you don't enjoy it, I think that's on you."

We take a break, Freddie inhaling and exhaling in time to the muffled music and me slowly crushing the sides of my lukewarm Strongbow can with my fingertips.

"You thought I was different now, and I am," I say finally. "I am. But maybe not in the ways you wanted. I don't think it's fair to expect me to have changed *just enough* to make you proud to be with me, but not *quite enough* to prioritize my own friends or say, 'No thanks, I don't want to follow you to a university that means absolutely nothing to me.'"

At this confession, Freddie's eyebrows spasm. I wait for him to tell me I've got it all wrong – that he's painfully proud to be with me and he'll do whatever it takes to keep us going forever, no matter what happens next year, no matter what Joshua thinks, no matter who we meet or what we do or where we go. But he doesn't. He just stands there, motionless, like he's all out of steam.

"I *like* socializing," I declare, and there's a new strength in my spine, holding me up like a flagpole, as I realize just how true that is. "I like hanging out with friends. Just … not yours."

There's a distant boo from Joshua's den, and Freddie winces at the sound. It's at that moment that I know for certain I've lost him, and that he's lost me. I felt it outside his house with Min, and at the RAU open day, and even at Brooke's party. *This isn't worth fighting for.*

Ever since we got back together, it's like we've been sledging down the vast green hill that Val showed us at RAU. We did it, and now we've reached the bottom, but neither one of us has the energy to climb back up to the top.

Freddie's open mouth hangs, helpless. He gestures from his body to mine, then back again. "How are we going to do this, Harl? How is it going to work?"

"That's the thing." I place the empty cider can on the top of Joshua's banister and take my first step down the stairs, away from him. "It isn't."

Seth texts me to say he found it impossible to get away from the monocle man and is still a few minutes away from Joshua's house as a result. He adds a capitalized SORRY! and a row of ghost emojis, followed by a crying face. I shunt the front door closed and stand outside anyway, gasping for the crisp air, teeth chattering in the cold while I rub at the tops of my arms. Even with my thickest coat zipped up around me, even with my woollen bobble hat on, my entire body is shaking.

Was that an argument, or a second, slightly less dramatic break-up? It *felt* like a break-up. It felt like one of those sad scenes from a movie, where the main characters finally realize what everyone around them has known for a while: that love alone isn't enough. And this time, the male lead doesn't chase after the woman. She doesn't want him to. He doesn't follow her down the stairs, grab her by the wrist, pull her into his arms.

He just lets her go.

"Are you ready," calls a voice in the gloomy distance, "to come rescue me from the local gravespotting society? If I see one more reminder of death this evening I am going to have an existential crisis or a panic attack." Seth's face comes into focus, and his smile is so wide his eyes have disappeared. "Maybe both!"

My shoulders relax at the sight of him, and the thought of Freddie gets squashed a little in my mind. "That bad, huh?"

"Harley," he says, breaking into a jog to speed up the last part of his journey. "I respect my friends' hobbies. I *support* my friends' hobbies. Does that mean I want to spend a sub-zero February evening staring at the tomb of a woman named Constance St Agnes just for the hell of it?"

Joy told me all about Constance St Agnes the night I first met her and Nate: Constance is a fan-favourite among the gravespotting community in our town – of which, it turns out, there are at least ten dedicated members. Constance was a woman who worked at her father's apothecary in the 1700s and, according to her gravestone, died at the tender age of twenty-two from *lethargie*. "Think of it as an eighteenth-century coma," Joy happily translated at the time.

"I remember Constance," I say to Seth now, returning the high five he offers me with one mittened hand. "That woman led a colourful life."

He shudders as he stands in front of me, letting ragged breaths turn into steam in the night air. "Hey, change of plan – what if we abandoned the cemetery idea? What if you came back to my house and showed me episode one of *Midsomer Murders*? Joy couldn't even be mad at us for that – it's literally *about* death."

The thought of being inside in the warm anywhere right now is appealing. The idea of returning to Seth's bedroom is, strangely, even more appealing. I'm just beginning to wonder whether I'd actually consider sitting on his bed this time – as opposed to returning as an awkward carpet-dweller – when the fight with Freddie creeps back into my mind.

"Thanks, but I kind of just want to go home now. Like, my home." I manage a weak smile. "It was a bad night."

"Of course," says Seth straight away. His nose is tinged with pink from the cold, like one of the Christmas-loving villagers from *The Grinch*. "C'mon. I'll walk you."

"Are you sure?" It's at least a half hour out of his way, but he simply *mm-hm*s me.

"I know karate. I'll keep you safe." He jolts his head back towards Joshua's house. "So what happened in there? What made your night turn out so bad?"

The worst argument Freddie and I ever had before today – except for our official break-up at the top of the Ferris wheel, I guess – was when he watched an episode of Marvel's *Daredevil* without me. He apologized (I'd been away on holiday with my mum; he hadn't been able to stand the suspense of not knowing what was happening in Matt Murdock's life) but I still felt betrayed for a few weeks. The days of *Daredevil* disagreements feel like a lifetime ago – as though the people from that memory don't even exist any more.

"The plan worked," I tell Seth as we walk. "Ours, I mean. But it just made things more complicated. We lied to Freddie. We lied to Gen. We tried to completely change ourselves, just so they'd want us."

It makes something new spark up inside of me: a deep, rib-crushing shame. At the time it was all so obvious – *Freddie says Harley is lacking; Harley tries hard to make up for the lack* – but now it just feels humiliating. Where did it get me? What was the point of any of it?

Seth bows his head and looks at the pavement in front of us, lit up by street lights. "I know. I don't like that, either. I mean, in some ways it's been good for me. I have a calendar on my phone now, Harley. A *calendar*! But you're right that it can't always be about bending over backwards for somebody else. Sometimes they have to bend a little bit, too." He tries to smile, but it doesn't come out right. "If Freddie won't do that for you..."

"He won't," I say, still full of the same courage from Joshua's house. "I know he won't. But that's what I'm saying – I never even gave him the chance to. I pretended he was getting this whole other version of me – this exciting version, like Bella. That isn't his fault."

Seth's head jerks up. "There's nothing wrong with the version he's got."

"You know what I mean."

"No, I really don't." He grunts out a puff of warm air. "I wish you'd stop trying to convince yourself that you two are supposed to be together. You're not."

I blink at this uncharacteristic negativity. "Excuse me?"

His long legs start to work up a pace as we reach the top of my road, and I struggle to stay with him.

"Don't worry about it."

"No, I do worry about it," I tell the back of his head. "Why is this any of your concern?"

"It's *my concern*," says Seth, swooping round to re-enter the conversation, "because I'm just as terrified as you are. It's like you think you're the only one who's afraid of change. You think that everyone else is born with some inbuilt lack of fear, and that you're the only person who has to be brave." He clenches his teeth, sending his jaw jutting out on each side of his face. I get a sudden, bizarre urge to tear off my gloves and paw at it. "Well, you're not. So, next year, while I'm living my scary new life alone in Liverpool, and you're off milking cows with Frederick just because it's safe, I hope you're happy. I'll be thinking of my old friend Harley, wondering what would've happened if she'd just dumped her boyfriend and written her damn book."

I narrow my eyes in confusion. "That's not what's happening here, at all. We talked about this – I can visit you in Liverpool, any time."

Seth scoffs, still speed-walking into the night. "Don't bother."

"Why are you being so mean?"

He tugs a hand through his hair. "Why are *you* being so mean?"

"I'm not *being* mean!" I yell, and the exasperation leaks out in my voice. "And even if I did go and milk cows with Freddie, this is what you wanted for me! So why would you care that I got it? Why is it so important to you that I stay away from him?"

"Why do you *think*?" Seth stops, and his entire body is

rigid, fixed to the ground. "Or do you not think about any of it? Is that just me? Am I just here for the pep talks and the comic relief?"

There's a hot, angry, breathy pause while I try to work out what he's telling me. *Do you not think about any of it?* I'm scared that I do – that I think about it in a way I shouldn't, that getting the urge to grab at the jaw of a fake ex-boyfriend and head on back to his bedroom is a terrible, terrible sign.

"You're my friend," I offer finally, in a hushed voice. It isn't a lie. It's the kindest, least inflammatory response I can muster right now – the only one that doesn't take everything Seth and I have done together over the last six weeks and immediately set fire to it.

"Great," says Seth bitterly. "Friends it is. I look forward to hearing more about Freddie's fascinating Minecraft antics at a time that suits you."

The sharpness of his retort catches me in the chest, so I hurl my own. "Well, you've never caught *me* complaining when you've been checking Gen's profile for the thirtieth time in a day, or yapping on about how beautiful and perfect she is, or Googling 'how to do a quiff hairstyle' when you thought nobody was looking."

"I Googled that *once*," he says hotly.

"Maybe one day I will write a book," I shoot back, "but I can tell you one thing: I sure as shit won't be dedicating it to you."

Seth's face hardens. "Well. I'm glad we finally got that cleared up."

He walks me to my door in silence, waits at the bottom of the drive for me to step inside, then disappears into the night.

30

The forest

What do you have for me today? asks my blank Word document, as the cursor blinks. *A poem? A short story? Or, given your current mental state, perhaps nothing at all?*

I've been writing most days lately, picking up inspiration from unexpected sources, like weeds in the garden or stars in the night sky or little old ladies on the bus. It feels messy – raw and sketched-up – but still like progress. Still like something.

After peering through the outside window like a stalker to confirm that Seth wasn't working this morning, I'm set up at a table in the coffee shop, accompanied by my laptop, a winter berry tea and a dull, relentless stomach-ache that kicked in the moment I slammed the door on him last night.

Do you not think about any of it?

His words bounce around desperately from one part of my skull to the other, like an air-hockey puck. At the start of all this, when he whirlwinded his way into the RDC classroom with his anxious pin-badge proposals, I couldn't see how he would slot into my life at all – but now it's the opposite. Now, I can't see a world of mine where Seth Whittaker doesn't feature in some large, unalterable way.

Seth doesn't get embarrassed when I don't laugh at a bad joke. He just says something like, *Damn, I think we need some better material over here* to the joke-maker, and they have no idea if he's with them or against them, which makes the whole thing even better.

He doesn't think I'm odd for liking the things I like, or hating the things I hate, or doing the things I do. He wants me to carry on writing. He wants my life to be big – sturdy – but it's not in the way that Freddie wants it. It's not because it makes him look better. It's because he thinks I deserve it.

Wren was right: we make a good team. Seth always shows up late and frazzled, and I always say something awkward and immediately think, *Not my finest work*, but it's OK, because that's what we do.

That's what we've been doing this entire time.

I take a sip of scalding-hot tea with my lips prised open and then, full of a new, confusing calm, I type.

Sometimes your dreams aren't loud and ever-present, like other people's. Sometimes they're small and uncertain – little acorns of potential, crammed next to each other in a sealed jar until you decide which one you want to plant.

I don't think there's anything wrong with that. Everyone makes out that you're supposed to have a plan – this perfect, linear dream life – but I don't know what my dream life is. I just know that I'm growing. I thought I wasn't – I thought I was a sapling, or a tree that had been planted too far into the shade by accident and would maybe just wither away. But I'm not that. I've grown strong without even realizing it.

I *feel* strong. I mean, I also feel the worst I've felt in weeks, but underneath all that there's a new core of steeliness. Two months ago, the thought of not knowing what was coming next would've been enough to destroy me. Now, I have no idea what's headed my way, and it isn't frightening like I thought it would be.

Harley Green refuses to drift through life any more, waiting for someone to grab her and redirect her path. Harley Green is done drifting, full stop.

I abandon the Word document, pull open a new browser

page, and type in "English literature and creative writing degrees". I don't bother to keep them local, or familiar-sounding. I don't check to see if they're within a certain mileage of RAU. I just go to work: opening new tabs, sifting through information, enjoying the growing hum of excitement in the pit of my stomach. I read about entry requirements and specialist genres and student libraries and guest lecturers and comic book societies and all kinds of things I never even considered before. Things I can choose for myself, now I want to.

When Freddie appears half an hour later, I don't even notice he's arrived. He coughs loudly, jolting me out of the zone I've absorbed myself in, and perches himself on the edge of the chair opposite, peering hesitantly over the top of my laptop screen.

"Hey."

He's wearing the sweatshirt he debuted when Seth and I saw him here weeks ago, the oversized bottle-green one with the thick varsity writing stitched on to it. The one that made me feel so distant and removed from his life.

I look at him today and I feel that way all over again, but it doesn't make me angry. It doesn't even make me sad. Instead, it's like I'm standing at the edge of a large, crowded forest, with trees inside of it so huge it'd be impossible for me to wrap my arms all the way around them. Freddie's there at the edge with me, holding my hand, and for the first time ever I don't want to cling to him, even though the forest is scary. I want to drop his hand and run, fast, into the unknown.

"I care about you," I tell him, snapping my laptop shut, and he frowns in confusion. "Maybe I always will. This isn't me saying that we can't ever speak again, or that being together was a mistake. But we don't suit each other any more, Freddie. I think we both knew that a long time ago."

Freddie takes his time stirring a sugar into his latte. "I think so, too." He licks his lips, purses them for a second. "Have you already told RAU? That you're not coming with me, I mean?"

"Not yet," I say, "but I will. You'll enjoy it more on your own. You'll get to go sledging with Val and do ten-mile hikes without me complaining the whole way."

The thought of that makes him laugh. "I'm not sure who we were kidding, expecting you to show up to a place like that. You're the least outdoorsy person I know."

I sit up straighter in my seat. "I am – same way you're the least wordy person I know. Doesn't make either of us bad people, Freddie. Just makes us different."

"No, of course." He pauses, tipping his chin into one hand as he rests an elbow on the table. "I'm sorry, Harl. Sometimes… Sometimes I feel like I don't really know who I am. It's like, you want me to be this old version of me, and sometimes I want that, too. But other people want a newer version, a different version, and it's hard to keep up."

"You want my opinion?" I ask, but it's completely rhetorical. "I think you need to stop caring about the versions other people might want. You've started to change who you are around everyone. You didn't used to do that."

"Ouch," says Freddie, though he still smiles, like he knows I'm right. "You know what I realized? I could never have a birthday party like Brooke's – one of those huge events, where you invite everybody you know. Everyone'd show up expecting a different Freddie. I wouldn't know what to do." He sighs. "You say you hate parties, but you'd never have that problem. You've always known exactly who you are."

"I'm a Victoria sponge," I tell him happily, even though he'll have no idea what I'm referencing. "Some may view me as unadventurous, or bland, but I don't see it like that. I know what I'm about." I echo Seth's words, feeling a pang of pride in my heart. "I'm a classic."

"Maybe I'd be one of those cakes with the sprinkles all over it," Freddie offers quietly, scratching at the back of his neck. "The hundreds-and-thousands cake: also kind of bland, but trying its hardest not to be and secretly hoping it doesn't get found out."

I shake my head. "I don't think you're bland. I think you're figuring it out, Freddie. We all are."

Something has shifted – I'm no longer seeing him as the confident, socially adept, beautiful universe of a boy I need to cling on to. Instead, I'm seeing him sitting here on a plastic chair, his whole life ahead of him, just as scared about it as I am.

"What do you think we'd be doing right now if we'd stayed together this whole time?" he asks me, and suddenly he's holding my hand, stroking at my thumb. But this time it's different. It doesn't feel like love. It feels like friendship. It feels like acceptance.

"Thursday morning? We'd be sitting right here, planning for university," I say. "You'd be telling me about some tractor-driving class you wanted to take, because that probably *is* an option, right?" Freddie shakes his head, but his face breaks into a reluctant smirk again. "I'd be trying my hardest to sound excited about it, even though I couldn't think of anything I wanted to do less. And then, in a few months, we'd move into our accommodation. I'd close in on you because I felt neglected. You'd distance yourself from me because you felt trapped. I'd stop myself from making friends or trying things because I'd be worried it'd take me away from you, and then I'd wonder why I felt so sad and small and lonely. We'd go through the next three years blurry, instead of fully immersed. And then we'd graduate. We'd start living in the real world and it'd be more of the same, and we'd always wonder if we could've made more of ourselves if we'd just peeled away from each other and started again separately." I swallow. "What do you think?"

Freddie blinks sadly. "More or less the same."

"None of this was a waste to me," I say, and the tears blur my view of his face. "You got me through *so* much, and I hope I did the same for you, but now it's time for us to go do something else. It's time for us to grow."

He uses his stroking hand to reach up my arm and leans forward to hold me. I rest my cheek on his head and try desperately to inhale the scent of his scalp before it disappears from me forever and becomes a faint memory – a story I will never tell the children I won't be having with him.

We stay there for a while, clutching on to each other, saying nothing at all.

When the bell rings for form-room Freddie coughs gently and we untangle from the embrace, both dabbing at our cheeks like we've just finished watching the saddest movie in the world. I extend my arms out to hug him and he launches into me, tightly gripping my waist.

"I hope you have the *best* life, Harley," he says, his voice muffled from the space between my head and my shoulder. "I hope it's exactly what you want."

For the first time, I know that it will be.

From: Harley Green (harleygreen12@gmail.com)

To: sluccini@leeds.ac.uk

Thursday 12 February at 20:40

Subject: Possible place on the English literature and creative writing course?

Dear Dr Luccini,

If you'd asked me a few months ago, I'd have told you I was happy – perfectly content – with applying to the same university as my boyfriend. We had this plan, where we'd both go to the same place, and we'd live together, and we'd basically start our adult lives ahead of schedule. I knew there wasn't any kind of English literature or creative writing courses at the university he'd chosen, but I told myself that was OK, because we'd be together. I felt like it would've been selfish of me to prioritize my future over our future.

And then, he told me he didn't want to be with me any more.

A lot has happened since, and I've learned a lot about myself, but the most important thing I've worked out is that I owe it to myself to take the opportunities I get. I feel like there's this giant snaking line in my mind, like propped-up dominos, full of all the women who came before me who'd have killed to have chances like these. Chances to do what they wanted with their lives.

What *I* want to do is write. I don't know what I want to do with that writing, but I know that I want to find out. I've attached a portfolio of my recent work – essays and poems and that kind of thing – and I'd be honoured to know you'd read any of it. There isn't exactly a style there, or not just yet anyway, but that's why I'm so interested in joining your course. I think I have some natural skills, and now I'd like to learn.

I know this is a long shot. I know you can't give random students who send random emails random places on your course. But what I'd like to say is: I really want this, and now I know it's what I want, I'm going to do whatever I can to make it happen. This is me, holding myself accountable.

Thank you for reading.

Best wishes,
Harley Green

31

The gamble

I've never entered the sports hall voluntarily before, but there's a first time for everything, so on Friday lunchtime I haul my backpack on, keep my hands gripped tightly across the straps, and set off in search of my former fake boyfriend.

Nate has advised me that Seth is likely to be in a PE-focused area of campus: Seth's going hard on the activities right now, he texted me this morning. He was talking about training for a marathon, which Joy is calling an obvious cry for help.

There's a group of girls in red side-striped hockey shirts leaving the sports hall, sticks tucked under their arms as they prepare to walk over to the pitch. I recognize one of them – Sienna, a long-legged goalkeeper – from my history class.

"Is there anyone in there?" I ask her, using my head to nod at the door.

"No," Sienna says brightly. "No clubs today. It's open if you want to practise, though – there's some sad guy in there playing badminton by himself."

I thank her, and pace forward into the building. When I reach the entrance hall – the same space we stood in with Gen and Jake a month ago, desperate to convince them Seth was a changed man – I pause for a few seconds in front of a circular window to the main hall, peering through it like a porthole to get the lay of the land.

The sad guy is still in here. He's facing away from me, furiously working his way through a pile of shuttlecocks on the floor next to him. A part of my torso – the bit underneath my ribcage, just above my stomach – tenses as I watch him serve. Each shuttlecock speeds through the air but then loses momentum and lands, dully, on the ground on the other side of the net.

I take a deep breath and push on the heavy green door, my heartbeat transferring to my ears as I realize how unprepared I am for an impromptu declaration of love. Maybe I won't need to say anything. Maybe I'll just pick up my own racquet, thwack the shuttlecock back to him as if to say, *Look – we really* do *make a great team*, and hope he picks up on the flimsy symbolism.

The noise of the door creaking open drags Seth away from his mission. He whirls round but flinches when he sees me, as though somebody's just prodded him in the chest.

"BUTTERFLY!" he bellows, as I step nearer to him.

I freeze. "What?"

He holds up his racquet, brandishing it in front of him like a hopeless weapon. "That's our code word, remember? Somebody says 'butterfly' and the other person leaves them alone."

"You're not allowed to use 'butterfly' to avoid difficult conversations," I remind him, but he doesn't budge. "Please, just *talk*. I don't want you to still be mad at me."

"I'm not mad," says Seth, marching towards the equipment station. "I'm humiliated. First, I yell at you on a moonlit walk home, then I ignore you for" – he checks his watch – "thirty-five hours, and *then* I walk in on you nuzzling your boyfriend in the coffee shop and have to awkwardly vacate the premises."

I follow him, shaking my head. "Freddie's not my boyfriend."

"Oh, sure." He dumps the racquet back into its cover, zips it up with force, then turns back to face me. "Until tomorrow, when the whole saga changes again and we all get invites to your *Doctor Who*-themed wedding."

"You're not hearing me," I say. "Freddie isn't my boyfriend. I was in the middle of breaking up with him when you saw us yesterday, because I realized that we aren't supposed to be together and that I want my life to be about more than him. And then I decided that my life *will* be about more than him. And then I emailed a course leader from the University of Leeds, to ask about their English lit and creative writing degree."

Seth takes a brief hiatus from the conversation to consider this.

"And *then*," I add, taking a tentative step towards him, "I kept thinking about how my friend Seth was right, about … pretty much everything."

He mirrors my movement, quick and clumsy. "I need to cancel the butterfly. Please. I immediately regretted the butterfly."

I nod. "Consider it done."

He sets his racquet down on to the floor and lets out a breath, then breaks into a wide, relieved smile – all teeth. All him.

"An *English degree*? Oh, you are not going to regret this. You're gonna be a writer, and we're all gonna turn up to Waterstones and point at your book on the shelf and say, *Why, yes, we* do *know acclaimed author Harley Green, what of it?*"

I fizz inside at his enthusiasm, but the reminder of our Wednesday night argument still heaves at my shoulders. "I'm sorry I said I wouldn't dedicate it to you. I will, if I ever actually write anything."

"And I'm sorry I said you were forbidden to visit me in Liverpool," he says. "Please, come visit me in Liverpool. I'll be the loud, weird kid with no friends and an improv shirt."

"You won't," I assure him. "You'll be the loud, weird kid with lots of friends, and I'll be one of them."

Seth smiles gently; one half of his mouth cranks up to the side and my entire body shivers. "What if you aren't?"

"I *will* be," I say. "Because I'll be at Leeds. Maybe. Eventually. If they let me in. I'm sure it can't be that far away from Liverpool."

"No," he says, and his face is suddenly serious. "You don't understand. I'm saying, what if I had lots of friends, but only one girlfriend, and it was you." He gulps. "Just you."

What if I had one girlfriend, and it was you. The question makes my heart feel like it's going to give out – it fills me with thoughts of Seth's golden forearms, of his blue-checked bedsheets.

My brain, always more hesitant than my heart, immediately comes up with more *what ifs* to add to the pile. What if being with Seth means I'm throwing my own self-development in the bin for the sake of a pretty, freckled face? What if it means I'm just jumping from one boy to another – catapulting myself from the good ship *Freddie* to the SS *Seth*, without taking any time on my own to work out who I am as a person? What if having a boyfriend at university messes things up for me, because I'm still – for some unknown, deep-rooted reason I'll probably unearth in Dahlia's therapy clinic one day – incapable of prioritizing my own needs over his? What if we grow apart, and then we lose each other, just like

Freddie and I lost each other at the start of all this? The thought makes me want to be sick.

I relay all these worries to Seth, except for the part about vomit, and he listens, calm-faced, centimetres away from me, as I speak.

"Yeah," he says simply, at the end of it all. "I guess you're right."

I blink at his easy retreat. "You guess I'm *right*?"

"Well, you are. Maybe we would be moving on a little too soon, and that wouldn't be ideal. Maybe we'd miss out on some opportunities when we got to university, because we'd be a couple. Maybe, eventually, we'd break up." He shrugs. "But here's another thought: maybe dating each other wouldn't be like dating those people before, because we're *not* those people before. Maybe we'd give each other space for deadlines and friends and hobbies and life, and maybe we'd be part of those things sometimes, too. And if we break up, well, then we break up. People do it all the time."

"That's so sad," I whisper, and he nods.

"I think so, too. Doesn't mean I couldn't get through it. I already did, and so did you. We could handle it." He takes one more step towards me so there's the smallest of gaps between my body and his, then picks up the very ends of my fingers to hold them gently, carefully, like a question. "We've already handled quite a lot."

The sensation of his skin on mine gives me the same visceral reaction I had at the party, when his hand made its way up my back and my spine whispered something incomprehensible. It's like a brand-new wanting, like an ache buried deep within my bones.

"You're a coffee cake," I blurt out, mostly to distract myself from the ache. "You're not to everyone's taste, and maybe sometimes people want something a little more run of the mill, but I don't, because I like you." I try to catch my breath. "And I *do* think about it. You're not just here for the pep talks, or the comic relief. I don't want you to show up early, or quiff your hair, or buy a Ford Fiesta. What I want is *you*."

Seth lets out a breath of laughter, resting his teeth on his bottom lip. "Well then. I guess that's really all that matters."

And then he kisses me. It isn't like the kiss at Brooke's party – nervous and sweaty and audience-focused. It's light and gentle, like he wants to make sure I'm into it, and then, when I've confirmed that I am, it's heavier. He places one hand on the back of my head, and the other on my base of my spine, which buzzes with gratitude again. We melt into it, letting the words we haven't said yet come out in a different way.

It's brave. It's scary, like anything good would be. It's world-changing.

From: Sara Luccini (sluccini@leeds.ac.uk)
To: Harley Green (harleygreen12@gmail.com)
Tuesday 17 February at 18:11
Subject: Re: Possible place on the English literature and creative writing course?

Dear Harley,
Thank you for your email. I must confess I read it several evenings ago and have meant to get back to you sooner than this, but I certainly kept it in my mind.

Firstly, well done you for making this decision. I think it's very courageous, and the kind of thing I wish I'd have done at your age. One divorce and two degrees later, I'm there, but it's never easy.

Although I'd love to be able to offer you a place with us to read English literature, you're right in assuming that those decisions don't lie with me – there's a rigorous and fair process in place to make sure everyone is given an equal opportunity, and we of course have entry requirements, which you will have to meet.

However, please don't be deterred by my words. If this is what you want – which you state very clearly that it is – then I suggest approaching our Clearing team in August, or applying next year. I know that might feel like a long time in the future, which I suppose it is right now, but if there's one piece of advice I can offer to you, it's this: you've got time.

Very much hoping to meet you in the future,
Sara

32

The stuff that scares you

The Recently Dumped Club's end-of-cohort presentation – open to friends, family and former members such as myself – takes place on a sun-tinged, blustery Wednesday. Dahlia has secured some space in the dance studio, sellotaped a large sign to the door that says PRIVATE SESSION IN PROGRESS, and decorated the entire room like she's hosting a large, unspecific party.

"Because nothing says, 'Congratulations on completing six weeks of group therapy following your devastating break-up' like a bright red balloon and a personalized cupcake," says Seth, but he still cradles his own cake like a baby chick.

"I knew it," says Lucy, arriving next to us with an overflowing plastic cup. Her kohl-rimmed eyes point accusingly at the merging of my hand and Seth's non-cupcake-holding palm. "Dahlia, didn't I say I saw them together outside of sessions? Didn't I *say* they liked each other?"

Dahlia pulls a kind but slightly uncomfortable facial expression that says, *I am the pretend adult in this situation; leave me out of your gossip, I beg you.*

Lucy sighs, deflated. "Well," she says. "I did."

"We did, too," says Joy, who's showed up with Nate to offer their support. She reaches over to pat Seth on the head and he wriggles away, like an indignant son. "But it took both of them a little while to catch up."

Seth takes a bite out of the pink "S" on his cake. "So, yes, Lucy, we are newly together. This glorious creature is now my girlfriend, and later I am taking her to the Botanical Gardens so we can look at the koi carp." He puts on his American accent, speaking through the remnants of the mouthful. "Ain't life grand?"

Lucy, visibly sickened by his unabashed optimism, slithers away.

"OK, folks!" yells Dahlia, slapping her hands together as she heads up to the stage in a pair of light-denim dungarees and a black roll-neck jumper. "Thank you so much for being here. Specially-invited audience members, you're very welcome – we just ask that you respect the privacy and safety of this room. Everyone speaking today has completed six weeks of group work with me via the Recently Dumped Club, and, as part of our healing process, they're being brave enough to tell us what they've learned throughout it."

She carries on talking as we all chew on our snacks, explaining the history of the group, that she's hoping to carry on running it next term and that any letters of support addressed to Mr Georgiou, the head of the psychology department, would be gratefully received.

"I'm here," hisses Bella, announcing her citrus-scented arrival and planting a kiss on my shoulder. She leans over me to tap Seth on the kneecap. "Fake Boyfriend, hey."

"Fun Bella!" whispers Seth, his mouth blooming into a smile. "Now that I'm Real Boyfriend, will we change my nickname? Or will it remain, for old time's sake?"

Bella swings her bag to the floor as she considers this. "The latter. It really rolls off the tongue."

"Thank you for being here," I tell her, and she nods, as if to say, *Duh. Where else would I be?*

Dahlia raises her voice, ready to kick off the proceedings. "Now, please join me in congratulating your friends and classmates!"

Everybody claps, and Dahlia puts a wobbly hand over her mouth, like she's going to cry. Behind her, a PowerPoint screen projected on to the wall says: I JUST GRADUATED FROM THE RECENTLY DUMPED CLUB. HERE'S WHAT I LEARNED...

Daisy is first up. Her auburn hair is pulled back into a thick ponytail and she presents the room with a wide, nervous grin as she shifts her weight from one foot to the other, clutching a scrap of paper that she reads from.

"Hi, I'm Daisy. I've learned a lot of things over the last two months – mostly that I'm not a failure just because somebody doesn't want to be with me any more. Being dumped isn't a reflection of my worth as a human being. It's just … something that happens, and I couldn't have controlled it. And it hurts right now, but I'm trying my best. I'm seeing my friends and going outside and taking care of myself as well as I can."

A girl in the audience shouts, "You're the best!" and Daisy's shoulders rise with bashful happiness. She scurries back down to her seat.

Lucy stands in front of the crowd next, tugging at the sleeve of her black mesh T-shirt.

"Lucy. Hi, whatever," she says, with her eyes on the floor. "I learned that just because someone says they want to be with you forever, *and* get married, *and* adopt a Cavalier King Charles Spaniel called Ozzy, that doesn't actually mean shit. And it can make you not trust people, because why would you when one of them lied to you like that. It feels like everyone you meet is just looking for something better all the time. And I don't know, maybe they are. But even if I don't meet someone new who wants to adopt a Cavalier King Charles Spaniel called Ozzy with me, I learned that I can just … adopt one myself someday. Like, nobody is going to stop me." She makes devilish eye contact with Dahlia. "It's my life, not anyone else's, and that feels … good."

Other members of the group get up to speak after Lucy – Reyan says that he learned to be kinder during this process, and to respect his ex-girlfriend's need for space. Oliver, red and solemn, says he learned that taking three days to reply to a text message probably isn't great relationship etiquette, which Seth claps especially loudly for. Maryam tells the audience that it's helped her more than anything to remember that someone who doesn't want to be with her any more probably *isn't* the great love of her life. Instead, they're probably just a chapter of it.

When it's Seth's turn to share, he takes a deep breath. "I learned two things from this process. Number one is this: we all play our own part in a break-up, but we aren't the sole reason it happened. And for some of us, it was probably helpful to remember the part we played, because we weren't able to understand what we might even have *done* in order to cause somebody to say they didn't want us in their life any more. But for others – like me – I already knew what I'd done. I knew I was messy, and late, and too talkative, and immature, and incapable of growing a beard, and all I wanted was to prove to my ex-girlfriend that she was wrong about me, because I knew I could change all those things."

He pauses to flip his blonde hair from one side to the other, scratching at the roots. "I mean, the beard didn't work. You can't force facial hair." There's a quiet laugh from the room. "But what I'm saying is: I already knew the part I'd played, and so all I did was *stew* on it. I tried to change myself into a completely different person, and I beat myself up for being who I was. And I feel sad about that now, because actually … I like who I am. I like him a lot. So, yes, we *do* all play our own part in a break-up, but it isn't ever a one-man show. I forgot about that."

Bella lets out a loud whoop as the audience claps, and Seth – uncharacteristically – looks a little flustered by the attention. He chews at a thumbnail. I blow him a kiss.

"What was the second thing you learned?" calls Oliver, speaking over the hum of onlookers.

"What?" says Seth. He catches my kiss and pretends to tuck it into his shirt pocket, then remembers himself and leans back into the public recognition, surrendering to a grin on one side of his mouth. "Oh. Stick it out with the cute, quiet, grumpy girl. She's worth it."

He doesn't wait for the rest of them to catch up with this declaration. He just stares directly at my pinkening face, takes a bow, and then leaves the stage.

At the end of the event, when everyone's had their say and it's time for us all to return to our cupcake-mingling, Daisy whispers something to Dahlia, who jumps up from her seat.

"Kind of putting you on the spot here, Harley," she says,

"so no pressure, but Daisy's just pointed out that you were a big part of the RDC, too. You might not have finished the course like everyone else did, but you've definitely learned a lot. Do you want to tell us about any of that?"

There's further murmuring in the audience while I reflect on the question. Dahlia's right – I *have* learned a lot. I might feel unprepared to share it, but that doesn't mean I can't.

And so I hoist myself up to my feet and take a step in the direction of the stage, ready to speak.

"I, uh … I left the RDC early, because my ex decided he wanted to get back together with me," I start. "And I thought that was what I wanted. I had this whole plan" – I make eye contact with Seth, who grimaces theatrically – "and it was all leading up to my ex finally wanting me again. But then, when he did, I realized he'd dumped me for a reason. He'd been right all along: that we needed to pull apart from each other and go our separate ways."

I try to ignore all the eyes on me, the loud lunchtime hubbub in the distance outside. "And the ironic part was, even though I thought being without him would leave me lonelier than I'd ever been, it didn't. I've made new friends." Joy and Nate grin from their seats next to Seth. "I've got closer to the ones I already had, and learned how important it is for me to cherish them." Bella winks at me over the sea of heads. "The stuff that scares me is easier to try now," I continue, "because I have good people next to me while I try it. So, I guess that's what I've learned. I'm enough as I am, but I'm also ready to find out what else I could be. It's both. *I'm* both."

And then, because I guess it's the kind of thing I do these days, I stay on the stage and allow myself to be applauded. I don't shy away from it. I don't worry about the heat burning through my cheeks, or the shakiness in my wrists. I stand rooted to the spot, knowing I am supposed to be here. I am as much a part of this universe as anyone else.

As the attendees pile out of the studio, we each take it in turns to hug/fist-bump/shake hands with/cry into the arms of Dahlia, who definitely deserves some kind of award for her role in all this.

"Thank you," I tell her, and she pulls me in towards her, lip wobbling. "You'll be an amazing therapist someday. Like Robin Williams in *Good Will Hunting*."

"God, I hope so," says Dahlia. She nods at Seth, then back to me. "Y'know, you two are very sweet together. Is it unprofessional to say that I always thought so?"

"I hope you don't think I'm abandoning my … journey of self-discovery, or whatever this is," I say, and I suddenly realize just how much I want Dahlia to think positively of me. "I'm still on it, I promise. I don't think it'll ever stop. I've just … got someone with me now. I've got Seth."

Dahlia shakes her head. "No way. If we've learned

anything through all this, I hope it's that healing isn't really something you *do* on your own. You do it surrounded by safe people, in the knowledge that they've got you, even if other people didn't."

Daisy and her friend call out to Dahlia, and she lays her hand on mine for a second. "Good luck, Harley. I think you're gonna be fine."

Seth, Bella, Joy, Nate and I wander out into the sunshine together, Joy clutching a plastic cup in one hand and Nate's pinky finger in the other, Bella bobbing along next to my shoulder and Seth on the other side tracing a pattern into the lines of my palm. Today, we're not looking for Gen and her dancer group, or Freddie and his Joshua group, or anyone else to change ourselves for. Instead, we've come together to make a new group, right here.

"You wanna do something tonight?" says Bella. She wraps an arm around my waist and lets out a satisfied sigh. "Pizza. Crazy golf. Soap carving. I don't care – you choose."

I freeze, terrified at the thought of letting Bella down again, but then I remember what Seth said, about things not having to be the same this time, because *we're* not the same this time.

"We have plans," I say, nodding at Seth, who squeezes my hand in encouragement. "Botanical Garden plans. But I'd love for you all to join them. We could go together."

I hold my breath for a second. I wait for this all to come crashing down around me, but it doesn't. Of course it doesn't. Nate grins, Joy nods and Bella just widens her mascaraed eyes at me as if to say, *Obviously.*

"Tell me, friends," says Seth, offering Bella an uneaten cupcake with a heart on it. "What are your feelings on koi carp?"

SEPTEMBER

Six months later...

33

The ending (but also the start)

September has always been my least favourite month. Like January, it's a month that forces new beginnings – and, for a change-hater like Harley Green, that isn't great.

But this September, things are different. Things are better. For starters, I'm standing with my cheek against Seth Whittaker's chest, while he wraps his unbuttoned plaid jacket around the both of us.

"You're so pretty," he whispers to the top of my head. "You smell like a bakery. How does a *person* smell like a bakery?"

I giggle into his collarbone. "Your guess is as good as mine."

"Uh, I hate to break up the smooching," calls my mum, who's already strapped up in the driver's seat, coffee in hand, "but we were supposed to leave twenty minutes ago, and

I have severe anxiety regarding the M1. Motorways are not at all calming for me."

"Say no more, Alice," says Seth. "The smooching is winding down."

He unwraps the jacket, unpeels himself from me and steps back a few paces, studying my face with unblinking intent. "I'm trying to take a photo of you with my mind, to sustain me until the next time we meet."

From my own spot, I return the gesture. I look at his freckled nose and his sea-green eyes and his ridiculous gym shorts, and I beg my memory to capture all of it.

"Two weeks," I tell him, like I'm reciting a magic spell, "with the chance to extend if we feel like we need more time to settle in before we see each other."

"Two weeks," he confirms, holding up his forefinger and middle finger to show me. "It's nothing, really. We've got through a lot worse."

"I'll miss you," I say, and the honesty of it makes me gasp under my breath.

Seth's jaw quivers. "I'll miss you so much. I'm going to literally ache, like an old man with a bad back."

I move over to him, thankful that my mum is currently pretending to be immersed in something on her phone, and reach for his hand.

"It's scary," he says, "not knowing what's coming next."

I nod, then surprise myself. "It's also *really* exciting, right?"

Seth squeezes my fingers. "You know it, Carly Dean."

I picture as many parallel-universe Harleys as I can, all showcasing a world of different futures. In one, I'm a writer, sitting at a computer desk with a blanket draped over my knees. In another, I'm an office hotshot, working in a shiny-floored London skyscraper before strutting out at the end of the day to drink cocktails in a pencil skirt. In another, I'm curled up on the sofa with a tall, blurry man, whose face I can't make out but whose hand rests on mine in a way that's safe and soothing. I see friends and trains and pets and tears and kisses and holidays and none of it looks any clearer or fuzzier to me. Any of it could happen. Maybe all of it could happen.

And so I get in the car. I kiss my boyfriend goodbye and then I clamber into the passenger seat, ready to begin my new life. I sit with cardboard boxes next to me, with pillows balancing on my lap, and I breathe it all in. And even though my heart is beating through my chest, even though I have no idea what I'm diving into, I trust that I can handle this.

There are a lot of uncertainties in life. Now I'm ready for them.

Acknowledgements

My first dose of gratitude will always go to my agent, Chloe Seager: a voice of calm and encouragement. Every time I hear from you my little heart soars – I am so happy we get to work together. Thanks also to everyone else at Madeleine Milburn Literary Agency, especially Kelly Chin, Valentina Paulmichl, Hannah Ladds and Hannah Kettles.

Creating another book with Scholastic has been a team effort, and a LOT of fun. Thank you to my hugely talented editor Polly Lyall Grant for suggesting twists and turns to the plot and helping to bring Harley, Seth and Freddie to life. Big thanks also to Karen Ball for jumping in to continue the editing process seamlessly, to Bella Haigh for editing support, to publishing manager Wendy Shakespeare (queen of grammatical trivia), and to proofreader Naomi Greenwood. Even more Scholastic thanks to marketing and PR gurus Tina Mories and Ellen Thomson, to cover designer Sarah Baldwin (I will NEVER be over the broken heart title!) and to Emma Roberts, copy-editor extraordinaire, who brings so much care to every project she works on.

Sending my appreciation to the bloggers, BookTokkers, booksellers and librarians who've championed *Red Flags*, whether via online posts, events, newsletters or (in the case of Waterstones Solihull) my first-ever on-shelf Waterstones recommendation! I hope you enjoy *Heartbreak Era* just as much.

Endless thanks and endless love to The Six, for many reasons, including the fact that referring to this friendship group makes me feel like Daisy Jones. I truly do not think I could function in the world of publishing without you. Thank you for being a safe space for us all to ask questions, share wisdom and have occasional tiny meltdowns.

To my friends and family: thank you for your support, and apologies for asking you intrusive questions about old break-ups in the name of research. Special thanks to my favourite gals, and to Tom, always, for being so excited for me when things go well and so ready to love me when they don't.

It would be criminal for me to write a book featuring a main character named Seth and not provide some form of thanks to *The OC*'s Seth Cohen, provider of the quick quips and pop culture-laden bromides I am so fond of. If you haven't seen *The OC*, please watch it. If you have, please watch it again. I myself will be leaving the DVD boxset in my will for some unsuspecting grandchildren.

The dedication at the start of this book was very nearly "*To the people who know what they're about*" – but that doesn't make much sense before you read the rest. So here's a second dedication, especially for those people: the Harleys of the world, who'd much rather be sitting inside reading a book. I am right there with you.

1

POPPY

When they can't handle the word "period"

My first-ever boyfriend was pretend.

I'm aware that this fact makes me sound slightly unhinged, but, honestly, I can deal with you thinking that about me. Maybe your opinion will improve if I tell you that this isn't about me having some compulsive lying habit, and that it is *actually* about me stumbling across the eighties film *The Princess Bride* seven years ago while my parents were having a dinner party.

Here's what happened: I'd been relegated to a bedroom with a large bowl of salted crisps and none of the usual television rules or curfews to contend with. If you haven't seen *The Princess Bride*, all you really need to know is that it starts on a farm, and that the man who works on the farm is named Westley. Westley has startlingly blue eyes and floppy hair that's regularly backlit by the sun, and from the moment I saw him on my parents' nineteen-inch television, I was obsessed. *Possessed.*

While my mum and dad served up homemade moussaka, *I* spent the rest of the evening drawing felt-tip interpretations of Westley with a sword, writing elaborate stories about Westley saving a sickly baby goat in the nick of time and then hotfooting it over to my house to ask me to raise it with him. It was the stuff at the start of the movie that *really* charmed me: when Westley's this quiet, mysterious farmhand, just wandering around being sweet and doing odd jobs for Buttercup the princess, and she's being sort of mean to him at that point, but it doesn't matter, because everyone can tell that they're meant to be together.

Anyway, when the dinner party had ended and I was supposed to be brushing my teeth ready for bed, I overheard my parents having an argument as they stacked away their dessert bowls in the kitchen.

"Ruth and Joseph asked about my interior design course and you couldn't tell them a single thing about it," said my mum. "How do you think it makes us look to people when I can recite every last detail about your damn job but you can't remember the first thing about me?"

"I said you were *enjoying* it," my dad replied. "I didn't know I was supposed to recite the entire bloody syllabus, Liz."

"Daniel, do you know how exhausting it is to always be the one compensating for your non-existent social battery? What if *I* just sat at the dinner table in silence? Tell me – what would happen then?"

I crouched there in my tartan pyjamas, eavesdropping from my regular spot at the top of the stairs, and you know what? I didn't feel sad, not like I normally would've done when they argued. Instead, I felt hopeful. There were people out there who'd committed too soon, I realized – people like my mum, who'd met my dad at sixteen, settled down shortly afterwards and now lived her life in a slightly resentful state with someone who clammed up at dinner parties. But as I'd clutched the television remote on that fateful Saturday evening, I'd seen first-hand that I didn't have to *be* one of those people. That it wasn't the only option available to me.

I made a promise to myself there and then, as an eleven-year-old: no matter how long it took, I would stave off a mediocre marriage and wait for my own Westley. Not necessarily a fairy-tale farmhand, granted, but someone who understood me, someone who found my difficult ways endearing, someone who just felt … *right*. I sprang up from the top stair, skulked back to my room and started to jot down exactly what this imaginary boy would be like.

~*~ POPPY'S DREAM MAN ~*~

The next day at school, I plucked the Dream Man list from my crumb-lined coat pocket and swore to my friends that this, right here, was what my future consort would be like.

"This boy," I told them all, as I led them to the library like a playground Pied Piper, "is out there for me. I don't know where he is and I don't expect to meet him any time soon, but I know for sure that I will not accept anything less. And neither should you."

They all followed suit – for one glorious lunchtime, the girls and I dug deep into our psyches, pulled out our pens and glitter glue, and manifested our ideal future partners together.

He'll make me laugh all the time.
She'll never talk over me while I'm
trying to say something.
He'll get on well with my friends, so
we can all hang out together.
He'll love swimming just as much as I do.

My friends, entertained as they were, left the library that afternoon with their creations tucked under their arms and forgot about the whole thing almost immediately. But I didn't. I was encouraged – bolstered, full of visions of my own perfect Westley-esque Dream Man. *I'm* so *glad we found each other*, I imagined him saying as he swept a rogue lock of hair away from my face, ready to recite a lengthy poem he'd written about me.

I knew it would all be worth it, some day. I just needed to wait.